Praise for The Fountain

"The Fountain is not your ordinary YA boarding school novel. With magic, mystery and romance woven together in just the right measure, it is sure to be a 'must read' with teens everywhere."

- Jacqueline Guest, author of Ghost Messages
and The Comic Book War

"Suzy Vadori does wonders with taking a simple theme - making a wish - and turning it into a wonderful novel of rich dialogue, memorable characters, and a few twists and turns, that will have the reader immersed in this mystery-laced read, bringing together both past and present, right and wrong, and of course, how one wish creates a ripple effect that may never be undone."

- Avery Olive, author of A Stiff Kiss
and Won't Let Go

"The Fountain is a very enjoyable book that can be read by readers from 10 to 100!"

- Kristina Anderson, The Avid Reader

The West Woods

Suzy Vadori

*For Patience,
wish for the stars!
Suzy Vadori*

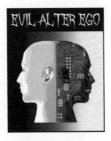

EVIL ALTER EGO PRESS

www.evilalteregopress.wordpress.com

Evil Alter Ego Press

www.evilalteregopress.wordpress.com

Published by Evil Alter Ego Press, 869 Citadel Drive NW, Calgary, AB T3G 4B8, Canada

The West Woods, Copyright © 2017 by Suzy Vadori.

Edited by Jeffrey A. Hite and Barbara Jacobson.

Cover by Jeff Minkevics, copyright © 2017 by Jeff Minkevics.

Interior design and layout by Michell Plested.

Print version set in Cambria; titles in Cambria, byline in Cambria.

Published in Canada

Printed in Canada

Library and Archives Canada Cataloguing in Publication

Vadori, Suzy, 1975-, author

The West Woods / Suzy Vadori.

Electronic monograph issued in EPUB and print format.

ISBN 978-1-988361-10-9 (pbk.).
ISBN 978-1-988361-11-6 (epub).

CONTENTS

CHAPTER ONE

No Retreat

Courtney had one foot out of the car door, with her body still firmly planted inside. Her throat tightened as the campus loomed before her. A dusting of snow graced the trees and roofs. Though she'd attended St. Augustus for ninth grade and half of the tenth already, it didn't feel like home.

The school's buildings were set well back from the road and Courtney stared at them now. The whole scene felt out of place in Massachusetts. She'd always thought the oldest building on campus could be a castle like you'd find in France or England. At one time, its coating of green ivy had fascinated Courtney, like it was being gobbled up by the vines. As the semesters had passed though, the plain red brick of the newer buildings seemed more in tune with the personality of the school she'd come to know.

Courtney sighed as she watched her dad walk away from the parking lot toward the dorm with her older sister Hanna. Winter break had ended too soon. "I'll wash your car every night if you reconsider?" she called out.

As if he hadn't heard her, her dad pulled the lapel of his suit jacket up over his face against the cold and continued walking toward the dorm. He didn't turn back. She wracked her brain for something else to offer, but came up with nothing.

After a long pause, Courtney hoisted her duffel bag from the car seat beside her up onto her shoulder. She pulled her long, bushy red hair out from under its strap. She could just stay in the car. Once her dad got Hanna settled in her room and returned to the parking lot, the two of them could go. Home. Courtney pictured his face turning a deep shade of red if she tried that. It wasn't going to be that simple. She'd argued her case all last semester, the entire winter break, then the whole car ride up here from Boston today. He hadn't given an inch.

Finally, she pulled herself off the leather seat of the car and stepped out into the staff parking lot where they weren't supposed to park. Jim Wallis regularly ignored No Parking signs. Besides, he wasn't planning to stay long. Courtney shut the car door with a satisfying slam.

Her dad and Hanna disappeared into the dorm entrance - Hanna's head bent over her phone as she walked. She was no doubt texting her friends, telling them she'd arrived, even though she'd see them as soon as she got inside.

Courtney walked fast as she crossed the lawn, her bag swinging against her back with every step. She'd have to hurry if she wanted to get in one more shot. She knew she'd lost this round, but maybe he'd give in by the summer if she had a convincing argument now. Taking the steps to the dorm entrance two at a time, she ran through all the possibilities.

Her dad waited in front of one of the plain doors in the hallway, his eyebrows knit into a frown.

"I've got to be getting back to the city, Courtney," he said as she approached. He took her bag from her.

"I can pack everything I have here really fast, Dad," Courtney joked as she fished her key out of her pocket and fit it into the lock. She'd done enough whining. Time to take a different angle.

"Courtney, you have to at least try to make it work here," her dad said firmly, following her into the small room she shared with her roommate, Margaret. "You were happy enough to come here last year. You'll like it again, just give it time."

The room smelled musty, as it always did when it had been shut up for a while. Memories of the first time she'd come to campus flooded in. Back then, she'd been full of hope.

She took her bag back from him and tossed it onto her unmade bed. Courtney cocked her head as it hit the blankets. Had her bed sat here like that the whole time she'd been gone, its sheets tangled up and exposed? Her face scrunched up as she looked over at Margaret's tidy covers, knowing the sheets underneath would be tucked into the mattress with hospital corners. She felt her dad's eyes on her. Turning toward the window, she took stock of her prison. Two and a half years left to serve, with no time off for good behavior.

Courtney held her mouth in a thin line. The Courtney her dad referred to had been a bright-eyed freshman. She'd been thrilled then to come to St. Augustus. It had turned out to be less exciting than she'd hoped.

Somewhere about an hour ago in the car, she'd thought he might agree to let her go home with him. But now, here they were.

"I know you loved it here, Dad," she said, turning and watching him carefully for any signs of weakness. "But I'd be the top runner at Harbor, including the seniors."

Harbor Heights was the Boston school she'd trained with over the break. She was faster than all of them.

Besides, being home was easier – more comfortable. She especially liked seeing her mom every day. Her mother had a busy social calendar, but still... she was home for meals and coffee in the morning. Once Courtney was back at school, she wouldn't get to talk to her mom much. Her mom didn't like to talk on the phone, and Courtney's dad handled anything to do with the school. Both of her parents were too busy to talk to her during the school year about much else.

The thought of leaving St. Augustus' starchy kilts and blouses behind made her heart sing.

Her dad shook his head. The corners of his mouth turned downward as he looked at his youngest daughter. If she didn't know better, she thought he might be about to cry. She hated to disappoint him.

"Courtney, St. Augustus can give you everything you want," he told her. "Swimming will look just as good on college applications as running. It doesn't matter much. If you swam as much as you ran, you'd probably get better." He looked at her with that expression he got sometimes. What was that expression? Courtney had never been able to figure it out. Dreamy, somehow – yet, disappointed. "You just aren't looking hard enough for what is *here*."

Courtney bit her lip to keep from raging at her dad. He was so out of touch. Her hands clenched at her sides. She'd heard this speech before and it didn't make any more sense to her now than it had the first time she'd heard it. St. Augustus was a school. Her dad talked about it like the buildings could live and breathe. He actually sounded pretty crazy once he got going. Courtney looked over at Margaret's empty bed, glad she wasn't here to hear him go off.

"Dad," Courtney said, taking a breath before plunging ahead, "it's not about the school. There's no track team here! I have been trying at swimming, I thought I'd get better..." Words spilled out, though they weren't telling the whole truth. Her heart hadn't been in swimming at all this year. She could do better.

"Hanna's going to have her pick of colleges," he reminded her. "You need to start thinking about that, too. With some work, you'll get there."

"Dad, my grades are good. I'll get into a good college," Courtney said. "Even if I'm at a public school."

She tried not to think too hard about Hanna graduating this year. The thought of being the only Wallis at St. Augustus was unnerving. Her dad's expectations would fall to her. She didn't mind living in Hanna's shadow, not really. It was better than being forced into the spotlight.

He didn't answer. For a few beats, their deadlocked argument hung in the air between them.

The room itself, with Margaret's bed only three feet from her own, seemed smaller than she remembered. Reality set in. She'd be staying. From her dad's tone, she'd be here not just this year, but until graduation. Her collarbone itched as she caught sight of the row of neatly pressed uniforms hanging in the open closet.

"You're just going to have to trust me on this one," he told her, breaking the silence as he placed a hand on her shoulder.

Courtney eyed him warily. His eyes were lit in a way that seemed out of place.

"St. Augustus is... special," he said, clearing his throat. "Courtney, there is no telling what you could accomplish, if only you'd open your eyes and go for what you want."

Courtney hated being mediocre, though not enough to want to train harder at something she didn't much like. Unwelcome hot tears waited like needles behind her eyelids. She dug her fingernails into her palms. Crying wouldn't work with Jim Wallis. She couldn't cry.

"Dad, I *am* going for what I want," Courtney answered, wrinkling her forehead. "What do you think I've been asking you for?"

"No, you don't understand," he said, shaking his head.

She followed her dad's gaze out the window. Why was he looking out of the window? This conversation was important.

"Courtney," he said, "pay attention. The West Woods are the key."

Courtney looked at her dad now, whose wistful gaze seemed

almost comical. He really said some crazy things sometimes. The woods were the key to what? What did that even mean?

"Dad, what are you talking about?" She asked, shortly. Her dad was a senator, and looking at him now, all Courtney could think was, it was a good thing his voters never saw him like this. He sounded positively flaky. "We're not even allowed in the woods."

"Ah, but did you ever wonder why?" he asked, suggestively. A smile played at his lips.

Courtney could only stare at her dad. She'd never ventured into the West Woods, though she'd run past them plenty of times. The thought of ever going in gave her the creeps, what with all the unruly branches. Especially in the winter time, when the trees were bare. Was there something more? If there was something he wanted her to know, he could just tell her.

"Dad, the West Woods can't make a track team appear," she said.

"You might be surprised..." he said, trailing off.

His smile had grown wider.

Why was he smiling? This conversation had gone seriously off the rails. She wasn't getting anywhere. Her dad was making less and less sense.

"I've maybe said too much already," he said to her, stepping back from the window. "But I'll make you a deal. You make an effort to find out what makes St. Augustus special. Do everything you can here to pad your college applications. At the end of the year, if you've done these things and you still want to leave, I'll consider it."

Courtney's heart leapt as she took in his wide eyes. He seemed sincere. She breathed deeply. There was a chance she wouldn't have to come back next year. She'd never actually thought he'd agree to let her leave mid-year anyway. This was about all she could have asked for.

"Uh, thanks, Dad," Courtney said quietly. She resisted the urge to look away from his intense gaze, nodding her head in agreement. She'd try anything to get home.

"Good," he said, moving toward the door. He had a small smile on his face, all that was left of his recent excitement.

He stopped at the door and opened his arms to embrace Courtney.

"I have no doubt you'll find it when you're ready," he told her, giving her a rare fatherly squeeze.

Courtney sank down onto her messy bed after the door clicked shut behind him, her mind going in circles. There had to be a way to make this work. If she did what he asked, he'd honor it, she knew that much about his character. But what did he expect her to find, and what would he accept as proof?

There had always been rumors about the school – its founder, Isaac Young, and his supposed curse or magic, the legend of the 'lucky' room... she closed her eyes, trying to remember what the stories were about. She'd never been that interested. What was it about the lucky room that was supposed to be special again?

Courtney shook her head. Those were just silly stories. He'd surely been talking about something else - something to do with the West Woods. She hadn't heard any stories about the woods.

She curled her feet up under her and lay down to nestle into her pillow. A calm feeling spread through her as she imagined herself at home in her own bed. As much as she liked Margaret, it had been nice to have her own room again over the break.

Her dad had gone to St. Augustus a long time ago. He wanted Courtney to find something – something that had been here, then. What if it was gone?

Whatever her dad thought was special about the school, if it was still here, she had time to find it. Another year and a half, to be exact. A groan escaped from her throat as she buried her face in the pillow. *The woods are the key*, he'd said. Had the woods been off limits all those years ago when he'd been at school?

The wheels in Courtney's mind turned, searching for a starting point. Hanna had been here longer. She seemed to love the school almost the same way their dad did... Did she know what Dad was talking about? Maybe he'd told her. Maybe he'd given her a clue what to look for.

Their dad had been a lawyer before he'd become a senator. He would expect proof.

What could she possibly use to persuade him she'd given this her all? If she could get him to see she'd unlocked whatever secrets he expected of her, he might let her leave. She had to be logical about this.

Suddenly not feeling tired anymore, she pushed herself up to a sitting position on the bed. She grabbed a notebook and a pen from her nightstand and pulled them toward her. Her goals should be bold enough to satisfy him - she'd have to pick things that felt beyond her reach.

Hands shaking, Courtney opened the notebook. She set her pen to the page and made a list in her messy scrawl.

Get Home List

1. *Master the secrets of St. Augustus – know more than Dad.*
2. *Win at swimming.*
3. *Make team captain.*

Courtney surprised herself that two of her three items were about swimming. Her dad had seemed focused on her making that work. If Courtney could show she'd accomplished what he wanted her to at St. Augustus, he couldn't argue she hadn't tried.

Team captain was usually reserved for a senior. But waiting for senior year was too long - she wouldn't have any time left to do track at Harbor. Surely it was possible to get it in her junior year. She made a mental list of the juniors on the team now – four girls. She ran through each one in her mind. There wasn't an obvious leader among them. It could happen. Courtney stared at the team captain goal she'd written down. If she did well enough at the swimming itself, maybe her dad would let her leave without becoming team captain.

She raised her pen to strike out the third goal, then hesitated. It was only a list. Nobody would ever see it, it was just something to shoot for. She didn't have to do it all. Instead of striking it out, Courtney doodled in the margin, letting her mind wander. She looked up at the door when she heard the jangle of a key being fit into the door's lock.

"You came back!" Margaret said with a laugh, swinging the door open and stepping inside.

"For now," Courtney conceded, closing her notebook and setting it on the nightstand, "but I have a plan."

"Of course you have a plan!" Margaret said, tossing her small suitcase on her bed and sitting down beside it. "You always have a plan," she teased. The perfect finish of Margaret's covers barely rippled where she sat, they were pulled so tight. "Happy New Year! Was your Christmas awesome?"

"Yeah," Courtney answered, "it was great to get away from here."

"You're so weird," Margaret said. "I'm soooo glad to be back! Everyone's down at the student lounge right now, let's go say hi. Is that a new hoodie?"

"It's from Harbor Heights," Courtney answered.

"Ooooo! Did you meet someone?" Margaret asked, her eyes trained on Courtney.

"No, nothing like that," Courtney answered quickly. She looked over at the notebook on her nightstand. She wasn't going to accomplish everything overnight. Maybe hanging out with the girls tonight would help her formulate a plan.

"Are you coming?" Margaret asked, her hand hovering on the doorknob.

"Sure, let's go," Courtney answered.

CHAPTER TWO

Hanna

Courtney and Margaret entered the student lounge, which was in a huge loft stretched over the lobby of the Main Building. A wide staircase curved up to the space, which could hold the entire student body comfortably. During the winter months, the lounge was where everyone gathered in evenings. Courtney liked to come during the day on the weekends, when the place was deserted, to read. Once the weather got better and the days were longer, the lawn was the more popular place to be.

Courtney caught sight of her sister Hanna, where she sat, as usual, in the middle of a large group of friends. Hanna was laughing whole heartedly at something, her head thrown back.

"I need to talk to my sister," Courtney told Margaret. "I'll be back in a minute."

Margaret made a face.

"What?" Courtney asked. "I'll be back, I swear."

Addressing Margaret's silent accusation that she might slip back to their room, Courtney handed over her jacket to Margaret. It was a thin form of insurance, but Margaret took it and didn't complain further when Courtney headed over to where Hanna sat.

Hanna's dark hair hung down the back of the leather seat – so different from Courtney's own frizzy mop. Courtney stood behind her sister's chair and cleared her throat.

"What?" Hanna asked, not unkindly as she turned toward Courtney. "Didn't you get enough family time over the holidays?"

The two girls usually gave each other a wide berth at school. Sometimes they went weeks without saying much.

Hanna's friends laughed, at Courtney's expense.

"I wanted to talk to you about Dad," answered Courtney simply.

"What about Dad?" Hanna asked, looking between Courtney and her friends. "Is something wrong?"

"No..." Courtney answered. She didn't want to talk to Hanna here. Courtney perched herself on the edge of Hanna's armchair so she wouldn't have to talk as loudly.

Thankfully, Hanna's friends had gone back to their conversation once Courtney had said there was nothing wrong.

"It's just," started Courtney, keeping her voice low, and trying to filter in her head how much she wanted to say, "he acts like there's some big secret at St. Augustus that will make me like this place more. I thought maybe you knew what he was talking about, and that's why you like it here so much." Her words sounded lame, even as she said them out loud.

Hanna's friend, Joy, stifled a giggle.

Courtney had thought they weren't listening.

Hanna nudged Courtney and stood up, taking a step away from her friends. Courtney followed her. "Courtney, let it go," Hanna advised her, squaring her shoulders to face Courtney. "I don't even know why you want to move home. You know, I wasn't really sleeping on the car ride today - I just closed my eyes so I wouldn't have to take sides in your bid to Dad."

Courtney blinked at her sister. She'd thought Hanna would be on her side.

"Honestly, I don't get you," Hanna told her. "Here, we have all the freedom we want. Home, we don't."

Courtney shrugged. St. Augustus didn't feel much like freedom to her.

"Well, he's made it clear I have to stay," Courtney mumbled, aware Hanna's friends had stopped their own conversation to eavesdrop. Courtney inched away from the group further and dropped her voice even more. She fiddled with the sleeve of her hoodie. She didn't really know what she'd expected her sister to offer. "I just thought I'd ask if you knew anything - anything more about the school than he's told me. He acted so weird about it, I thought maybe he'd talked to you about it, too."

"Figure out what Dad's talking about?" Hanna asked, scrunching up her forehead and giving Courtney a funny look. "I almost never know what he's talking about, Courtney."

"Thanks, anyway," Courtney said, smiling thinly. "I just thought... It's just that you have everything here, Hanna." She could hear the desperation in her own voice. "You're doing what Dad wants me to do. I thought maybe the school..."

"There's no magic pill, sis," Hanna told her, taking a step back toward the table and picking up her latte. "Study. Work hard. Hang out and make friends with kids in your grade. That's it."

The part about kids in Courtney's grade was a clear dismissal. Somehow, she'd hoped her sister would have better advice.

"Dad talks about the magic of St. Augustus, but there's no such thing," Hanna assured her, pity written on her face. "As for college, I wouldn't worry about it. Your grades are good, and whether you like it or not, our dad's a senator - that helps your college applications. Maybe that's the silver bullet he's hinting at."

"Oh," Courtney replied flatly. Her stomach stirred. Hanna had gotten into every college she'd applied to. Courtney highly doubted their dad had anything to do with that. Did she think Courtney wouldn't get in without their dad intervening?

Courtney looked up at the high ceiling of the lounge and

blinked, trying to clear her head. She couldn't think of anything else to ask her sister, though she wasn't yet ready to go see her friends. To return to the monotony of the school's routines.

Courtney didn't believe in magic, of course. Surely their father didn't, either. Courtney looked back at Hanna's face. Was that a twitch at Hanna's eye? Maybe she knew something after all.

"Hanna?" Courtney prompted.

"I'll come find you," Hanna told her firmly. It was a second dismissal.

Courtney's spirits lifted slightly as Hanna turned away from Courtney and stepped back toward her friends. Courtney stared at her sister's back for a moment before turning away herself. Hanna knew something.

CHAPTER THREE

Dared

"Nice of you to join us," said Violet, as Courtney returned to the group of sophomores after leaving Hanna. "No books to read in your corner tonight?"

Courtney flopped down into an armchair, landing on top of the jacket she'd given to Margaret as collateral.

Violet meant no harm, but Courtney wasn't in the mood. Violet was one of her oldest friends – their parents had been friends since before the two girls were born. Courtney had begged her parents not to make her room with Violet when they'd come to school last year. Violet had always been the first one to break the ice in a crowd, while Courtney took more time to warm up. She could be a little much.

Tonight, Violet wore a mauve top with a poofy purple skirt. Her leggings were white, but even they had large purple dots scattered from top to bottom.

Violet's outrageous style and excessive use of purple in her wardrobe always made Courtney smile, though it had made a lot more sense when they'd been nine than it did now.

"Margaret is trying to encourage me to socialize more," Courtney said, addressing Violet's jab. More than a dozen of their classmates sat nearby, all talking over each other about what they'd done over the holidays. The din was disorienting.

"Well, you should socialize more!" Margaret chimed in. "In fact, Violet, I've decided we're going to get Courtney a boyfriend this semester."

"Sounds like fun," Violet answered, with a pleasant twinkle in her eye.

"Great," said Courtney, with a weak smile. Her friends were always trying to 'help' Courtney with something or other. She found the easiest way to make them give up was to ignore their meddling.

"Does anyone here know much about Isaac Young or the West Woods?" Courtney asked, speaking loudly to include anyone nearby.

"What does that have to do with you getting a boyfriend?" Violet asked, her face falling.

"Violet!" Courtney exclaimed, swatting Violet hard on the leg. Violet had said that loudly.

"The West Woods are scary," piped up Jules, a perky girl also in tenth grade. She sat on her boyfriend Jake's lap a few seats away from Courtney.

"Well, they don't scare me," said Jake, laughing. "It's just a bunch of trees."

"Then, I challenge you to a dare!" Jules replied, giving him a playful punch on the shoulder.

"Ooo, Truth or dare!" Violet exclaimed, clapping her hands together. "Yes, let's!"

Courtney looked around the student lounge. Truth or dare was her cue to leave. Reading in her room was even better than reading in the corner of the lounge, when Margaret wasn't there.

"Okay, Jake – Mr. Tough Guy," Jules said, reaching over to tousle his blond hair. "I dare you to run into the West Woods, do a loop and then come back."

Courtney froze as she registered Jules' suggestion, though it seemed silly, now that she thought about it, that students were banned. It was just a bunch of trees, and it was right on the edge of campus.

"Hey," Jake protested. "Why am I the only one who has to go?"

"Because you're the one who said you weren't scared," Courtney answered, surprising herself.

A sly smile spread over Jake's face.

"Well, then I dare you, Courtney, to come with me," he stated, crossing his arms across his chest and looking right at her.

Courtney blinked and looked around the student lounge. These were the most words that Jake had ever said to her. There were no teachers in sight, but it was the first night back from break – there were still students arriving even at this late hour, and a few parents hanging around the dorms. The teachers were probably too distracted to be watching the woods. Jake would be with her, she wouldn't be alone.

"Because you're the one who asked about the woods in the first place," he added.

"Come on, Courtney, live a little," Violet urged her. "The teachers won't miss you, they don't even know you're here!"

The chatter in the larger group suddenly went silent. All eyes were on Courtney.

Courtney looked around the lounge. There didn't seem to be anyone in charge. She'd already made up her mind to go, but didn't want to seem too eager. A nervous energy spread through her as she nodded her head and pulled on her jacket. Her dad had practically told her to go to the West Woods. Getting started on her quest to find her dad's secret seemed much better than staying here and listening to Margaret and Violet plan how to get her a date.

Courtney glanced toward the exit. It was a dark January night, though it wasn't yet late. She and Jake would have to cross the campus lawn in full view of the Main Building. Courtney felt her heartbeat throb all the way up in her throat. Any night in the past she would have turned this dare down flat. Tonight, she felt different. If they didn't go now, she might lose her nerve.

Courtney's legs shook slightly as she stood, whether from excitement or fear didn't matter to her at that moment.

"Let's go," she said, meeting Jake's gaze.

Jake's face broke out into a wide smile and he hopped to his feet as well.

"Courtney," Margaret said in a low, urgent voice, grabbing Courtney's arm. "You don't have to go."

"Yes, she does," Violet said laughing, pulling Margaret back. "She's been dared."

"I'm good," Courtney answered, gently removing Margaret's hand from her arm.

Margaret let out a squeaking sound that sounded suspiciously like a whimper.

"Ready?" Jake asked her as she joined him at the top of the winding staircase that led out of the lounge.

Courtney took a deep breath and nodded as the group erupted in a supportive cheer. Heads all over the student lounge popped up and looked their way.

Courtney scanned the room for Hanna. She saw her right where she'd left her earlier, though her back was to them. Courtney turned toward Jake.

"Shh," Jake told the group in an urgent whisper. "You're going to get us busted."

Despite Jake's request, the group of sophomores crowded against the balcony railing to watch them leave the building. The lawn and the distant woods were visible through the large leaded windows that stretched from floor to ceiling in the foyer.

Courtney winced at how exposed they'd be, but followed closely behind Jake as he bounded down the steps and out the front door.

"We should probably run, so we're not gone too long," Jake said to her, after waiting for her at the edge of the lawn. "Let me know if you can't keep up."

Courtney laughed. He didn't know her very well. She could keep up.

The unlikely pair sprinted across the frost crusted grass. There wasn't enough snow on the ground to leave footprints, Courtney thought. She let Jake lead. If they ran behind the West Building on the way to the woods, they'd at least have some cover. Courtney was grateful the teachers' residence was tucked on the other side of the Main Building. They weren't in their line of sight, at least.

"Don't go behind the West Building," Jake called over his shoulder. "If they can't see us go into the woods, it won't count."

Courtney had almost forgotten the dare. She didn't much care if she got credit for it, though she adjusted her game plan accordingly.

Closing in on the West Woods, Courtney looked back over her shoulder, half expecting to see a teacher or Giles the caretaker running after them. There was nothing but the warm glow of the Main Building spilling out onto the lawn. Jake plunged into the trees without looking back. Courtney was close behind him.

As they passed the tree line at the edge of the woods, Courtney imagined crossing an invisible barrier, as if breaking through the tape at the finish line of a race. They hadn't found a path, exactly – the trees were tightly spaced and it was difficult to keep running. Jake showed no signs of slowing, so she kept as close behind him as she could, holding her arms in front of her face to keep stray branches from hitting her eyes.

Courtney nearly crashed into Jake as he came to an abrupt halt.

"What do you think, did we go far enough?" Jake asked, his breathing ragged. He turned to face Courtney.

Courtney also struggled to catch her breath, but not from the run. Her canvas runners were soaked through, her hands stung with scratches from the branches and she was standing in the West Woods with a boy from the football team who'd dared her to be here. They still had to get back without being seen. She felt alive.

She nodded her head, taking a deep breath to steady herself. There was no time to explore tonight, but she could come back. This hadn't been hard - she could do it again. Her dad had said the West Woods were the key. She would come back.

Jake swung himself around a tree trunk and headed back toward the campus.

Courtney took a few steps deeper into the woods to touch the same tree trunk Jake had just circled before turning to go back - somehow it seemed important to go as far as he had.

The woods seemed darker on the way back. She lengthened her stride to catch up to Jake, who'd pulled ahead. Just as she glimpsed the campus lights through the trees, her foot hit a pile of wet leaves and skidded forward. She lost her balance and felt herself fall. It all happened quickly as the leaves under her right foot gave way, trapping her leg knee-deep in a hole.

Courtney yelped in surprise.

In a moment, Jake had doubled back and was at her side.

"Are you okay?" he asked, squatting down to her level. "What happened?"

"I'm okay, I think," Courtney answered, wondering if she was. "But my foot's stuck in this hole. Give me a hand?"

Jake hoisted her up out of the hole and Courtney tested her weight on the foot that had been trapped. She'd turned her ankle, but it didn't feel too bad. She could probably walk.

The flashlight from Jake's phone stung Courtney's eyes as she blinked to see what she'd fallen into.

"Odd," Jake said, poking at the hole with a stick. "It looks like some kind of trap."

"A trap?" Courtney repeated, kneeling beside him and helping to clear away the leaves with her hands. Her hands ached with the cold.

"Maybe not a trap, but it's lined with wood, see?" Said Jake pointing to the inside of the square opening. "Looks like there was a cover over the top of it, but now it's rotted through. It could be a box?" He pulled up a square piece of soggy plywood that had a giant hole in the middle where Courtney's foot had broken through.

Courtney looked down at where she'd fallen, curiously. His light didn't help much, throwing odd shadows into the hole. Before she could think better of it, she reached her bare hand down to feel around. She felt Jake's breath on her neck, as he leaned in over her. Courtney's hand closed around a solid bundle.

She pulled the small, lumpy mass out of the hole and held it in front of Jake's light.

"It's filthy, leave it," Jake told her, his nose wrinkled.

Instead, Courtney had already started unwrapping the lengths of dirty cloth wound tightly like yarn.

"It's a tiny mummy!" Jake said with a laugh, looking at the coil of rags on the ground.

Working as quickly as she could with her numbed fingers she pried the tight cloth apart. As she got closer to the center, the cloth looked cleaner. It had maybe once been green, but had faded with time. Something solid slipped from the bundle and fell quietly into the leaves.

"Ah!" Courtney exclaimed, diving down to rummage for whatever had fallen.

Jake panned his light back and forth across the area as she searched.

Courtney felt something hard and cold and grabbed it. Holding it under the light, she could see it was something made from aged metal.

"It's a key," Jake announced flatly.

CHAPTER FOUR

The Key to Everything?

"Why would someone bury a key?" Jake asked Courtney, unimpressed.

"I don't know," said Courtney, her voice wavering from the cold. Her hand shook as she took the key and tucked it into her jacket pocket.

Her dad had said the West Woods were the key. Had he literally meant a key? Courtney shuddered. She didn't believe in coincidences. What did this key have to do with her dad? Was twenty-five years long enough to rot a wooden box? Maybe. More likely it had been there long before his time. Had he known? She wiped her grimy hands on the outside of her coat.

"Let's go, it's freezing out here," Jake said, standing up. "We've been gone too long. Can you walk?"

"Yeah, I think I can walk," Courtney answered, as she stood up shakily and brushed off her jeans. "But I probably shouldn't run."

"Okay, we can walk," Jake said as they picked their way back through the trees toward the lawn.

As they reached the edge of the woods, a figure came running toward them.

"I guess Jules couldn't wait for us," Jake said with a laugh.

"What took you so long?" Jules called at them.

Courtney didn't miss the accusatory tone.

Jules jumped into Jake's arms when she reached them.

He reached out to catch her, laughing.

"What happened?" she demanded, poking him in the chest, and giving Courtney an unfriendly look.

Courtney was thankful for the dark, to hide the muddy state of her clothes. They couldn't have been gone more than fifteen minutes.

"Courtney hurt her ankle, so we had to stop," Jake said, kissing Jules full on the lips. "You worry too much."

Jake set Jules on her feet and offered Courtney his arm to help her walk.

"You're limping," Jake said. "Let me help."

Courtney gratefully accepted his support. Her ankle throbbed.

Jules clutched Jake's other arm tightly and the trio headed toward the pools of light coming from the Main Building.

A few of Jake's friends had made their way outside, crowded around outside the heavy main doors.

"We thought the ghost of Isaac Young got you guys!" Jeff, one of Jake's buddies called to them as they approached. His voice echoed in the night air.

Courtney looked around the lawn before reminding herself that they were allowed to be on the grass. She could have hurt her ankle anywhere, if they had to explain. It didn't have to have happened in the West Woods. She felt her shoulders relax a little as they reached the stairs.

Courtney used the railing as well as Jake's arm to climb up to the Main Building – she didn't want to push it.

"Nah, we went clear to the other side of the woods and back," Jake said, dropping Courtney's arm as they reached the top.

"Yeah, sure," the boys said as they slapped Jake on the back and followed them into the building.

They hadn't seemed to notice the state Courtney was in.

"Are you okay?" Margaret asked, rushing down the steps from the lounge as Courtney entered the foyer. "What happened? You're all muddy."

"I fell in a hole and twisted my ankle," Courtney told her, pulling the key out of her pocket to examine it in the light. "And I found this."

It was a very large, old fashioned key, as large as Courtney's hand. The metal it had once been peeked through in a few spots, but the rest was rusted over almost completely.

"What's it for?" Margaret asked, looking down her nose at it.

"I have no idea," Courtney admitted, looking at the key in her hand. Whatever it was, it looked like it hadn't been used in a long time.

"C'mon," Margaret said, tugging Courtney up the stairs to the lounge. "Let's go show Violet."

"Truth," chose Jeff as they arrived at the seats they'd been in earlier. He apparently hadn't missed a beat after rejoining the group.

"You missed a few dares," Violet told them by way of explanation.

Courtney groaned to herself. The game was still going. She should have had Margaret help her to her room instead of coming back.

"Okay, okay," said Rhoda, who'd clearly challenged him. "Did you, or did you not cheat on our history midterm in ninth grade."

Margaret giggled as she sat down next to Rhoda.

Rhoda swam with them, though Courtney wasn't as friendly with her as Margaret.

"Um, can I still pick dare?" Jeff asked sheepishly, sending the group into fits of giggles.

Clearly, he'd cheated.

Courtney edged herself to the fringe of the gathering, leaning on the chairs she passed for support. This game was ridiculous.

"I dare you to slide down the banister into the foyer!" Jeff challenged another.

The dare was accepted, and another of Courtney's classmates slid down the curved banister into the foyer, in plain view of everyone who cared to watch. Courtney looked around, but the game seemed to be going unchecked. Where were all the teachers tonight?

She looked again at the key, which she still held. Her hands were smudged with dirt. The game seemed to have turned into chaos, she should be able to slip away unnoticed, though she might need Margaret or Violet's help to get back to the dorm on her ankle.

Courtney tried to catch her friends' attention, but the spotlight was on them and they weren't looking her way. Margaret revealed she would be a horse if she could be any animal and Violet admitted her first crush had been on a friend of her brother's. Courtney yawned and sank down on the armrest of one of the chairs. She was ready for bed, but she'd stick it out until there was a lull in the activity and she could get some help. She could wait a bit.

It was Violet's turn to challenge, and Courtney looked up from the key in her hands to see Violet staring straight at her.

"Truth or dare?" Violet asked Courtney.

Courtney's heart sank. What was Violet up to?

"I'm just leaving," Courtney said, shaking her head wildly as she pushed herself unsteadily to her feet.

"No, no," Violet insisted, coming over to give Courtney her arm for support. "You can't leave when it's your turn. It's against the rules. Choose."

Courtney gritted her teeth. Whatever it was had better be quick.

"Dare, I guess," answered Courtney, tucking the key into her coat pocket. "But it has to be something I don't have to move much for," she clarified.

"Okay, then I dare you to kiss…" Violet said, looking around the circle, "Ethan!" she proclaimed, pointing across the circle at Ethan Roth.

Courtney felt all the blood drain from her face. The room seemed to stop as she stared open-mouthed at Violet. *What?*

She looked around. Nobody else seemed to be protesting. Was this even allowed? All her earlier excitement at trying something new had fled. This was a really bad idea.

"No," Courtney stammered.

"Oh, come on," Violet teased.

Titters erupted around the circle.

"Just kiss him, then I'll help you back to the dorm," Violet assured her.

Courtney looked around at the rest of the group, her gaze resting on Ethan, who had a half smile of amusement on his face. He could refuse the dare.

She looked to Margaret for support, who smiled at her encouragingly and came over.

Margaret tugged Courtney's coat off.

"It's really dirty," Margaret whispered to her.

Courtney let Margaret take her jacket. She was too stunned to protest. Was this their plan to get her a boyfriend? Her cheeks warmed. Ethan was nice enough, but…

"I'll take truth," Courtney heard herself say, her voice cracking slightly. She avoided looking in Ethan's direction.

"No!" Violet protested, taking Courtney by the elbow and guiding her over to where Ethan stood. "You picked dare – can't change your mind!"

Courtney stared at Violet, her mouth agape. *What the hell?*

"It's time you dated," Violet hissed in her ear, nudging Courtney forward. "Ethan's perfect for you."

Courtney looked over at Ethan, who hopped to his feet,

apparently accepting his fate. He took a step forward toward Courtney. Courtney reached up to smooth her hair. She took a deep breath and considered her choices. She'd been in the West Woods tonight. Her dad had told her to embrace St. Augustus.

Yes, Courtney decided. Nobody else seemed to think this was crazy. She could do this.

Ethan grinned where he stood. He didn't look as nervous as she felt. He didn't look completely disgusted with the idea, either, Courtney told herself.

Violet blew a bubble with her gum and let it pop on her face. No help there.

This would be... an adventure, she told herself. Like the woods earlier. Courtney looked at Ethan as if he had the answer. She could do this – and then she could go to bed, let her ankle rest, and leave this crazy day behind.

She stood in front of Ethan now and looked up – he was several inches taller than her. The chatter in the group had stopped and she could hear her own heartbeat, pounding in her ears. She was close enough to notice how soapy and clean he smelled. Her hands and knees were covered in mud. Everyone was watching.

How hard could it be? Courtney's gaze locked with Ethan's. This didn't seem hard for him.

The circle of their classmates was surprisingly quiet. If someone had catcalled just then, she might have turned and hobbled away. She knew she didn't have to do this. Yet, she stayed.

Her stomach tightened. Courtney pictured the kisses she'd seen a hundred times on TV. She took a deep breath and closed her eyes, leaning in. As she felt Ethan come closer to her, she parted her lips and tipped her head up to meet him. The moment they met in the middle, his warm, dry lips surprised her. He pulled away quickly, pushing her slightly so she took a step backward and stumbled on her bad ankle.

Margaret was there to catch her.

The circle erupted in hoots of laughter.

Courtney's eyes flew open as she looked at Ethan, who wiped his mouth lightly on his sleeve. She'd done it. Her insides tickled. She'd fallen, but she'd completed the dare.

Courtney clutched Margaret for support as she smiled at Ethan a little, grateful he'd not made this into a big deal.

"Uh, sorry," Ethan stammered at Courtney, looking down at the ground. "You surprised me, there."

The whole group around them howled with laughter. Everyone in the student lounge looked their way. Courtney looked around, confusion swirling in her head. They were laughing. They were laughing at Ethan and her. Or, were they only laughing at her? The kiss had been so quick. She replayed the moment where their lips had touched.

Courtney's cheeks flamed hot as the sinking realization set in. She looked around the circle at her classmates, some of whom had tears streaming down their faces. Ethan's lips had been dry. She'd gone in for a dramatic, soap opera kiss.

"Courtney, it's late, I'm heading to bed. Did you want to come?" said Margaret, was guiding her by the elbow.

Courtney's heart hammered in her chest, though she nodded at Margaret.

"Goodnight!" Courtney called to Ethan loudly. She blinked at the sound of her own voice. Where had that come from?

"Come on, Courtney," Violet said. She'd appeared at Courtney's other side, propelling her lightly toward the door.

"Ms. Krick!" Margaret exclaimed, stopping in her tracks.

As the threesome shuffled away from the group, they'd come face to face with the elderly teacher.

Ms. Krick's gray-white hair was pulled tightly into a roll behind her head. Her small frame only seemed marginally taller in the sensible gray heels she wore.

"What's with all the racket, Miss Wallis?" Ms. Krick asked her, straightening her thin frame.

"Uh, nothing Ms. Krick," Courtney stammered, looking back at the group. How much had Ms. Krick seen and heard? Miraculously, the group they'd just left were suddenly on their best behavior and looking anywhere but in Courtney's direction. "I... I was just leaving."

"Well, keep it down," Ms. Krick addressed the group behind the girls, narrowing her eyes.

A scattering of snickers reached Courtney's ears.

Ms. Krick whipped around to glare at the other side of the circle. The outburst stopped abruptly. With one last withering look, Ms. Krick walked slowly through the middle of the gathering and continued to the other end of the lounge.

Taking their cue, Courtney, Margaret and Violet made a beeline toward the stairs. Courtney put more weight on her ankle than was advisable.

"You are so brave!" Margaret whispered to her on the way down the stairs. "No way I could have kissed him in front of all of those people."

"Ethan was so surprised," Violet giggled as the three left the foyer.

Courtney shot her a withering look.

"What?" Violet laughed. "What were you doing, anyway? Jake said it looked like you were trying to eat him."

"Thanks," Courtney mumbled, as she tugged open the door to the dorm.

"Violet, shush!" Margaret hissed.

"Sorry!" Violet called to Courtney, who'd shrugged off their support and pulled ahead of them in the hall. "I won't laugh again, I promise!"

Courtney barely heard her as she arrived at the door to her

room. The kiss with Ethan hadn't gone well, but who cared? Truth or dare was a silly game. Ethan was nice, but Courtney hadn't really given him a second look before tonight. Besides, she had work to do. She had her list to work on. If leaving campus had been a priority before, it was doubly so now.

"Courtney, I'm sorry," Violet told her, panting from the effort of walking so quickly. "I thought you'd like kissing Ethan. I mean, who wouldn't? Remember you agreed to let us find you a boyfriend?"

Courtney had most certainly not agreed.

"I wouldn't have..." Violet continued. "I mean I didn't know you were – er – going to do that! All you had to do was kiss him, not swallow him whole." She broke off into a fresh fit of giggles.

If Violet was trying to give her a pep talk, it wasn't working.

"Violet," Courtney said, putting her hand on her friend's arm, "it's fine. It was just a dare." She wished Violet would let it go.

"Ethan would be great for you," Violet continued. "He might even join you on your crazy morning runs. He's sporty!"

"Thanks," Courtney replied, an edge creeping into her voice. "If you like him, you're welcome to him. I'm good if you girls want to go back," Courtney told them, opening the dorm room door.

"I'll just walk Violet to her room," Margaret said, her voice a little unsteady.

Courtney nodded and stepped into the room. Violet's room was just a few doors down. Margaret was giving Courtney space. It was appreciated.

Courtney walked to the window and looked out toward the West Woods. The outline of trees was barely discernible in the dark. She'd been out there, and she'd found a key. She'd also kissed Ethan Roth tonight.

A giggle escaped from Courtney. She'd kissed Ethan Roth – kissed him very badly, in fact. No matter. She'd know better now when she kissed someone for real.

CHAPTER FIVE

Run, Run Away

Courtney's eyes flew open the next morning to the annoying buzz of her alarm clock. Expertly, she whipped her hand out from under the covers and switched it off.

She looked toward the bed on the other side of the darkened room as the previous evening's events flooded back to her. Margaret stirred a little, though she didn't open her eyes.

Bracing herself for oncoming pain, Courtney pointed and flexed her right foot under the covers – surprisingly, it felt okay.

"Cooouurtney," Margaret moaned, pulling the covers up over her head, "what time is it?"

"It's early, go back to sleep," Courtney answered, swinging her feet over the side of the bed and putting some weight on her offending foot.

"Can you at least get a less annoying alarm?" Margaret groaned, peeking out from under her duvet. This was the second year the girls had roomed together and they weren't the best match, schedule-wise.

"Sorry," Courtney said, laughing lightly.

Deciding her ankle was good enough, Courtney quickly tied her hair into a ponytail and got dressed without turning on the lights. Margaret would go back to sleep – she always did.

Courtney reached under her bed for her running shoes and pulled them on roughly. Her weak ankle smarted as she stuffed her feet in, but quieted down once she'd done the laces up snugly. Accidentally closing the door more loudly than she usually did, she slipped out into the dim hallway.

The chill in the air hit her face with a slap as she stepped outside. New snow covered the stairs and the lawn. Little enough that it would be gone once the sun was up. The sun came up this time of year just as she returned from her morning runs – the sunrise a beautiful reward for her effort. The fresh coat of white powder mixed with ice crunched under her shoes as she made her way, at a slow jog, to the edge of campus. Her breath hung in white clouds, glowing under the street lamps as she exhaled. Once she got going, the cold didn't usually bother her. She was happy to see that the sidewalks had already been cleared.

Courtney sniffed at the chilly air as a familiar acrid smell wafted from the ground. Her nostrils flared as she checked the bottom of her shoes. A good smear of dog poop lined the bottom of one, its freshness leaving a wet sheen jammed between the treads.

Ugh. Courtney's nose wrinkled with distaste. Her family had a black lab named Coal, and though he was a part of their family, she'd never warmed to picking up after him. Vigorously, she scraped her shoe against the new fallen snow, which provided little resistance.

Resigned to the fact she'd have to clean it better later, she fit her earbuds into her ears and started the GPS on her phone. She'd decided she would do a slow loop toward Evergreen's center and back. No point pushing it today, with her ankle only at half-health.

Each song on her running playlist was selected for its steady pace. While she ran, she rarely thought of anything but putting one foot in front of the other. This morning, though, something was off. She skipped past the first song, then the next, trying to find a rhythm. After her encounter with Ethan last night, there'd been little else on her mind and she'd thought a run would help, despite her injury. It wasn't working.

Had her dad been right that she was the one not taking advantage of what she had? The question had nagged her all night. The woods were the answer, she played in her mind. *The answer to what?* Courtney slowed down. If she turned now and ran back past the campus, she could check out the woods and still be back in time to get ready for class.

Her music was interrupted for her GPS to report her unusually slow pace. She'd only gone one mile. This run was a write off anyway, she reasoned, though she made no change to her course.

Evergreen's Main Street opened up before her as she approached. Her regular route went down one side, then back on the other, though she probably shouldn't go as far as she normally would. She spun on her good foot and headed back in the direction she'd come from. Before she knew it, she'd run right past the campus. Every step she took now brought her closer to the West Woods. Her gut stirred. What exactly would she do when she got there? Could she actually go in?

She mapped out what she knew of the woods in her mind as she ran. The place where she'd found the key with Jake was far from the road she was on. Courtney slowed as the dark trees of the woods took shape ahead on her left.

Walking now, she surveyed the woods. The trees were set back about ten feet from the sidewalk. They were so close, she'd only have to venture a few steps. Yet she didn't veer from the pavement. Keeping her course, she watched the shadows between the trees curiously. It was too dark to see much. She stopped on the path, staring into the woods.

A whistling sound rang from above as the morning breeze echoed through the bare tree tops. Courtney felt gooseflesh break out on her forearms under her jacket. She could go into the woods another day, she told herself. She had plenty of time.

Feeling release at her decision, she turned back toward the campus, intending to retrace her steps.

"Ohhh," Courtney exclaimed, looking up to see the pink glow of dawn shoot up from the horizon in rays of light. Sweat dripped down her brow from her moderate exertion, growing clammy with the cold.

Clutching her phone, she didn't bother trying to capture a picture. Sunrise was much better in person. She watched the sky change slowly until the pink light diffused into a haze that covered the sky. Courtney inhaled through her nose, feeling cleansed somehow from the thoughts that had clouded her mind when she'd set out.

She glanced quickly to her right. The woods were still there, looking less ominous as the sun began to flood the sky. She pressed stop on her GPS, curious how far her altered route had taken her. Courtney frowned at the running app. She must have run further than it said. She touched the map button again to reveal the traces of where she'd been. She blinked three times at the screen. Her route was recorded, but the thick green line was broken. Long gaps showed a sporadic path. Her GPS wasn't showing her whole run. Weird.

She used her fingers to zoom in for a closer look. It had traced her path into town and back, until she reached the West Woods, where it stopped... The hair on Courtney's arms prickled. She looked toward the woods, then back at her phone. The sections missed were in front of the West Woods.

She stared at the screen for what seemed like minutes, until a spiral appeared in the top right corner, indicating an update. Watching the green line fill itself in, Courtney laughed out loud. The screen had refreshed and her route loaded in front of her eyes. The path looked just as it should. Why wouldn't it?

Feeling limp with relief, Courtney stretched her arms above her head, just as she heard a rustle coming from the trees next to her. She froze. The sound grew louder. Something low to the ground was heading toward her. Courtney looked toward the woods, then back at the campus. Before she could decide how to react, a blur of fur tackled her to the ground.

Courtney screamed as she was knocked onto the pavement, beating her assailant with her fists in front of her face. Warm wet spread across her fists as the intruder littered her with sloppy dog kisses. She relaxed a little as she realized the white and gray puppy posed no real threat. She tugged at his collar to pull him off her. An uncomfortable chill rocked through her. The damp on the ground seeped through her clothes where she sat. She pushed the strange dog aside and sat up. The small husky nuzzled her leg playfully, his leash lolling to one side.

"Are you lost?" Courtney asked the pup, her fear subsiding. She grabbed hold of his leash.

"Sorry!" called a voice coming from the woods.

A boy about her age, with hair as orange as her own, burst through the edge of the trees and scooped the puppy up in his arms.

"Are you okay?" he asked Courtney. "He ran into the woods and I couldn't catch him," the boy explained, breathless from his chase. "Then he ran out again."

Courtney nodded, rubbing her elbow where it had struck the pavement.

"The trees are really thick in there," the boy continued. "It makes it hard to chase him. He's just a pup. He doesn't like being on a leash, He got free and then he just ran..."

"No problem," Courtney said, pulling herself up to a kneeling position beside the puppy. "He's cute. Playful." She reached out a hand to the pup.

"He's Husk, I'm Cole," Cole extended his hand.

"Courtney," she replied, accepting the boost to get her on her feet. Her legs buckled a little as she put weight on her injured ankle. It stung again in a way it hadn't when she'd been running. "I have a dog back home... his name is Coal," she blurted, reaching down to give her ankle a poke.

"What?" Cole asked. The freckles on his nose wrinkled with his quizzical expression.

"It's true," Courtney said, straightening up, "but coal, like black coal."

"Oh," Cole said, seeming to turn over this information in his mind. "You go to St. Augustus, right?" Cole asked as he caught Husk's leash. "I saw you a few times out running before Christmas, near my house. Husk joined our family just a few months ago and he's been waking me up early. You run fast."

"Um, Yeah." Courtney answered, hoping she didn't seem too full of herself. She did run fast.

"I go to school in town," Cole added.

"Evergreen High?" She asked.

"Yep," He answered, nodding. "Tenth grade."

"Me too," Courtney answered, pleased. She would have guessed he was at least a junior.

"Sure is a beautiful sunrise," Cole said, standing facing the brightening sky.

Courtney took in the deep oranges and pinks that now spread across the whole horizon. Wispy clouds drew the light out into horizontal shapes. She leaned heavily to one side, favoring her sore ankle.

"Are you hurt?" Cole asked, his brow furrowed. "Husk and I will walk you back. Do you need help?"

"I'm fine," Courtney answered quickly, looking away from the painted sky and testing her ankle again by shifting more weight onto it. She could walk.

"I just moved to Evergreen from Rhode Island this fall," Cole said, as they started toward campus. "Husk likes to wake up early – we walk most mornings. That's when I've seen you running."

Courtney stole a look at Cole. She'd never seen him in the mornings, but she rarely paid attention to anyone once she got going. He had a nice smile. His teeth were straight and very white. His cheeks were ruddy from his chase through the woods.

"It's great you're so disciplined," Cole added quickly. "I've been meaning to start up again, but Husk is still too little to go far..."

"Seems he's ready now," Courtney said, laughing at Cole's puppy weaving in and out of their legs as they walked.

"Yeah, I guess – if you'd like some company on your runs?" He replied, giving her a sideways look.

Courtney sized Cole up. He'd said he lived in town - new to town. If she met him for a run in the dark morning, it wouldn't be weird, would it? Besides, Husk was pretty cute.

"You don't mind getting up this early?" Courtney asked, hesitantly. Her gaze found his and she looked at him curiously.

"I'm up anyway," Cole said, pointing to Husk with a laugh. "But really, I come to watch the sunrise. It's beautiful how it illuminates the St. Augustus buildings. It looks almost magical."

There was that word again. Magic.

"The buildings?" said Courtney, tilting her head and squinting a little toward the sun. "Really?"

"Well, to me, I guess," Cole said with a small laugh. "Since we arrived in town I've been fascinated by the Main Building. It's such a mix of architectures – gothic, with Victorian influences for sure. I've never been inside, though – what's it like?"

"The inside?" Courtney asked, raising her eyebrows. "Well, it's plain, I suppose – except for the foyer. The ceiling in there is painted, with gold leaf beams. It's pretty cool actually, I've just never really thought about it."

"I've heard about the frescos on the ceiling," Cole said, nodding his head, "I would love to see them." He looked at Courtney expectantly.

She looked back toward the campus.

"Maybe another time," Courtney said. "It's a little early to be bringing someone into the school, most everyone's still sleeping."

"Oh, of course I didn't expect to see it right now," he said, quickly, "just that I'd like to see it sometime."

Courtney relaxed a little.

The first pause in their conversation seemed long.

"So, are we running tomorrow morning, or what?" Cole asked, fiddling with Husk's leash shyly.

"Sure," Courtney replied, watching Cole's face as he smiled at her. What was she doing? She liked running alone. That was mostly the point.

"Tomorrow morning, then, same time?" he asked. "Or, do you think you'll be able to?" he added quickly, gesturing to her ankle.

"I'll be fine by then," Courtney answered confidently.

"Great," Cole said eagerly. "Husk and I will watch for you and join you on your way into town."

"Sure," Courtney answered. She took a sideways look at him. He didn't look like much of a runner. He didn't seem athletic, at all. Still, he had a certain charm. If she didn't beat her personal best every run, that was okay with her. She found she wanted to see him again. Husk hopped playfully around Cole's legs. Dogs were good judges of character, weren't they?

They'd reached the edge of campus. Husk scampered on and off the small snow banks in an excited dance.

"Am I, I mean..." Cole trailed off as he stopped on the sidewalk and looked up at the Main Building. "Am I allowed on the campus? I've never been sure."

"Well, maybe not at this hour," Courtney laughed, imagining Bessie, her house mother, if she saw Cole walking with Courtney across the lawn. No, she'd see him tomorrow. "But I will show you the foyer some other time, if you'd like."

"That sounds great," Cole answered, his face splitting into a wide grin. "Okay, well then I guess I'll see you in the morning."

"Sure," Courtney answered, reaching to give Husk a quick rub behind his ear. She turned and took a step toward the campus, to realize too late her legs had been ensnared in Husk's leash. He'd managed to wrap it around her as he'd bounced between the sidewalk and the snow. Courtney leaned smack into Cole. His quick thinking caught her and saved her from hitting the pavement for a second time that morning.

"Whoa," he said, bracing her arms with his, "are you okay?"

The pair stood facing one another, their arms held as if at a seventh-grade dance where the chaperones made sure you didn't dance too closely together. Courtney felt a little dizzy as she looked up at him. He was a good head taller than her – even taller than Ethan, she thought. Courtney hoped he couldn't smell the faint odor still coming from her soiled shoe.

Looking into her eyes, Cole slowly slipped his arms down her back to her waist until he held her in a casual embrace. Courtney felt her back tingle from his touch through her thin running jacket.

After a long moment where they both stood grinning stupidly at one another, Courtney found her voice.

"Yeah," She said softly, and then cleared her throat slightly. "I'm fine."

Cole still smiled widely at her.

Courtney's stomach did flip flops as she looked at him, looking at her.

They'd somehow moved their bodies closer together, until she could feel their hips touch.

Suddenly, Courtney felt a rise of panic. Was he going to kiss her? Her mind flashed back to the night before, to her sort-of-kiss with Ethan. But then Cole released her and crouched down to unwind Husk's leash from her legs. The moment was gone.

"So, uh," Courtney stammered, looking up toward the dorm. The darkness was all but gone, and there were no trees or other cover between where they stood and the Main Building.

It wouldn't do at all for Bessie to see her standing out here at this hour with a boy. She liked the freedom of her runs. She didn't dare go out in the dark this early at home – Boston was a little different than sleepy Evergreen. Freedom. Just like Hanna had said. Maybe it wasn't so bad.

"See you tomorrow?" she asked. She shook out her ankle. It seemed about the same as it had when she'd started out that morning.

"Absolutely," Cole answered, closing the gap between them to grab her hand and give it a light squeeze, before dropping it again.

"Great," Courtney answered, her voice much higher and more enthusiastic than she'd meant it to be. With a small wave, she turned and jogged across the campus toward the girls' dorm without looking back until she reached the entrance.

Taking a peek in the direction she'd left him as she pulled her keys out of her jacket pocket, she saw he still stood at the edge of the lawn.

He lifted a hand in a wave to her and she could see even from the distance he was still smiling.

She waved back, turned her key in the lock to the dorm and pulled the door open more clumsily than she would have liked. She didn't know if he still watched her, but didn't dare look back again.

Her heart hammered in her chest as she walked lightly down the dim hallway toward her room. She had some sort of date tomorrow morning – with a guy with the same name as her black lab. It seemed a good sign.

The hallway of the dorm was still quiet. Smiling, she carefully opened the door to her room. Thin morning sun peeked through the closed blinds. Not surprisingly, Margaret was still asleep.

Courtney stood beside Margaret's bed for a moment. Margaret probably wouldn't stir for another half hour or so, then she'd scramble to breakfast so she wouldn't be late for class.

Courtney hugged herself. She was going to see Cole again. She grabbed her things and headed down the hall for a shower, whistling softly under her breath.

CHAPTER SIX

The Rest of Monday

Courtney walked into the cafeteria a short while later feeling light, despite having to favor her right foot a bit. As Courtney approached their regular table after getting some breakfast, she squinted to see what Violet was doing - something with waving her arms in the air. Only Violet was there that morning. The rest of the table was empty.

Courtney's mood deflated as she realized what Violet was up to. Her hands in the air, Violet mimed one hand dramatically eating the other. Violet was making fun. Courtney had almost forgotten her kiss with Ethan.

"Give it a rest, Violet," Courtney told her with a confidence she didn't feel as she reached the table. Violet sometimes needed a firm hand.

As Courtney sat, she took a discreet look around the surrounding tables. Thankfully, she didn't see Ethan. She'd never noticed where he usually sat in the cafeteria. She'd never much noticed him at all, she realized. She gave her head a shake. There was no good reason to start noticing him now.

"If you must know," Courtney said, returning her attention to Violet, "I've met someone else." Courtney winced as the words popped out of her mouth, matter of fact. Okay, maybe a little too soon.

"Who?" Violet asked, looking doubtful. She'd stopped making her hands reenact Courtney's moment in the spotlight.

"Someone," Courtney answered, peeling back the lid of her yogurt. "Don't worry - I'll let you know if it turns into anything." Why had she said anything? Cole was - well, there was nothing to tell - yet.

Pulling her spoon slowly around the edge of her yogurt cup, she scraped out the last vanilla bite and swallowed it down as she got up to go. "I've got to get going."

Violet lifted her hands up and swallowed one with the other in farewell. She wore a good-natured grin.

Courtney stuck her tongue out at Violet as she left her sitting at the table. Despite the mortifying implications, Courtney chuckled a little to herself as she walked away. If Ethan was mad because of what had happened last night, she'd have to deal with it. But she had to give Violet points for the way her mind worked.

Outside on the path toward the West Building, Courtney passed Mr. Chase, her math teacher. He gave her a strange half-smile with a small wave.

Courtney whipped her head around after he passed and watched him walk on. The look he'd just given her - was she just being paranoid? It wasn't possible he knew about her being in the West Woods with Jake, was it? Courtney's heart raced a little faster as she studied his gait. It wouldn't be good if he knew about her failed kiss with Ethan, either - or her meeting Cole on her run that morning, probably while curfew was still in effect. She relaxed her clenched jaw as she realized Mr. Chase wasn't turning around and coming back. Maybe his smile was simply a smile, but that was quite the list of things she'd just thought of. She'd never realized how easy it was to break school rules. She really shouldn't make a habit of it - she didn't like the feeling of worry she felt worming around in her gut.

Hugging her arms to her chest, she walked quickly toward the West Building. The wind was icy, she needed her winter coat. Instead, she wore her thin running shell.

Cole's smile popped into her head as she neared the building. It warmed her to remember. He didn't seem like much of a runner, despite what he'd said. Thankfully, he didn't go to St. Augustus - he'd never even been on campus he'd said. He couldn't be subject to its rumor mill, could he?

She paused at the threshold to the West Building. Were people actually talking about her kiss with Ethan? She practiced shrugging her shoulders at nobody as she stepped inside. *What?* She'd say. *Yeah, of course it wasn't a proper kiss, it was just a dare.*

Ethan was in her next class. Would he talk to her?

Courtney took a deep breath and entered the classroom, scanning. Her heart leapt into her throat as she located Ethan at the back. He looked up as she entered, his eyes wide. Courtney drew a sharp breath. What if he laughed at her, or worse, yelled? She hadn't moved from the doorway. He could even be mad at her. Yes, he was probably mad.

As their eyes met, Ethan's expression melted into a lopsided smile. He gave Courtney a small nod of his head, then went back to whatever he'd been writing before she'd walked in.

Courtney breathed out but didn't move until she was jostled out of the entryway by other students trying to get in. There wasn't going to be a confrontation. Of *course* there wasn't going to be a confrontation. Why had she worried about that? She slunk into her desk two rows over from Ethan, taking out her books and appearing busy. He was letting it go. She could do that.

Once class got going, Courtney relaxed a little as Mr. Garrison, her history teacher, droned on about The Great Depression. She opened her notebook and saw the list she'd written the night before.

It had been a confusing twenty-four hours.

Courtney fiddled with her pen as she stared out the second story window of the classroom. Mr. Garrison's room was in the West Building, the building closest on campus to the West Woods. A flock of birds circled the woods, swooping down to take roost in the uppermost branches of its trees. They looked different somehow today. Maybe she'd never really noticed them before.

She was suddenly aware the class was quiet.

"Courtney, are you with us?" asked Mr. Garrison, his voice breaking the silence.

Courtney looked down at her notebook and mumbled that she was.

"Good," he said simply, resuming the class.

Her mind wandered to Cole. They didn't have much of a plan for meeting up in the morning – not the way Courtney liked to plan. He'd said he'd seen her running before, he must know she ran the same route, at the same time each day. That morning, that had seemed sweet, but it could also be a huge red flag. Serial killers had been known to track women's running schedules. Had Cole staged the meeting this morning, in order to meet her?

Courtney felt suddenly cold. She was probably being ridiculous.

Besides, Cole had a dog, she reasoned to herself. That made him normal, didn't it? He'd watched the sunrise. A serial killer wouldn't have done that, would he? Psychopaths didn't have feelings, wasn't that it? He was just normal. There would be houses full of people all around them. There was no reason to make the situation into something it wasn't, just because she was having a crazy week. She looked down at her page to see she'd sketched a thick heart with her pen around Cole's name in the margin. She tilted her head to one side and drew a jagged line right down through the middle of the heart.

"Now class, remember Ms. Krick will be visiting our classroom later this week to talk a little about the history of St. Augustus. It was built in the middle of The Great Depression and has historical significance that ties in with our study of the 1930's."

A low rumble went through the classroom. It was bad enough most of them had Ms. Krick for English. To have her during history, too, wasn't anyone's idea of entertainment.

Ms. Krick played favorites, and Hanna had been one of hers. By extension, Courtney had an easy time in her class. Besides, she was coming to give a talk on exactly the topic Courtney's dad had challenged her to learn about – the school. Maybe this could be good.

CHAPTER SEVEN

Aftermath

"Are you doing okay, Courtney?" Margaret asked, in their dorm room later that afternoon. "You're like a million miles away or something. Are you upset about the dare? I don't think it's that big a deal."

Courtney frowned at Margaret. She hadn't given the dare another thought after seeing Ethan. She wasn't upset about it.

"Well, what's wrong then?" Margaret probed. "For what it's worth, I haven't heard anyone talking about it."

"Thanks," Courtney muttered, gathering up her laundry and throwing it into her hamper.

"Maybe you need more sleep," Margaret said. "Stop getting up so early. Skip your run for a day or two. Didn't you hurt your foot?"

"No," Courtney answered, shaking her head slightly and pulling her covers up over her pillow. There, she'd made her bed - even if the day was mostly over. "Tomorrow morning I'm actually running with a friend, so I can't skip it. And my ankle feels fine." She'd all but forgotten she'd even hurt it.

"Who's the poor soul getting up that early?" Margaret asked with a pitying laugh.

"His name is Cole," Courtney told her, looking around for her jacket to make the trek to the Main Building. "He lives in town."

"Wait," Margaret said, her mouth hanging open a little. "You run in the mornings with a *guy?*"

"Not usually," Courtney said with a small shrug, "this will be the first time."

She'd had this secret all day, and it felt good to let it out, though she hoped Margaret wouldn't ask too many questions. She didn't know the answers. She'd considered rescheduling the run for after school, but she didn't have any way to contact him. She didn't even know his last name.

At least now somebody knew she was meeting him, though it wouldn't do her much good if she needed someone to find her. Courtney shuddered.

"You're going on a date?" Margaret said, her jaw now halfway to the floor. "That's, well, that's great, Courtney - where did you meet him? No wonder you were so upset about the dare with Ethan, you should have just said. But you haven't kissed this guy yet, right? Because if you had, it would have gone better with Ethan."

Courtney took no notice of her roommate's flustered rambling.

"Hey!" Courtney exclaimed, suddenly realizing her winter coat probably wasn't hiding somewhere in her room. "Margaret, did you happen to grab my jacket last night? You took it from me before..."

"Oh, sorry, no..." Margaret told her, frowning. "We left so fast. We can go by and see if it's there?"

"Let's go later, I'm hungry," Courtney said, reaching for her Harbor Heights sweatshirt.

"Sorry," Margaret said again.

"Don't worry about it," Courtney said, meaning it.

"Hm," Margaret mused as they left the room to head to the cafeteria for supper. "Technically, your runs are before the end of curfew. You're off campus, and with a boy. Bessie would kill you."

She nodded her head with an exaggerated eye roll, toward Bessie's room at the end of the hall from where they came.

"I don't think there's a morning curfew," Courtney said. Was there? The thought had never crossed her mind. Bessie had never said anything about Courtney going for runs before it was light, though it was possible she'd never noticed.

Bessie wasn't great at her job. Getting caught on a run by Ms. Krick was much more likely. That woman seemed to be everywhere.

CHAPTER EIGHT

Alone

Courtney opened her eyes the next morning to her clock glowing 5am – a whole hour before she had to get up. She tucked her comforter under her chin and rolled over toward the wall. Something had pulled her out of her deep sleep. She'd been dreaming, she realized. Cole had been there.

She smiled to herself as she thought of his awkward stance. Interesting that he was a runner – she wouldn't have guessed.

He might be anything. Courtney felt an uncomfortable flutter rising in her chest. She hoped she was a better judge of character than she was giving herself credit for.

At 5:45am, Courtney still lay in bed staring at the wall. She reached over to shut off her alarm before it had a chance to announce her imminent rise. For once, she didn't have to disturb Margaret. She'd probably need a few extra minutes to get ready, anyway. This wasn't just another run.

Usually, she wore a running shirt a few days in a row before washing. She gave the shirt she held a sniff. It didn't smell like roses, but it wasn't bad. She shook her head lightly. No, she could do better.

Easing the top drawer of her dresser open as quietly as she could, she grabbed her favorite running top – one the green color of her eyes, with racerback straps. She lightly tossed the black one she'd worn the day before on top of the laundry hamper. Stealthily, she let herself out of the dorm room and padded down the hall to the restroom in her bare feet, her arms full.

Courtney set her bundle of clothing down on the bathroom counter and looked in the mirror. The flannel pajamas she wore did nothing for her complexion. Fluorescent lights above the counter gave her pale skin a translucent glow, highlighting the puffy area under her eyes. Courtney splashed water on her cheeks, pinching them to pink them up. She ran her wet hands through her hair, pulling it back off her face.

Was this a date? She studied her hair in the mirror, its curls springing their way out of their confines.

She'd already been in the bathroom longer than she usually was before a run. There was no time for a shower, much less to wash her hair. There was nothing worse than wet hair freezing in the frigid winter air. Why was she even considering showering before a run? This wasn't a date, she reminded herself, shaking her head. It was a run. She didn't need to do anything special. Still, she reached for her toothbrush and put an extra squeeze of toothpaste on its brushes for good measure.

Courtney smiled at herself in the mirror, inspecting her newly brushed teeth.

She'd never actually been on a date. And before this week, she'd never kissed anyone, either, though she was pretty sure her kiss with Ethan didn't count. Courtney turned her face to the side and opened her lips the way they must have been as she'd kissed Ethan. Even just doing it in the mirror with nobody around to see, her lips looked mortifying.

Courtney pushed aside her misgivings. She had to get going or she'd miss meeting up with Cole. Her first kiss hadn't been a real kiss, her first date probably wasn't even a date. It had been quite the week.

She pulled on her running gear quickly, smoothing the fitted athletic shirt down over her leggings. Maybe she should have picked a longer shirt – one that covered her rear end better. There was no time to find another one now.

She lathered on extra deodorant – three passes under each arm.

Courtney fit her phone into the pocket on her jacket sleeve and then put her jacket on. Turning to check herself over one last time in the mirror, she was pleased to see her rear was now mostly covered by the jacket. Courtney flashed a smile at herself, with disappointing results. She looked too enthusiastic.

"Hi, Cole," She said out loud, trying out a shyer smile in the mirror.

Courtney gave her head a shake. It was time to get going. She tucked her things into a cubby on the wall by the showers and headed out.

A wave of trepidation swept over her as she stepped out onto the lawn. Far from feeling routine, it suddenly seemed very odd this morning to be awake and outside the dorm when it was still dark. She looked over to Bessie's window, but it was all shadows, with the curtains drawn.

She took a deep breath, then grabbed onto one foot and pulled it up behind her. Courtney stretched one quad, then the other. What was she waiting for? At least the route she'd be taking was well lit. She was being silly, of course. She didn't know anything about Cole because she'd just met him. People didn't tell each other everything they'd ever want to know the first time they met. If they did, there wouldn't be anything to talk about later.

She started off toward the sidewalk across the lawn at a slow jog, watching her feet hit the uneven ice on her path. They hadn't picked a time to meet, but she was later than she was most days.

"Hi, Cole," she said out loud to herself again. She frowned. It still sounded eager.

Courtney ran the half mile to the start of the row of houses at a comfortable speed, then slowed to a jog. As she listened for the sound of Husk's paws, she realized she hadn't started her music.

It wasn't as cold this morning as it had been the day before - Courtney couldn't even see her breath. She looked from one side of the street to the other. It was still dark between the puddles of light cast by the street lamps.

She felt her gut twinge at the thought of seeing him again. He'd seemed different than the boys she knew from St. Augustus – more interesting somehow. Was he really any different? He lived in a real house instead of a dorm, for one – that was different. He probably had a great family that the two of them would hang out with all the time. There was Husk, too. If they saw each other more, she'd be able to visit his house sometimes to get away from the sterility of the dorm. It probably had a nice comfy couch, with a big screen TV they could waste hours watching.

She was getting ahead of herself. This was only a run. She hadn't been invited in to lounge on his couch. Maybe it wasn't even all that comfortable. Did he spend so much time watching TV that he was woefully out of shape? Suddenly her throat tightened. What if she liked him, but he wasn't a good runner? What if he wanted to run with her every day, anyway? She'd have to tell him.

All the windows on the street were dark, but she looked carefully at each one anyway as she passed. A breeze bristled through the trees overhead. Most mornings it was a welcome sound, but today it was a sorry replacement for Husk's bark. She was barely jogging now as she waited for Cole to appear. Her rhythm felt lopsided – off somehow.

Courtney reached the end of the block. She'd passed all the front yards on the street, but hadn't seen so much as a car driving by. She squinted down the road toward the shops and commercial part of Evergreen. Half-heartedly, she headed that way and jogged the loop around the silent shops, the Closed signs at Luigi's Pizza, the library and the corner store all hanging crookedly in their windows. The bakery at the end of her run had a few lights on at the back already, delicious smells wafting out. These were the familiar sights, sounds and smells that had always fueled Courtney's runs, but that morning they only highlighted that she was out here by herself, while she wasn't privy to what was going on behind closed doors. Courtney turned around.

Any hint of excitement she'd felt earlier had drained by the time she'd doubled back. Realization had sunk in. It was clear Cole wasn't coming. Courtney jutted out her chin and got going as fast as she could, staring straight ahead of her. She should have known. No guy actually wanted to get up before dawn to run.

So, why had he suggested it? Courtney didn't let her gaze waver. For all she knew, he'd gotten up early anyway and watched her now from one of the darkened windows she passed, laughing.

Courtney thought back to the moment she thought they'd shared the day before and winced. She'd thought he might kiss her.

She shook her head as she remembered the details of that moment. Husk had pushed them together, she recalled. It hadn't happened because Cole had made it happen. Maybe for Cole it was nothing more.

Her temples pounded as she ran. Had he asked her on this run to be cruel? Tomorrow, she'd find a new running route. Maybe run back toward the woods instead of into town.

As she touched her GPS to confirm her pace, a bark came from the house just to her right. Courtney felt the cloud hanging over her lift a bit, and slowed to a walk. She looked up at the house the bark had come from and saw a light come on in an upper window. Turning her head, she practiced her smile, her lips feeling dry as they pulled back from her teeth. She ran her tongue over her lips to moisten them and tried it again, focused on the front door of the house she'd stopped in front of. It was a blue two-story, with a wooden fence around the yard. In the center of the fence was a low gate that she looked over, trying to get a glimpse inside the house.

Did she have a right to be mad? Should she tell him she'd thought he wasn't going to show? He'd missed most of the run, but she'd let him off the hook, she decided. It was early in the morning, after all. Cole and Husk could walk her back to campus if he wasn't up for running – they'd talk. Courtney suddenly wished she'd planned something to talk about. What would they talk about?

She shook her head. It would be fine. They hadn't had any trouble coming up with things to talk about yesterday. She could just ask him about himself. He could do the talking. She didn't like to talk much when running, anyway – if they ran at all.

Courtney leaned forward into a lunge to keep herself warm. She shifted her weight to make sure her right ankle got a chance to move. She looked again at the lit window expectantly.

Courtney had stretched both legs out and moved on to her arms when the porch light finally came on. Courtney licked her lips again and directed a smile toward the door. Excited barking could be heard coming from behind the closed door as a shadow appeared. When the door swung open, a dog came bounding down the steps and ran to the gate, yapping happily at Courtney and rolling in the shallow snow accumulated at the edge of the yard.

Courtney stared at the dog, her mouth hanging open. Maybe Cole's family had another dog. This dog had dark curly fur. His tongue hung out of his mouth with drool dripping. This dog was most certainly not Husk. Courtney's smile faded as she looked back to the doorway.

An elderly gentleman waved to her, though he looked confused. Courtney quickly dropped down on one knee to tie her shoelace - a plausible reason to be stopped at the man's gate at that hour.

From her squatting position, she peeked through the fence slats at the man. His dark skin couldn't have been more unlike Cole's freckles. Besides, this man looked far too old to be Cole's dad.

Still crouched low to the ground, she looked up and down the street. A few lights were on by now, but there was no sign of Cole.

Courtney took a few deep breaths before recovering and unfurling back to her full height. She reached around her neck for her headphones and plugged them into each ear.

"Bye," she called to the man on the porch, who was watching her with interest.

Courtney pumped the volume buttons on her phone. Music filled her ears and she let her mind go blank. The first rays of dawn spread at her back and stretched around her body, glowing at the edges of the shadow cast on the sidewalk before her. She took a step toward her own shadow, that stretched long on the pavement in front of her. As the bass from her running mix filled her, she put one foot in front of the other and did her best to outrun it.

She hadn't misunderstood him. She was sure of it.

Courtney was breathing hard, but she didn't want to stop. She knew she wouldn't stop until she reached the dorm. She heard nothing but the music. Each step crashed into the sidewalk as she ran.

CHAPTER NINE

X Marks the Spot

For once, Margaret's eyes flew open when Courtney let herself into their room after her run.

Courtney's stomach tightened. The one day Margaret didn't sleep in. Of course, it had to be today. Courtney's ears throbbed with the music she'd already shut off. She could feel a headache brewing.

"Hey," Courtney said, smiling thinly, "I'm going to grab a shower." She reached into the closet to grab a blouse and kilt for after.

"Soooo?" Margaret said, sitting up in her bed, grinning from ear to ear. "Can he run?"

"No idea," Courtney shrugged. She wasn't in the mood to play twenty questions. "He didn't show."

"Ouch," Margaret said, sitting forward.

"It's fine," Courtney answered. She didn't know what else to say. "I'm sure he had a good reason." She wasn't sure of that at all, but she wasn't interested in discussing it just now. "Gotta go, I'll fill you in later," Courtney said, heading for the door. Margaret wouldn't get out of bed and follow her at this hour, would she?

She heard Margaret flop back down on the bed dramatically behind her.

Good, Courtney thought, she wasn't getting up. She could tell her more later. Or, more likely she wouldn't. She hadn't totally forgiven Margaret's implicit participation in daring her.

Courtney opened the door to the hallway and hopped back in surprise.

Hanna stood in front of their door, wearing a bulky gray zip-up hoodie. She held the unzipped front of the hoodie closed with one hand.

"Oh, you're up," Hanna said in a low voice. "I was just trying to think how I was going to slip this under your door."

Courtney couldn't remember the last time Hanna had visited her room - certainly not this year. They stood in Courtney's open doorway a moment, looking at each other.

Hanna drew something long carefully out of her sweater.

Courtney blinked at it. It looked like a rolled-up poster. Or at least a very old rolled up sheet of paper with something that looked like coffee stains on it.

"Hi Hanna," Margaret called half-heartedly from her bed.

Hanna didn't answer Margaret, but indicated Courtney should shut the open door.

Courtney closed the door behind her and stepped out into the hall.

Once the door was shut, Hanna looked from side to side, then up and down the hall, then back at Courtney. She held the rolled-up paper out in front of her and handed it to Courtney with two hands as if she were awarding her a hard-earned college diploma. "Dad gave it to me at the beginning of this year," Hanna explained in a rush. "He said to keep it hidden. He claims his class took it from Ms. Krick in their senior year. They pulled a senior prank."

"And they never returned it?" Courtney asked, an uneasy feeling stirring in the pit of her stomach. "Are you supposed to return it?"

Courtney stared at the paper in front of her, but didn't reach for it. Her dad had stolen this from Ms. Krick.

"Don't ask me," Hanna said. "Take it. I don't want it. If there's a senior prank this year, I don't know about it – and don't want to know about it. I've had to keep it hidden away."

"Why are you giving this to me?" Courtney asked.

"You asked about the school," Hanna said with a shrug. She darted her eyes around the hall. "I want to get rid of it anyway. I have my college acceptances. I definitely don't need to get caught with something Dad stole years ago."

"Well, I don't want to get caught with it, either!" Courtney blurted. Why should she take a risk that her sister had decided was too great?

"Well," Hanna said, "Dad told me I had to give it to you when I graduate anyway. He says it belongs on campus." She hesitated, looking at Courtney.

Courtney narrowed her eyes. She took the roll from Hanna and held it in front of her as if it could burn her.

Margaret peeked her head out of their dorm room door. "Everything okay out here?" she asked, yawning. "What's that?" Margaret asked, pointing at the roll Courtney held.

Hanna backed away from the roommates toward the seniors' section of the dorm.

"Keep it hidden," Hanna said, addressing them both. Then she turned and walked away.

Courtney watched her sister's back intently. Hanna had acted like she'd just unloaded a heavy burden. What did this decrepit paper have to do with what their dad had told her to find? What did her sister know?

Courtney felt Margaret's weight as her friend leaned on her and stifled a laugh into her shoulder as the roommates re-entered their room.

"Shh..." Courtney said. It really wasn't early anymore, but there still wasn't any sign of life on the floor.

Courtney pulled a sleepy Margaret back into their room and shut the door.

"Your sister is such a drama queen," Margaret said. "Everything is always so serious with her. She looked like somebody had died."

Courtney looked at her roommate with a thoughtful expression on her face.

"Oh god," Margaret gasped, her face suddenly ashen. "Sorry, *did* somebody die?"

"I've no idea," Courtney answered, unrolling the thin paper slowly as it cracked with age in her hands. "Not that I know of, anyway," she added.

Courtney stretched the paper gently to its full size – about the size of the map of the world she had in her room back home. She held it up to the sunlight that shone through the split in the room's curtains. The sun's rays passed through the back of the oversized page, making the translucent white parts glow.

"It's a map," Margaret said flatly, yawning at Courtney's shoulder.

Margaret moved over to crawl back into bed.

It was definitely a map. The St. Augustus campus was drawn across the page - one with much more open space than Courtney remembered. The Main Building was unmistakably marked as St. Augustus in flowery lettering.

Courtney blinked as she looked closer. The map only had three buildings on the campus – The Main Building, the teachers' residence, and another small structure at the southern edge of the West Woods. The map was old. Really old. Besides the buildings, the map was covered in small designs, barely noticeable. Courtney moved closer. The designs seemed to be small drawings, glowing translucently through the paper.

Each spire and stair was detailed on the drawing of the Main

Building. Courtney recognized the trees flanking the stairs – much smaller trees than were there now.

The buildings looked in order, but the tiny drawings that glowed in the sunlight followed no obvious pattern. There were hundreds of them - small trees and flowers, among other things. Courtney ran her finger over one of a chubby baby. A cupid? The drawings seemed like nonsense, each only an eighth of an inch tall, scattered around the map in seemingly random clusters. Courtney tilted the paper toward the light coming from the window, but that only made the tiny icons all but disappear. What did they mean? She rolled down the bottom right corner a smidge further to get a good look. The map was dated 1932. When had St. Augustus opened its doors?

Courtney shouldered her way past the half-open drapes and pressed the map flat against the window.

"Turn out the light!" Margaret moaned.

Courtney glanced over her shoulder. Margaret had pulled her pillow over her face and rolled toward the wall. Courtney turned back to the map.

Sunlight had filled the translucent icons and made them more prominent. The woods were there - detailed trees were hand drawn with sepia ink. Where had she and Jake gone into the woods the other night? Courtney braced the corner of the parchment with her right elbow and traced a path with her finger to the place they'd entered - near where the West Building was now. Tiny icons littered the area.

"There," Courtney said aloud, pointing at a spot near the edge of the woods. They'd been somewhere near that tree, not too far in. Courtney's index finger explored the glowing markings surrounding the area where they'd completed their dare.

Her finger stopped on a small image – a box. Courtney's breath hitched. The key had been in a wooden box. It was still in her coat pocket. She'd left her coat in the student lounge. She studied the drawing of the Main Building and found where the student lounge should be. There were glowing symbols of a book, a tree and a painting in the general area of the lounge, but no key. She followed a path with her eyes from the lounge to the school office, skipping over the icons in the way, until she saw it. The key. There was an outline of a key in the office. They'd forgotten to look for her coat at the lounge last night. Her coat – and the key - could be in the lost and found at the office! Courtney's neck prickled. Why had she thought the key would be on the map?

Just then, Courtney's fingers slipped and the map snapped itself shut into its coil at the same moment as Margaret's phone jingled to life with her morning alarm, on the bedside table under the window.

Courtney looked over at Margaret, who seemed to have gone back to sleep - she didn't make a move to shut off the alarm. Courtney knew Margaret would hit the snooze on the phone two or three times before finally getting out of bed.

The office wouldn't open for another hour. She needed to think – and she needed to hide the map.

Courtney pulled an edge of the map with care to tighten the tube it made. The elastic she released from her ponytail pinched her hand. She was more careful as she snapped it around the fragile paper.

Courtney looked at her sleeping roommate. It was truly unbelievable how much Margaret slept. She picked gingerly through her hamper, intending to hide the map underneath her clothes. Wrinkling her nose at the sweaty mess waiting to be washed, she thought better of the idea and instead tucked the rolled-up map in the closet, behind a broken umbrella she'd been meaning to toss.

She reached up to ease a crisp St. Augustus uniform off its hanger then let herself quietly out of the room, heading down the hall to the showers.

CHAPTER TEN

Lost

Courtney checked the time on her phone and adjusted her kilt. There were still a few minutes until the office was supposed to open, but when she rounded the corner, she could see through the open office door that Miss Samantha was already at her desk.

Miss Samantha's pink face cracked into a wide smile as her eyes lit on Courtney standing beside the door to the school office.

"Good morning, Courtney," she said, nodding her head at Courtney in a friendly way. "Do you need something?"

Miss Samantha's smeary lipstick had made its way onto her teeth.

"I forgot my coat in the student lounge the other night," Courtney answered, averting her eyes from Miss Samantha's caked-on lipstick. "I'm hoping it's made its way to the lost and found."

"Well, you're welcome to look dear," Miss Samantha told her.

Courtney's gaze flicked to the heavy wooden door of the main office and her heart sank. If the old key she'd found had once opened a door at St. Augustus, surely the lock had been replaced by a modern one. The key could be a dead end.

"The lost and found is over in the corner, why don't you see if your coat is there?" Miss Samantha answered, busily arranging papers on her desk.

Courtney looked over at the pile in a wooden box at the back of the large room, near Headmistress Valentine's office door.

"Thanks," Courtney murmured, heading over.

"You might have to dig a little," Miss Samantha called over her shoulder. "I opened the office early, and Jeff Moore was in here half an hour ago looking for something. He took everything out - it won't be in order."

Courtney's pulse quickened. What had Jeff been looking for? Had Jake told him about the key? The map had shown a key here, but it could already be gone. She'd left the map back in her room.

"He loses something at least once a week," Miss Samantha said, clucking her tongue and shaking her head.

Crossing the room quickly, Courtney eyed the pile of junk in the box with distaste. It gave off an odor she'd rather be done with quickly. Gingerly, she moved a plastic water bottle balanced precariously on the top, then pulled out a pair of football shoulder pads, holding her breath. They smelled of old socks and moldy cheese, all rolled into one. If they'd been Jeff's, maybe he'd opted to leave them. A swatch of brown the color of her coat was visible and Courtney pulled at it soundly, releasing the garment from the mess. She would have to wash it before it could be worn.

She felt the coat pockets for the key and frowned. Twisting the limp fabric around in her hands, she felt for the pocket openings. Both pockets were unbuttoned. She fished around inside each with her hand, one at a time. They were empty, and so was the lapel pocket on the inside, where she sometimes tucked her phone. Could Jeff have found her key?

She turned all three pockets inside out. The light-colored lining of one of the side pockets was streaked with brown and black. Courtney stared at the thick residue the key had left behind.

A tickling sensation brushed the back of her hand. Courtney

dropped her coat on the floor in surprise. She looked at her hand and cried out. A small spider made its way across her pale skin. Courtney quickly trapped him between the thumb and forefinger of her other hand and dropped it on the ground, her stomach churning. This box hadn't been cleaned, in, well... maybe ever.

"Did you find your coat, dear?" Miss Samantha called to her in a singsong voice.

"Not yet," she called back, toeing her dropped coat toward the shoulder pads on the floor to hide it.

Courtney wracked her brain. She'd been the only one interested in the key. She didn't remember Jeff even seeing it. It was here, somewhere. Courtney thought back to the previous night at the student lounge. Who had she shown the key to? Her eyes narrowed. Ms. Krick had been in the lounge that night. Courtney had spoken to her just before she'd left without her coat. A hot feeling spread across the back of her neck. Had Ms. Krick found her coat, and the key? If the map had been important to her, would she be interested in an old key as well? Courtney thought she knew the answer. The key had been on the map – Ms. Krick's map.

With new fervor, Courtney knelt beside the lost and found box and got to work. As gingerly as possible, she lifted each item quickly, shook it and tossed it into a growing pile of discards on the floor. Hoodies, beanies, scarves, and the odd dirty sock she moved pinched between her fingers, but no key. Courtney hadn't had the pleasure of losing anything else in the year and half that she'd been at St. Augustus. As she neared the bottom of the box, she vowed if she ever lost something again, it could stay lost.

The box was almost empty. The light in the corner of the office was dim, so Courtney felt around the bottom of the box until she felt something hard. Something she'd had in her hand before.

"My goodness, Courtney," Headmistress Valentine said as she approached from behind, making Courtney drop the key. Its clatter echoed in the nearly empty box. "Did you lose something?"

Courtney looked up with dismay at the headmistress and then back at the pile of discarded things she'd made, which she hadn't realized blocked the headmistress' office door.

"Headmistress, I'm so sorry," Courtney said, with a quick glance down at the key she'd dropped, now clearly visible in the middle of the box floor. Deciding, she turned back to the pile.

"I was looking for my coat," she declared, snatching it up from the bottom of the discarded pile, "and here it is."

"Oh good," Headmistress Valentine said, staring at the eclectic pile blocking her path.

"I'll get that cleaned up," Courtney said quickly, grabbing a large armload of the offending items and lifting them back into the box. She lowered them right down, bending unnaturally low to grab the key from the bottom of the box. Gracefully, she palmed the key into the waistband of her kilt, which had been rolled up to shorten her skirt. She hoped it was snug enough to hold until she could get it into her backpack.

Courtney leaned over again to grab the next load, feeling the hard metal key against her waist shift as she moved.

"How's your father doing?" Headmistress Valentine asked, standing over Courtney. She didn't move to help with the transfer of the mess, instead just watching Courtney work. "We haven't seen him around campus much lately, though we really appreciate his support."

"Yes, he loves St. Augustus," Courtney replied, forcing herself to smile. She eyed the few stray items still littering the floor. She couldn't lunge down to get them without showing the headmistress her back, and the key protruding from her beltline, which stuck out over her blouse.

Courtney eyed her coat, which she held in her hand. Somehow, it didn't feel like hers anymore - it had just had an unintentional vacation with all these smelly, unwashed things. Standing upright, she slipped it on, one arm at a time, trying not to cringe. She pulled the tail of the coat down over the key. The smell of the garment's neglect assaulted her nostrils. Courtney took shallow breaths.

"It really is quite an honor for your dad to be asked to head the admissions committee," the headmistress continued. "I know he's very busy, but we do need an answer from him by the end of the month."

Courtney positioned her body away from Headmistress Valentine, not wanting to flash her if her skirt rode up as she squatted down to move the remaining items. Had her dad not replied to the invitation? He'd had mentioned the admissions committee invitation, but she didn't remember if he wanted to be on it or not.

"I'll tell him," Courtney answered.

"Has he mentioned anything about the admissions committee to you, dear?" Headmistress Valentine asked.

Most of the students were terrified of the headmistress, but she'd always reminded Courtney of a stray puppy. She was tall and thin, and a little homely looking. Her dark hair was usually in a tight bun on top of her head. She was the kind of lady who could almost be pretty if she'd only smile more.

"No, he hasn't said anything," Courtney lied.

"Well, would you be sure to ask him for me when you speak to him," Headmistress Valentine asked. "I've emailed and called, but I really don't want to pester him."

Headmistress Valentine looked stuffy in her navy skirt suit. Under her jacket, she sported a crisp white St. Augustus uniform blouse. None of the other teachers wore St. Augustus uniforms and Courtney was sure that Headmistress Valentine didn't have to, either. The school really was her life.

The warning bell buzzed through the office. Courtney was

about to be late for class.

"Sure," Courtney answered, tossing the last stray sock on top of the pile, "but if you'll excuse me, I really need to get going."

"Of course, dear," Headmistress Valentine said, leaning against the doorframe of her office, smiling at Courtney but making no move to go in.

Courtney's first class was in the West Building. She'd have to run to make it – but the key, which was still tucked into her skirt - would fall if she ran. Placing one hand awkwardly on the small of her back over her smelly coat, she walked as quickly as she could to the door of the office. As soon as she was in the hallway, Courtney broke into a run. Her loafers pinched her feet as they hit each tile. She had to let go of the key to crank open the heavy front doors of the Main Building. As she let go, it slipped loose and fell out the bottom of her kilt, jangling on the slate floor.

"What's that?" Margaret asked, appearing beside her.

"Nothing," Courtney said quickly.

Margaret lifted an eyebrow at her - she wasn't fooled.

"It's just the key I found in the woods the other night," Courtney explained in a low voice, picking it up.

"You think it opens something here?" Margaret asked as they went out onto the lawn.

"I do," Courtney answered as the girls started to jog toward the West Building.

"Crap," Margaret muttered, checking her phone. "My new year's resolution was not to need any late slips."

"Well, let's go then," Courtney said, pulling Margaret by the hand and sprinting across the lawn. Their loafers slowed them down a bit, and Courtney's ankle reminded her it wasn't one hundred percent, but they entered the West Building just as the late bell rang.

They stepped inside Mr. Garrison's history classroom, only to come face to face with Ms. Krick.

"Miss Margaret," Ms. Krick said dryly to Margaret, "tardy again. Do you have a slip?"

Margaret shook her head no.

Courtney shifted her weight on her feet in front of Ms. Krick, who addressed solely Margaret. This must be the day Ms. Krick was here to talk about the history of Evergreen – and St. Augustus. Both girls breathed heavily from their run.

"Oh, they're fine," piped up Mr. Garrison, crossing the room toward them and waving an arm toward the desks. "Girls, take your seats."

Ms. Krick's eyes flickered.

Courtney looked away, flashing a grateful smile at Mr. Garrison for his rescue as she sat at her desk.

Ms. Krick glared at Margaret, but must have thought better than to challenge Mr. Garrison in his classroom, because she let it drop.

"Ms. Krick is kind enough to share her formidable knowledge of Evergreen and the founding of St. Augustus as it relates to our study of the 1930's," Mr. Garrison announced. "Please give her our thanks." He led the class in a round of applause.

Courtney slipped out of her still-smelly coat and dropped it on top of her backpack. She leaned over to get her notebook, and then stuffed the coat to the bottom of her book bag. She tuned back in to what Ms. Krick was saying, introducing the town and St. Augustus. Suddenly, these were topics she was keenly interested in.

CHAPTER ELEVEN

History Lesson

It felt strange to have Ms. Krick at the front of their history class, as if it were English class instead. Courtney watched Ms. Krick as she paced in front of the class during her lecture. Courtney wondered just how old the teacher was, as she watched the soft skin under her chin wag as she walked. Courtney's dad made it sound like Ms. Krick had been old even when he'd been in her class.

"Seven founding families are credited with establishing Evergreen town," Ms. Krick rattled off the list of the families. The Young's were not among them.

Courtney had given up scribbling down who controlled the mill, the bank and whatever else had failed during that time. Town families. What did a mill do again - make paper? Courtney clicked the end of her pen a few times, watching as the nib popped in and out. She didn't really know anyone from Evergreen itself - except Cole, if he even counted, since he hadn't lived there long. Besides, it wasn't like she knew him all that well.

Apparently, he didn't want to know her, she remembered.

Rubbing her temples, Courtney tried to focus her attention back to the lecture.

Ms. Krick looked right at her just as Courtney yawned.

Courtney met her gaze and tried to turn the yawn into a weak cough, covering her mouth with her fist. She was only catching every third word or so now. The lecture hadn't been as interesting as she'd hoped. Mr. Garrison had slipped out into the hall and hadn't come back. Courtney looked at the classroom door, which he'd left ajar. If he wasn't even going to listen to the lecture, the chances of the details showing up on a test were slim.

Courtney looked around the classroom at the silent students. The class looked defeated – much as they did when they were in Ms. Krick's English class. Mr. Garrison's interactive style made history class fly by. This hour had felt like three.

Courtney dug her fingernails into her palms, to prevent the yawn from coming that she felt building again. She looked down at her notes page, which only had a few sentences for the last half hour's information.

"Isaac Young was the key to Evergreen's revival during the depression," Ms. Krick rambled.

Courtney relaxed her hands and reached for her pen again, suddenly paying attention. Ms. Krick had used the word key. Courtney narrowed her eyes at Ms. Krick. Was it possible this old teacher had the answers?

Courtney had landed in Ms. Krick's English class two years in a row. She was boring, but she really did go easy on Courtney. It was widely known Ms. Krick favored alumni kids, but she embarrassingly went out of her way with Courtney – casually mentioning to her something that might be on the midterm, or give her "suggestions" for topics on Courtney's assignments. Courtney always got top marks in Ms. Krick's class, though she knew others struggled.

Courtney had always assumed Hanna had paved the way for this extra treatment, though she thought maybe now that her dad had a hand in it. She thought of the map she'd hidden in the closet of her room. Did Ms. Krick know Jim Wallis had kept it all these years?

Courtney looked quickly down at her backpack. How long had the key had been in the woods, encased in layers of dirt? Ms. Krick couldn't have ever seen it, could she?

She reached down to her backpack and squeezed the outer pocket where she'd put it earlier. The key's hard form greeted her - it was still there. The map had led her to it. What did that mean? For all she knew, it could be someone's old hidden house key, lost, but no longer needed. The symbols on the map could have been there just for decoration. The key in the office could very well have been a coincidence. Yet, Courtney felt sure it would lead her to whatever her dad expected her to find.

Courtney looked out the window toward the woods. Gloomy clouds blocked the sun and made them seem ominous. A few flakes of snow swirled through the air. She'd tuned out again. Courtney gave her head a quick shake - Ms. Krick might say something important – something that could help her. She put her pen on the page and resumed recording the lecture. Writing down what Ms. Krick said would at least keep her focused.

"...Isaac Young's proposal to build St. Augustus came out of nowhere, and at first the town council resisted. Isaac was unknown to the area, and gave no explanation as to why the school should be built here. Later, it was found Isaac had lived with his mother, Alexandrina Young, on the St. Augustus property as a child, though that was only after his death, when he willed the land to the school. His childhood home was built just past the south end of the West Woods."

Courtney tore a jagged hole in the page she wrote on with the tip of her pen, she was writing so fast. Isaac Young had lived at the south end of the West Woods. There was a house there on the map. She kept scribbling on the page, trying to get it all down. Finally, there was something that might help.

"Evergreen didn't trust Isaac Young. He was unknown and it

was rumored his money had come from bootlegging. Which was true, by the way. He'd controlled several distilleries in New England before the prohibition, and he continued to supply many towns with alcohol through an underground network, even after it was introduced."

Courtney sat up in her seat. It was as if Ms. Krick's whole face had transformed. Something she was about to say seemed important.

"There were letters written that protest the construction of a school for wealthy children, during a time when the town should focus on stabilizing its banks and food supply."

Ms. Krick paused, looking down her long nose at the class.

Courtney held her breath. Did Ms. Krick really see the students that way? The way she said the word 'wealthy' was loaded with judgement. Courtney had never thought of her family as wealthy, though she supposed they were.

Ms. Krick had walked to the window and stared out, just inches from Courtney's desk. "Isaac Young founded St. Augustus against many odds," she said. "'Rum running', as it was called, was widely accepted and not much different than liquor distribution today. Yes, Courtney?" Ms. Krick turned toward her.

Courtney hadn't realized she'd let out such a long breath.

"I, uh..." Courtney felt the eyes of her fellow students on her. She wanted to know more about Isaac Young - much more.

"Did you have a question?" Ms. Krick prompted.

"Um, wasn't alcohol illegal during the prohibition?" Courtney managed. Courtney's lame question hung in the air. Ms. Krick had already said it was widely accepted.

Ms. Krick waved her hand dismissively.

"Barely," Ms. Krick answered, walking toward the center of the room.

Courtney searched her thoughts for a way to keep the conversation going. Isaac Young had been a criminal - or at least somewhat on the edge of the law. There had to be something to that.

"But, how did he convince the town to build the school?" Courtney blurted out. Courtney was keenly aware of the stares she was now getting from the other students.

"He owned the land. And he brought cash," Ms. Krick answered, without missing a beat. "He didn't need their approval, not really. They couldn't stop him, so much as slow him down. But in the end, the jobs to make the school a reality were sorely needed."

Courtney searched her mind for more questions to ask. She wanted to keep Ms. Krick talking.

"The protests were silenced by the jobs created building the school," Ms. Krick said. "Isaac Young always paid his bills on time, and was known for his generosity with the workers. He would often overpay."

Ms. Krick looked almost triumphant. It was as if she were telling a story much more personal than something that had happened nearly a century ago.

"Once the building was underway, though," she went on, "and Mr. Young established he was good for the payments, the town thrived." Ms. Krick paused, somehow savoring the moment. "The building took nearly three years to erect, the stone for the Main Building being cut from the hill beyond the West Woods." Ms. Krick opened her arms wide in the direction of the woods, to show where the stone had come from.

The bell rang to signal the end of class. Ms. Krick looked startled to hear it.

Courtney reached down to pack up her backpack. When she looked up again, Ms. Krick stood beside her desk.

"Come to my rooms after supper," Ms. Krick told Courtney in a forceful whisper. She reached out and firmly grabbed hold of Courtney's forearm. "I'll finish the story."

Courtney looked down at Ms. Krick's grip on her arm, her eyes wide. She was close enough to feel Ms. Krick's hot, stale breath on her face, to see the teacher's small pupils behind the watery film on her eyes.

Courtney's stomach tightened. She'd always assumed the teacher's residence was off limits to students. It had never occurred to her to visit. The few teachers that lived on campus had rooms in a large house on the eastern side of the lawn.

Courtney nodded. She would go. This was what her dad had asked of her - to learn the secrets of the school. Finding out what Ms. Krick knew about Isaac Young seemed a good place to start.

CHAPTER TWELVE

Gossip Girls

"Man, Courtney," Margaret complained at lunch, "why do you even bother sucking up to Ms. Krick? She already thinks you're like, a princess or something."

"What did I miss?" asked Violet, piping in.

Violet neatly cut her Salisbury steak into triangular shaped pieces. She wore a long, purple beaded necklace that she must have gotten for Christmas, over her starched white blouse.

"Nothing," mumbled Courtney, somewhat regretting having been so eager in history class. She'd attracted Ms. Krick's attention, though she wasn't sure it was the positive kind, as Margaret implied.

"Ms. Krick is just an old bat," said Violet. "Don't bother with anything she tells you. How did your date go?" Violet prompted, leaning forward.

Courtney glared at Margaret.

Margaret just shrugged.

"If she told you about the run, she also told you he didn't show," Courtney answered, resigning herself to the fact that telling Margaret was usually the same thing as telling Margaret and Violet. The three friends didn't have many secrets from one another. She supposed she hadn't told Margaret to keep it quiet.

"Yeah, did you find out why he didn't show up?" Rhoda asked, putting her tray down on the table across from Courtney.

"Margaret!" Courtney exclaimed. Had she told the whole school?

"What?" Margaret said, eyes wide, looking between Violet and Rhoda. "I only told Violet."

"That's true," Violet confirmed, nodding. "I told Rhoda. And... I guess I told Lynette too, she was there."

Courtney sighed. Word travelled fast. Lynette was Violet's roommate. She was also on the swim team with them, but Courtney didn't generally confide in her any more than she would tell something important to Rhoda. Courtney probably wouldn't have minded so much if Cole hadn't stood her up.

"Don't get upset," Violet told her, patting Courtney's hand patronizingly. "I'm just doing a little damage control for your show with Ethan the other night. People need something else to talk about."

Courtney pulled her hand away gently. Violet was probably making the rumors worse, as was her tendency. She looked over at Margaret for help.

"Sorry," Margaret told her, taking a swig of her milk, "but Violet has a point. If we're going to get you a date this year that actually shows up, eating Ethan Roth's lips needs to get buried by other gossip, and fast."

Courtney winced at Margaret's characterization of her kiss with Ethan.

"So, how *was* the date with running guy?" Hailey chimed in, joining their table.

Courtney's mouth dropped open at Hailey's comment. Hailey was a freshman that Margaret had befriended.

"See?" Violet said with a laugh and nudging Courtney in the ribs, "I didn't tell *everyone* he stood you up, just that you were seeing a guy from town."

"He didn't show up?" Hailey asked, the confusion on her face matching Courtney's own.

Courtney had managed to keep her mind off Cole for most of the morning. She'd been so amped to see him, and then...

Courtney pushed her chair back. She needed to clear her head.

"Girls, thanks," Courtney said, "but I don't need help."

"Don't be like that!" Violet called after her, "I didn't tell anyone else he stood you up!"

Violet's voice rang through the cafeteria, loud enough for anyone to hear.

Courtney looked from side to side, but the kids at the other tables weren't watching. Violet's announcement dissolved into the din. She shook her head as she left the cafeteria. Violet was impossible.

CHAPTER THIRTEEN

Invitation

The rest of the day had dragged on, with English class last period. The animated Ms. Krick of this morning's revelations about Isaac Young was gone without a trace, replaced by Ms. Krick's signature monotony. She said nothing about her invitation to come to the residence later, and Courtney didn't dare bring it up with other students around.

After supper, Courtney took a deep breath as she stepped onto the walkway for the large house where the teachers lived. She'd never come this close to the teachers' residence before. She'd been invited, she reminded herself, pushing aside the nagging feeling she was entering somewhere she didn't belong. She climbed the steps of the wide front porch one at a time. Her footsteps echoed.

Up close, the house was even more expansive than she'd realized. Brick lined the main level, wooden siding wrapped around the top. It was a plain, but functional, house that ran deep into the campus lawn. Courtney wondered how many teachers lived here? She thought most of the younger ones lived in town. Some of the teachers who lived in town had families – lives even. Courtney felt a pang of empathy for Ms. Krick, who seemed to have neither of these things.

Courtney stopped short as she reached the oversized wooden door. A shudder ran up her spine as she looked at its owl-shaped door knocker, glowing ominously in the light of the porch lamp. She looked back over her shoulder. This side of the campus was far enough away from the Main Building that the artificial light didn't touch it. There were no street lamps.

The windows in the house were completely dark. Maybe Ms. Krick had forgotten she'd invited her here – she certainly hadn't mentioned it when she'd seen her in English class. Had Courtney misunderstood? Her stomach churned. She could tell Ms. Krick she'd gotten sick when she saw her tomorrow. Yes, she could tell her tomorrow.

Courtney shuffled her way back to the edge of the porch and looked toward the glowing lights of the Main Building. A bitter wind blew tonight. The student lounge would be warm. She could curl up in her corner and read a book. Or better yet, read in bed. What she really wanted, though, was to be able to read tonight in her big double bed in her own room in Boston. She'd be giving up if she didn't at least see if Ms. Krick had anything helpful to offer.

Turning back toward the residence, Courtney gritted her teeth and put her hand on the brass door knocker. Instead of knocking as she let it fall against the door, it drifted down without a sound as the door swung open. Courtney gaped for a moment at the open entrance before stepping slowly inside.

She found herself in a dimly lit hallway, with a row of doors on either side. She looked from door to door. This felt a lot like running down Cole's street that morning without knowing which house was his. Which door belonged to Ms. Krick?

The heavy front door swung closed behind her, sending an echo through the hall. In the following silence, Courtney heard a sound from the back of the house. Good. Ms. Krick had heard her come in. Courtney started toward the sound.

As she neared the door, she strained to hear what television program was playing from within. She raised her hand to knock, but the door swung open.

"Giles!" Courtney exclaimed.

"Can I help you?" Giles asked, sharply. He stood in the door of what looked to be his apartment, clearly not expecting to see a student. "Headmistress Valentine isn't in, if you need her."

He nodded his head toward a door across the hallway.

Courtney gaped at the door he'd indicated. Headmistress Valentine lived there? Of course, Ms. Krick wasn't the only staff member who lived in the house. But Giles, the caretaker, sharing a house with Headmistress Valentine and Ms. Krick?

"Ms. Krick asked me to come!" Courtney blurted out, her voice too loud.

Giles gave her a hard look then motioned for her to follow him as he moved out into the hall and disappeared deeper into the house. He snapped on a light when they reached the end of the hall. Courtney blinked against the brightness.

"Matilda's rooms are upstairs," he said, starting up a narrow stairwell at the back of the house.

Courtney fell into line behind Giles, staying close. He climbed quickly, and she followed. At the top of the flight, Giles pulled a cord on the ceiling and a dim, naked bulb sprang to life, hanging by a single wire from the high ceiling. More doors greeted them on this floor. The house felt very quiet. Courtney realized there were probably apartments for many more teachers than currently lived here.

Giles turned and stepped to the left.

"Her rooms are at the top," he said to Courtney, gesturing to yet another staircase. "Mind you lock the front door when you leave."

"Uh, thanks," Courtney said, peering up the short staircase.

She hadn't realized the house had a third floor. She looked back, but Giles had vanished. Somewhere from deep in the house she heard a door close firmly.

Courtney took a deep breath, turned back to the staircase and started up. Giles would surely tell Ms. Krick she'd been here, so there was no point in turning back. She took a step forward. Each wooden stair creaked under her feet.

She reached the top of the stairs, where there was a brown door, with an owl shaped knocker, matching the one she'd seen on the front door of the house.

The stairwell was close and musty. Courtney's heart pounded as she let her imagination get the better of her. Ms. Krick had invited her here. She grabbed the knocker firmly and gave it a solid rap. Courtney stepped back, reacting to the noise it made.

Hearing no signs of life inside, Courtney put her ear to Ms. Krick's door. Maybe the teacher wasn't even home. Her ear, however, was met with an atrocious screech coming from within the apartment. Courtney instinctively jumped back, grabbing the railing to keep from tumbling down the stairs. She looked up to see Ms. Krick at the open door, holding a stringy black cat. The cat howled so loudly that Courtney felt her whole body tense.

"Oh, don't mind Oscar," Ms. Krick said, restraining the cat by hugging him close. She was clad in one of her signature drab skirts and blouses, though a threadbare orange cardigan had replaced her usual blazer.

Courtney stared at the strange pair.

"He's just not used to having visitors," Ms. Krick said, nuzzling her face into the ugly mess of fur on the cat's back before letting him down on the floor.

Oscar stood his ground beside his master's feet.

Courtney was surprised to see Ms. Krick wore green striped socks pulled over her pantyhose.

Oscar sniffed at Ms. Krick's toes without taking his eyes off Courtney, the intruder. His four paws sat unevenly on a sea of unmatched squares of carpet that covered the floor of the apartment.

"Come in, child," said Ms. Krick.

Courtney placed one foot onto the odd mosaic of carpet squares, which extended as far as she could see into the room, even under the overstuffed couches. She recognized the coffee table and end tables scattered around the room. Their style was identical to what the students had in the dorm. Courtney stopped a few feet into the apartment. The footing was tricky, with the carpets' uneven seams threatening to trip her with every step.

"Isaac Young himself lived in this apartment during the construction of St. Augustus," Ms. Krick told her, heading into a kitchenette just off the main room. "Can I make you some tea?"

"Uh, sure," Courtney answered, though she wasn't sure at all. The apartment smelled of mustard pickles, making her nostrils cringe. Courtney's gaze followed Ms. Krick as the ancient teacher busied herself making tea. Stacks of dishes lined the countertops of the small space, so every inch was covered.

"I try to keep the place as original as possible," said Ms. Krick, who had managed to find the kettle, teacups and teabags without opening a single cupboard. "The carpets are to protect the floors from getting scratched by the cats. They're samples. They give them for free at the store to see if they'll match your house. Can you believe the luck? It took me years to collect enough. I'm sure they don't really expect to ever get them back."

Courtney looked around, eyes wide. She highly doubted Isaac Young had lived with all this clutter in his space. At least three pairs of shining cat eyes gleamed at her from around the room. One fat tabby sat perched on a stack of papers, licking his paws. Short towers of loose leaf paper and binders peppered the corners of the space.

"Thank you for coming, Courtney," said Ms. Krick, returning from the kitchenette with two steaming cups of tea.

The apartment wasn't dirty, not exactly – but the kitchen was so full of stuff she was sure it hadn't been properly cleaned in a dog's age. What possible reason could Ms. Krick have for bringing her here? This apartment had been Isaac Young's. That at least was interesting. There could be something here.

Courtney took the teacup Ms. Krick held out to her. She sniffed at the liquid inside. Ms. Krick had crossed in front of the couch and shooed an orange cat off the overstuffed cushion nearest to where Courtney stood. She patted the seat beside her for Courtney to come and sit.

Courtney's hand trembled, causing the hot tea she held in front of her to teeter dangerously close to the rim.

"Come, dear," said Ms. Krick. "I won't bite."

Courtney shuffled carefully toward the couch, studying her feet as she walked. Oscar leapt up into Ms. Krick's lap.

"It's like an obstacle course in here," Courtney mumbled under her breath.

Courtney sat gingerly at the edge of the couch. She made a show of blowing on her tea to cool it, though she had no intention of putting it to her lips. It smelled of black tea leaves. She drew in a deeper breath. The strong tea was a welcome mask to the rest of the stale air surrounding them.

"Do you know why I asked you to come?" Ms. Krick asked gently.

Courtney stared at her English teacher. She hoped she was here to learn whatever history of St. Augustus would get her a ticket to public school. But she couldn't say that.

"I've given that lecture every year since I came to the school twenty-five years ago," Ms. Krick told her quietly, pausing to take a sip of her drink. "Every year I watch. I watch for a student who *knows*."

Courtney's jaw dropped.

"Hmmm," crooned Ms. Krick. "Just as I thought. So, what do you think you know?"

Courtney absentmindedly took a sip from her teacup, then

gagged as she realized she'd decided not to drink it. Slowly, she brought the cup to her lips a second time and parted her lips slightly to let the liquid dribble back into the cup. Ms. Krick didn't seem to notice. Courtney scraped her tongue with her teeth to try to rid her mouth of the tea remnants.

Ms. Krick thought Courtney knew something. What was she supposed to know? Was this about the map? Courtney's dad had been cryptic. She really didn't know anything at all, though she did have a key.

"I'm not sure what you mean, Ms. Krick," Courtney answered, setting her teacup down on a side table with a shudder. Good, her voice sounded even. Not at all like the panic she felt rising inside her. Alarm bells were going off in her head. Her body seemed to think she was in danger, firing up the sweat glands in her palms. Courtney wiped her hands on her lap. Oscar glared at her from his perch on Ms. Krick's skirt. Courtney wasn't in any *real* danger here, was she?

Ms. Krick seemed un-phased, watching Courtney.

"You know more than I thought," Ms. Krick said. "You know about the magic."

Courtney's heart skipped a beat. What was she talking about?

"Isaac Young?" Courtney asked, without thinking. She was here to get information. She might have to give a little to get some back. Courtney blinked rapidly. She'd always thought Ms. Krick was a little crazy – now she knew for sure. She darted her eyes around the cat-filled apartment. It would only take her a moment to reach the door. Coming here had been a very bad idea.

"Yes, Isaac Young," Ms. Krick confirmed, nodding her head.

What about Isaac Young? Courtney's head swam. She'd only pretended to know what Ms. Krick was talking about. What could she say now?

"So, I suppose you know about the fountain, then?" Ms. Krick probed. "I always wondered how much your father had figured out."

Courtney's heart raced. Her father. Is this what he'd been trying to tell her? Surely Ms. Krick didn't mean actual magic? Jim Wallis didn't believe in magic, did he? Courtney's mission was to convince her dad she'd found whatever secrets he believed the school held. She had to keep Ms. Krick talking.

"I'm not getting any younger," said Ms. Krick. "It's been years since an alumni kid came through this school who showed any interest in the history."

Courtney held her breath.

"Twenty-five years I've waited to unlock the secrets of the school. Courtney, with your help, this year could be the year. I don't have many left."

Several beats passed while Courtney's thoughts stuttered. Help Ms. Krick? She didn't know anything. Ms. Krick was supposed to be helping her, not the other way around.

"I'd been starting to wonder if the fountain was real," Ms. Krick continued. "But I'm sure your father and his friends found it."

Courtney snapped to attention. Ms. Krick needed to talk to her dad – though he hadn't helped Ms. Krick when he'd been a student. Had he been asked? It seemed obvious to Courtney that working together with Ms. Krick was against the spirit of what he'd asked her to do – the deal they'd made. How much could she find out from her teacher before she realized Courtney wasn't planning to share. She shifted uncomfortably on the cat-hair covered couch.

"How can I help you?" Courtney asked, smiling sweetly while her insides sank. She felt like she'd just made a deal with the devil.

"Isaac Young was a charmed man," Ms. Krick began. "Everything came easily to him, if you know what I mean."

Courtney nodded her head as if she knew what Ms. Krick meant.

"A little too easily," Ms. Krick continued. "There is evidence this school will give back to those who seek help."

Ms. Krick paused.

Courtney held her face in what she hoped was a neutral expression. Had Isaac Young created a charity? Like some sort of scholarship? Her brain raced to try and keep up.

"Among other things," Ms. Krick said, "he left a wishing fountain."

Courtney tried to appear nonchalant. This conversation was starting to sound like nonsense. She'd come here for answers. Ms. Krick had already assumed Courtney, and possibly her dad, knew about some fountain.

Courtney nodded her head in agreement, her thoughts swirling.

"It is said its powers know no limits," Ms. Krick said, becoming animated. "I've searched high and low. I'm beginning to think the fountain won't let me find it."

Courtney felt she could have laughed, if she wasn't so horrified at what Ms. Krick was saying.

"I know the students find it," Ms. Krick continued. "I've felt the changes their silly wishes make." Her face puckered as if she'd just sucked on a lemon. "It's my turn."

A chill ran up Courtney's spine. Whatever this was, Ms. Krick was serious about it - about a wishing well. It was Ms. Krick's turn for what, exactly? She blinked at the elderly teacher, not sure what she was expected to say.

"And it can be your turn too," Ms. Krick continued. "We can find it together."

Courtney nodded her head again involuntarily. Was this what her dad had challenged her to find? Had Ms. Krick told him this same far-fetched story? More likely, her dad and his friends had thought there was something real to find - like Ms. Krick was tracking some sort of treasure - but not this. Had her dad, like

Ms. Krick, been chasing some silly dream all this time?

"Good. More tea?" Ms. Krick asked, standing up and brushing off her skirt before heading for the kitchenette.

Courtney got up. She'd had enough. There wasn't anything she could do to help - and Ms. Krick clearly needed help - lots of it. She started toward the door, but Oscar blocked her path.

"No, thanks, I'm not thirsty," Courtney managed to say.

Oscar let out a low hiss in Courtney's direction. Ms. Krick busily fixed herself some more tea in the kitchenette anyway. Maybe she hadn't heard Courtney protest.

Courtney looked toward the door. She could just leave – but what if Ms. Krick's far-fetched story was exactly what her dad wanted her to know? This could all be some kind of crazy test. Her dad had always liked puzzles.

"So, where is this fountain you mentioned, and why do you need my help?" Courtney asked, still standing near the door.

"You haven't seen it?" Ms. Krick asked, sounding disappointed. "Oh, I thought you had."

Courtney felt her cheeks flush. "Why would I have seen it?" she asked, throwing up her hands. "You're talking about a magic wishing well? Sorry, Ms. Krick, but this is all a little crazy."

So much for playing along.

"I thought your father had told you," Ms. Krick answered, simply.

Courtney shook her head.

"He and his friends definitely found it that spring..." Ms. Krick said, her voice fading as she faced Courtney. "So many secrets they had."

Courtney had one hand on the doorknob, braced to leave.

"I once had a map I thought might help, but it's gone," said Ms. Krick.

"Where did it go?" Courtney asked, her heart beating in her throat. That part, she could shed some light on. Should she?

"It was taken the year your father graduated, but I suspect it's long gone," Ms. Krick answered, sitting resignedly in a rocking chair.

"And you think my dad took it?" Courtney asked in a tone she hoped didn't give him away. She took a step back into the apartment. This was just getting interesting.

"Oh no, Jim wouldn't have done that," Ms. Krick answered, simply. "One of his friends, maybe. David Roth, Steve, or Mariam – rest her soul."

"She's dead?" Courtney blurted.

"Oh yes, but unrelated to the fountain, of course," Ms. Krick added, quickly.

Courtney blanched. Why would someone's death be related to a fountain?

"One of them climbed right up the drain pipe outside that window over there," Ms. Krick said, gesturing to the alcove in a corner of the apartment. "They broke in through my window to get the map. I never could prove which one of them it was."

Courtney looked at her teacher. Why did Ms. Krick think Courtney could help her?

"I need you to take me to the fountain," Ms. Krick told her, her voice filled with purpose.

"Me?" Courtney asked, suddenly understanding why she'd been asked here. "Why me? I don't know anything about a fountain."

"Because you believe," Ms. Krick replied.

"Believe in a magic well?" Courtney asked, choking at the thought. "I don't." She shook her head back and forth. "This is nuts," Courtney said, edging toward the door.

"I can help you find what you're looking for, Courtney," said Ms. Krick. "I've spent 25 years tracking Isaac Young."

"If you know all about him, you don't need me!" Courtney exclaimed. She felt as if her head was being squeezed. First her dad - now Ms. Krick.

"I've come close to finding it," Ms. Krick said. "But it's always eluded me, only showing itself to the students. I'm running out of years and I believe you can lead me to it."

"I can't," Courtney stammered.

"That's a pity," Ms. Krick said, with a cluck of her tongue.

They were interrupted by a scratching sound at the window.

"Perhaps you should see this," Ms. Krick said, cocking her head to one side, and heading over to a rounded front corner of the apartment.

Heaving open the wooden window frame, Ms. Krick leaned out of the window.

Courtney's hands shook. She needed to get out of here. It was okay to abruptly leave if the person you were visiting was off their rocker, wasn't it? She looked over toward Ms. Krick and the window and heard herself cry out in alarm.

Ms. Krick had her whole upper body out of the window, her feet no longer touching the ground.

Forgetting her trepidation, Courtney rushed over to the window and grabbed hold of Ms. Krick's legs, pulling her back into the room. A flat tar papered roof sat just below the window sill. Ms. Krick wouldn't have fallen far if she'd lost her balance, but she was so old she'd probably snap in two. Courtney pulled her back inside and let out half of the breath she'd been holding.

"No, no," Ms. Krick said, brushing Courtney away from where she still held onto the teacher's legs. Ms. Krick leaned out the window a second time, almost climbing onto the sill.

What was the old lady up to? Courtney gave her head a shake. She needed to get out of here, not worry about her teacher's safety. Yet, she didn't move.

There were plenty of students who would love the chance to push Ms. Krick out a window, Courtney figured, observing that it wouldn't take much force. Instead, she waited impatiently for

Ms. Krick to come back inside.

Ms. Krick's head re-emerged only moments later, backing herself into the apartment. One of her arms was the last to emerge from the open air, extended in front of her. On her long, bony hand perched a plump, brown owl.

Courtney gasped instinctively, lifting her hands to her face. This apartment was full of surprises, none of them good. It was a veritable zoo.

"This is Izzy," said Ms. Krick. "He's been visiting my rooms practically since I started teaching."

Courtney spread out her fingers that covered her face, peeking through the gaps.

Izzy rotated his head and locked gazes with Courtney. Slowly dropping her hands to her sides, Courtney looked at the puffy owl then back at Ms. Krick. She felt frozen to the spot. She'd never seen an owl this close before, though he looked just like the renditions of the school's owl mascot, come to life. What did Ms. Krick mean for her to do? It was as though Courtney was expected to know - expected to think this meant something.

"What do you think, Izzy?" Ms. Krick asked the bird.

Izzy cooed and jutted his head as if he were imitating a turkey.

"That's what I think, too," said Ms. Krick.

Courtney watched Ms. Krick and the bird, still unwilling to move. He seemed tame enough, but what if her movements upset him? Was he likely to fly at her? His beak looked sharp.

Ms. Krick stretched her hand back out of the window and let Izzy drop down to the roof surface on the outside. Shuffling his feet around in a circle, he turned his body back toward the window. Izzy's claws clicked against the roof surface. His eyes focused on Courtney.

"Close your mouth, Courtney. Owls are not uncommon around here," said Ms. Krick. "Although, Izzy is uncommonly smart. He sees everything that goes on at St. Augustus. He's particularly fond of sunrise. I don't often see him at night. Perhaps he wanted to check you out."

CHAPTER FOURTEEN

Distance

Courtney had raced across campus very fast, even for her. She needed distance from the teachers' residence – from Ms. Krick. There had been an owl. Ms. Krick had called it by name. What had she called it again?

Courtney slowed to a quick walk once she was heading down the hallway to her room. In her haste, she'd forgotten to lock the door to the teachers' residence, as Giles had asked her to. She only hesitated for a moment. She wasn't going back.

The door to the dorm room she shared with Margaret was ajar and Courtney entered without a word of greeting.

"Courtney!" Margaret exclaimed, jumping up. She knocked her laptop on its side on the bed where she sat. It was switched on, glowing in the semi-dark room. "Where have you been?"

"You'll never believe it," Courtney mumbled, only vaguely acknowledging her roommate and made a beeline for her closet. Digging under the umbrella and fallen coats at the back, she pulled out the rolled map Hanna sister had given her.

"Were you out with that guy from town?" Margaret asked.

"What?" said Courtney, whirling around.

Margaret's mention of Cole brought her back into the now.

Margaret lay on her bed, tummy down and legs wagging in the

air behind her. She closed the screen to the laptop and blew a large, pink bubble with her gum. Courtney winced as Margaret popped her bubble with her fingers.

"Gross," said Courtney, nodding at the gum now on her friend's hand. "But no, this has nothing to do with Cole." She waved the map near Margaret, but not close enough so she might grab it with her sticky hands. "Look at this."

Margaret put her laptop right side up again, then swung her legs around to a seated position on the bed. She reached over to take the map from Courtney.

"Your fingers have gum on them!" Courtney exclaimed, slapping Margaret's hand away from the map.

"Ow," Margaret said, pretending to be offended. "Is that your sister's map?"

"It's Ms. Krick's map," Courtney corrected her then realized her mistake. "Actually, it's Isaac Young's map."

"Are you still trying to suck up to Ms. Krick?" Margaret asked. "Wasn't today's class enough?"

Margaret wasn't taking this seriously. Sharing the map with her might have been a mistake.

"I just came from Ms. Krick's apartment," Courtney said, unrolling the map and watching Margaret cautiously.

"What?" Margaret squealed, "Yuck! What was it like?"

Courtney narrowed her eyes at the parchment she'd stretched out in front of her.

"Margaret, can you hit the lights?" Courtney asked.

"Tell me about Ms. Krick's apartment!" Margaret demanded. "What were you doing there?"

"Of course," Courtney said. "But could you get the lights?"

Margaret frowned, but padded over to the light switch by the door. With one flick, the room was brighter.

"They're gone," Courtney gasped, staring at the paper in front of her.

"Tell me what's going on!" Margaret whined, still standing by the light switch.

"The symbols," Courtney replied, tracing the parchment with her fingers. "There were symbols all over this map. They're not there anymore."

"Courtney, you're not making sense," said Margaret, folding her arms.

Courtney's eyes traced the map. The teachers' residence was off to the left, the east side of campus. The Main Building was there, too, though just as when she'd first looked at the map, the West Building, the Sports Complex and the newer boys' dorm weren't there.

"There were symbols," Courtney said hurriedly. "Didn't you see them the other day?"

"I didn't see anything," Margaret told her, furrowing her brow. "I was trying to sleep. You opened the curtains, and the light was so bright..."

A wave of hope washed over Courtney. Of course! She'd held the map up to the window. It needed light. She stretched the map so the overhead light fixture threw its rays onto the backside of it. Its paper glowed with the warmth of the bulb, but only the brown sketches adorned the paper. Courtney threw the map down on her bed.

"Gah!" she exclaimed.

"Okay, Courtney," Margaret told her, placing her hands on her hips. "Fill me in."

CHAPTER FIFTEEN

Crazy Talk

To her credit, Margaret had taken it all in stride. Out loud, the story of Courtney's visit to Ms. Krick seemed even more bizarre to Courtney than it had in her head.

"So, she actually thinks there's some sort of magic fountain?" Margaret asked.

Courtney sank to the floor, leaning her back against the bed. She nodded slowly. It had taken her twenty minutes to explain everything she'd experienced so far, but really, that was the crux of it.

"And she has a pet owl?" Margaret asked.

Courtney nodded again. Not a pet, exactly, but close enough.

"And your dad, he told you to find out about it all?" Margaret continued.

"I think so," Courtney confirmed. "Ms. Krick's words seem to fit what my dad was talking about."

"Maybe if you tell your dad what you found, he'll let you go home," Margaret added. "Not that I want you to go home, of course," she added quickly. "But if it's what you want."

"I don't think that's it," Courtney replied. "He doesn't think much of Ms. Krick. He even stole her map." Courtney gestured to the parchment sitting on the bed. "Still, I'll give him a call and see what he says. I really don't want to have another conversation with Ms. Krick. My skin is still crawling."

"So, do you think Ms. Krick is a witch?" Margaret asked, snapping her gum between her teeth.

Margaret's question was in jest, Courtney knew that. Yet something about it nagged her.

"Margaret, can you look up owls that are native to this area?" Courtney asked, sitting down on Margaret's bed and handing her roommate her laptop.

CHAPTER SIXTEEN

Sunrise

Courtney lay awake long into the night. Everything she'd learned only posed new questions, giving no answers. She'd called her dad. She could tell she was on the right track, but he just told her to keep looking. He'd seemed amused. He didn't answer anything directly.

"A fountain?" he'd asked. "Why, what have you learned?"

Talking to him had only generated more questions. It was clear he had no intention of helping her.

"Don't worry, you'll know when you've found it," he'd told her.

Big help he'd been. She was even more confused about his involvement in the whole process than she'd been before she'd called. Had he ever found the fountain Ms. Krick described? When Courtney had asked him about it a second time, he'd only laughed and told her again the school had a lot to offer. He'd treated her questions the way she'd seen him do a million times in interviews when he couldn't tell the press what was really going on.

From the sounds of Margaret's deep breathing on the other side of their room, she was asleep.

Margaret thought the whole story was crazy, Courtney knew. She'd treated it like a bit of a game, but she'd been listening. She and Courtney had stayed up late, talking through everything Courtney had learned. It had helped.

Searching online, they'd found some pictures of owls common to the area. The ones they saw could have looked like Izzy, as far as Courtney could tell. The troubling part was that Wikipedia claimed those owls had an average lifespan of 15 years. Ms. Krick had been teaching at St. Augustus much longer than that. Perhaps she'd been exaggerating when she said Izzy had been visiting that long. Or maybe there was a second owl.

Or, Courtney reminded herself as she wriggled around under her covers, trying to get comfortable, Ms. Krick could be completely delusional. The thought had crossed Courtney's mind more than once.

Still, Courtney's dad believed there was magic here, too. And he wasn't crazy, was he?

Courtney closed her eyes for the umpteenth time, but all she could imagine was Izzy, staring at her. Not exactly a recipe for sweet dreams. Could an owl really be as tame as he'd seemed? He even seemed tamer than the cats in Ms. Krick's apartment.

Another thing they'd learned from Wikipedia was that owls were supposed to sleep during the day. They were nocturnal. Courtney could have sworn Ms. Krick had said he didn't visit at night.

Still unable to block his eyes from her thoughts, she pulled the covers up over her head. Yet the day's events continued to play like a movie reel in her mind, over and over. It was a puzzle she was meant to solve.

Courtney woke with a start the next morning. The first rays of light peeked through the edges of the drapes, dancing on the beige walls of their room. Courtney stared at the straight lines of light reaching onto the far wall, by the closet. Ms. Krick had said Izzy visited at sunrise. Maybe sunrise had something to do with it.

Courtney hadn't bothered to put the map away in the closet the night before, preferring to keep it close. She retrieved it from where she'd tucked it behind her headboard and unrolled it hastily, holding it up to the thin beam of light stretching into their room. She was rewarded for her effort. Anywhere the sunlight touched, icons glowed through the paper. The rest of the map remained dark.

Her hands shaking, she let the map snap shut and fall to the bed. Jumping to her feet, she reached over and pulled back the drapes. Orange-tinged sunlight poured into the room.

A loud groan came from Margaret's side of the room.

"Look!" Courtney exclaimed. Margaret would forgive her for the wake up once she'd seen what Courtney had found. She reached over and excitedly pulled the covers from her roommate's face. "The symbols. They're back! It's the sunrise!"

"What?" Margaret asked, rubbing her eyes.

Courtney stretched the map so Margaret could see it without getting up.

"They're here now," said Courtney. "They need sunrise. Or, sunlight anyway, I'm not sure."

"Well, *I* need sleep!" Margaret cried, pulling her pillow over her head.

"Sorry," Courtney said, lowering her voice to a whisper. She knew this wasn't the first time she'd disturbed Margaret this week.

Courtney dug around in the top drawer of her desk and retrieved a roll of scotch tape. Smoothing the wrinkles out of the map as best she could, she lightly tacked its corners against the window.

The symbols didn't seem to form any sort of pattern, except where the center of the West Woods was virtually littered with them.

"That's got to be where it is," Courtney whispered in Margaret's direction. She hoped her hushed voice would annoy her roommate a little less, but she also wanted Margaret's help. "Will you come with me?" she asked, crossing to stand beside Margaret's bed. Somehow, going out on her own that morning seemed like a bad idea.

Margaret didn't answer, though she stirred a little.

She would come, Courtney thought. She just maybe needed a minute to wake up. Adrenaline coursing through her body, Courtney turned her back on Margaret and the map and yanked open the top drawer of her dresser, almost tugging it right off its tracks. She pulled on her running clothes in record time. Tying her hair back with an elastic, she looked over at Margaret, still in bed.

"Are you coming?" she asked, not as quietly this time. She reached over and gently shook Margaret's foot through the covers.

"Where?" Margaret groaned.

"To find the fountain!" Courtney exclaimed. "It's got to be there, in the woods!" She stood close to the map and put her finger where the concentration of symbols was thickest. Right in the middle of a clearing, a tiny fountain shape glowed. "Do you see that?" Courtney asked in Margaret's general direction, as she reached under her bed and pulled out her running shoes.

"You're going running?" Margaret asked, her eyes now mostly open. "I'm *not* going running."

"We just have to make it *look* like we're running," Courtney told her. "In case we get caught."

She waited a moment, but the sunrise would be gone soon.

"Are you coming?" Courtney asked.

"Running?" said Margaret, laughing without moving from her position in her bed. "Heck, no!"

Had Margaret not heard anything she'd been saying? Courtney

tapped her foot as Margaret yawned dramatically, stretching her arms over her head.

"We're not *actually* going running, Margaret! We're going to try to find the fountain," said Courtney, impatiently. "It's in the woods."

"We can't leave campus at this hour," Margaret protested.

"Sure, we can," said Courtney, her arms folded against her chest. "I do it all the time. Get dressed. Hurry, the sun is almost all the way up."

She reached over and offered her hand to help Margaret. She complied by rising out of bed and going to her dresser. Her eyes were barely open, but at least she was moving.

Courtney found Margaret's runners buried deep in the closet and threw them at her roommate. She then took a snapshot of the map with her phone. Crimson light of the sunrise spilled through the symbols.

Moments later, the two girls silently left the room and burst out onto the lawn.

"C'mon," Courtney said, breaking into a jog.

"I thought we were only pretending to run," Margaret complained, walking quickly behind her.

"Well, you took so long to get out of bed," Courtney said over her shoulder. She picked up her pace. "We don't have much time. I don't know what the sunrise means, but it seemed to work on the map."

To her credit, Margaret kept up, jogging easily alongside Courtney. She wasn't a runner by choice, but they had to do lots of dry-land training for swimming and she was in decent shape.

"Last night you didn't seem to think much of the fountain," Margaret remarked as they hit the sidewalk at the edge of the campus lawn. "Now you want to find it?"

"That was before sunrise could make glowing symbols appear on a map that regular light couldn't," Courtney answered, taking her phone out of her pocket and opening the picture she'd taken earlier. She had to know if there was something to all of this. "It looks like there's a spot right in the middle of the woods that doesn't have trees. That's where we're going. If we make a straight line from right about here, I think we'll hit it." Courtney pointed to the line of trees near the sidewalk.

The girls slowed to a walk as they came to the edge of the woods. Courtney looked over at Margaret, who shrugged. She seemed up for it. Courtney gave her a quick nod, then the girls plunged forward, moving branches together to clear the way. There was no discernible path, but the trees were evenly spaced and there wasn't much underbrush.

The light was still dusky under the canopy of the woods. Courtney felt chilled. If there was some sort of magic fountain in these woods, why hadn't Ms. Krick found it? That part bothered her the most.

"How much further?" Margaret asked, in a forced whisper.

Courtney consulted the picture of the map on her phone.

"Should be up ahead," she answered, looking down at her soggy running shoes. They were covered with half-melted snow and wet muck, just as her canvas shoes had been the night she'd gone into the woods with Jake.

The trees seemed to get more thinly spaced and the girls could walk a little faster, their hands leading the way by moving the spiny branches. Courtney swore under her breath as a long branch of dead wood snapped off in her hand. She didn't want to hurt the trees, but they had to hurry.

The trees abruptly gave way to a glen with long, frosty grass and a smattering of snow drifts. In the center of the clearing stood a large stone fountain.

"Whoa," Margaret said, with a low whistle, stopping in her tracks. "There really is a fountain in here."

The fountain looked like it had sprouted from the grass, the vegetation around it was so overgrown. White stone cracked with age was meticulously carved into a basin, with a tower gushing water down in the center. Its edges were rounded with time.

Courtney found herself quickly at the fountain's side, peering into its clear water. Scattered coins littered the bottom of the basin. "How is the water so clean?" Courtney wondered aloud. Stone on the outside of the basin was stained with moss and cracked, but inside the water was clear. Mist sprayed from the center tower, landing on her cheeks as a warm fog.

"Now what?" said Margaret, her voice seeming far away.

Courtney turned to see her roommate still standing at the edge of the clearing, snapping photos of the fountain with her phone.

The sun was over the horizon now, its thin beams peeking through the trees to the east, casting lines on the water. As Courtney watched ripples form in the basin, a noise overhead made her look up.

"Izzy," Courtney gasped.

An owl just like the one Ms. Krick had brought into her apartment flapped his way into the clearing and landed on the tower of the fountain.

"Is that Ms. Krick's owl?" Margaret asked in a hoarse whisper.

Courtney shrugged. Izzy was the only owl she'd ever seen up close. It could be him. She felt rooted to where she stood, watching the owl. He was so still he could have been part of the fountain. Were owls dangerous? He hadn't seemed dangerous in Ms. Krick's living room. The owl looked back at her. Courtney knew what she needed to do.

"What if he tells Ms. Krick we were in the woods?" Margaret asked, louder this time.

"Don't be ridiculous," Courtney answered, not breaking eye contact with Izzy. "He's an owl." He couldn't communicate with Ms. Krick. Could he?

With a flap of his wings, Izzy took flight and flew off away from the school.

"See?" Courtney said, relaxing a little. "He's not even going to Ms. Krick's." She looked into the sky in the direction he'd gone, somehow feeling she'd insulted him.

"I think I'm ready to go back," called Margaret. "We'll be in big trouble if Ms. Krick comes here."

"Not yet," said Courtney. Ms. Krick had spent years trying to find this fountain. It couldn't be as easy as it seemed.

"What, then?" Margaret asked.

Wasn't it obvious?

"We make a wish," Courtney answered, looking back at the fountain.

"No way," Margaret called loudly, coming in closer to Courtney. "This whole thing is too creepy. I'm not making a wish. That's just what Ms. Krick wants us to do. What if it's a trap?"

"I really don't think Ms. Krick's ever seen the fountain," Courtney replied. Ms. Krick had made that clear, and Courtney believed her. If she had seen it, she wouldn't need Courtney's help. Courtney fished around in her running coat pocket and found a penny, as well as the list she'd made about the deal with her dad. She unfolded the list and read it again. There was no harm in asking for help. In fact, it seemed perfect. The quest her dad had started her on would help her get home.

"*I wish for the strength to go after everything on this list with all I've got!*" Courtney declared, flipping her coin into the basin. The coin plummeted to the bottom of the water without a sound, settling on the stone alongside the other hopeful coins that had been tossed in before it.

Courtney couldn't remember the last time she'd wished on a coin. She smiled. Whatever this strange fountain was, she was willing to believe it might work. What was the harm in that?

"How is this thing even running, without pipes or electricity?"

Margaret asked. "What's pumping the water?" She ventured closer and walked around the fountain in a slow loop, as if sizing up an opponent.

"Fountains have been around since Roman times or something, silly," said Courtney. "They must not need all that." Margaret was completely missing the point.

"Maybe," Margaret replied, not looking convinced. "But I don't get how Ms. Krick hasn't found it, if she's been looking. It wasn't that hard."

"Maybe teachers aren't allowed in the West Woods, either?" Courtney offered. The truth was, she wasn't thinking about Ms. Krick at all. She felt like a weight had been lifted from her. She was ready to tackle her list. The bones of a plan formed in her head, as if they'd been there all along. She could start right now.

"We should get back," Courtney said, starting to walk toward the edge of the clearing. As an afterthought, she pulled a second penny from her pocket. "Want to make a wish?" Courtney asked, offering Margaret the coin.

Margaret shook her head forcefully, her eyes wide.

"Suit yourself," said Courtney, pocketing the coin, "but we can't stay." She turned and walked briskly back the way they'd come.

"There's a sort of path leading that way," Margaret said, pointing to a gap in the trees in the direction of the campus.

"That probably leads right to the lawn," Courtney said, looking where Margaret pointed, but only for a moment, since the lawn looked too exposed. "Better to go this way, less chance of getting caught." She barreled back into the trees. They had swim practice starting soon. She had some work to do and she didn't want to be late.

"Courtney, wait up!" Margaret called from behind her.

Courtney slowed down, though she didn't want to.

"What did you wish for?" Margaret asked her, looking at her strangely.

Courtney waited a beat. How could she explain? It was complicated. She reached into her pocket and pulled out the list, handing it to her roommate without a word. Margaret unfolded the list and stood still while she read it silently. Her brow furrowed.

Courtney watched her for a moment, then turned and kept picking her way out of the woods, putting distance between her and Margaret. She didn't want to hear Margaret's judgement. She already knew it was bad.

"Seems harmless enough," Margaret called to her. "But, you know, you could do all these things on your own."

Courtney nodded, but didn't slow down. She was sure she could.

CHAPTER SEVENTEEN

I Believe

"So, what are you going to say to Ms. Krick?" Violet demanded of Courtney after swim practice. They had a full table for breakfast.

"I don't know," Courtney answered, picking at her cereal. She wasn't hungry at all. Truth be told, she hadn't given Ms. Krick another thought. She'd been so focused at swim practice she'd even surprised herself. They hadn't been timed, but Courtney was sure her times had been up there with her personal best.

"I can't believe you drank her tea! Blech!" said Rhoda.

Courtney gave Margaret a withering look, as her roommate was deep in conversation with Lynette. How had Margaret managed to share everything about Courtney's visit to Ms. Krick's so quickly? She certainly had a gift. Courtney smacked her gums a little. She'd almost forgotten about the tea, but now its bitter taste was all she could think about. She had no desire to try anything ever again that was made in Ms. Krick's unkept kitchen.

Even Margaret was at breakfast today. She only got up early enough to join them when they had early swim practices. Otherwise, she'd still be lounging in bed. Courtney hadn't explicitly told Margaret her visit to Ms. Krick's, and the wish and everything else was a secret, but still – she hadn't expected her to tell everyone they knew. It seemed private, somehow. She wasn't ready for her well-meaning friends to challenge her about her sudden belief in magic.

"Guys, c'mon, it's just legend. Nobody believes it," Courtney said, addressing the whole table of girls. She hoped they'd drop it. Then she'd be free to figure out what she thought, on her own.

"I'm confused," said Violet. "How did you make so many wishes? That's not how a wishing well works."

Courtney looked at the clock on the wall at the far end of the cafeteria. The gym would still be open for another half hour before classes started. She could still get in a workout if she left now. She knew she'd need to build more strength if she wanted to make any serious improvement to her swim times. Running helped her calves, but did little for her upper body strength.

"No, silly," Margaret explained, sipping at her mango juice. "Courtney only made one wish. But she wished for a list that had a bunch of stuff on it." Margaret produced the list from her pocket and held it up. Courtney reached over, but wasn't quick enough to grab the piece of paper before Lynette plucked it from Margaret's hand, out of Courtney's reach.

"Team captain?" Lynette asked, reading from the list out loud. "You barely even practice. You're going to have to kick it up a notch."

The competitive edge in Lynette's voice shone through her comment. Courtney let her outstretched arm fall. They'd seen the list now, anyway. Well, let them look. Courtney took a deep breath. She was going to achieve everything on that list. She didn't need their permission.

"I'm actually going to hit the gym," Courtney announced.

She stood up and stretched her arms above her head. A good workout was exactly what she needed to get this day re-started.

"What?" Margaret shrieked. "Is it even open this early?"

Courtney had English class first period with Ms. Krick. Surely, the decrepit teacher wouldn't bring up her quest for the fountain in front of the whole class. Courtney didn't want to be alone with Ms. Krick, maybe ever again. That was the trick. She had no intention of telling Ms. Krick she'd found the fountain. Margaret was right. Courtney could master all the items on her list without a magic fountain.

Ms. Krick wasn't in her right mind, and Courtney didn't need her. She'd show her dad she'd tried, on her own. Courtney snatched the list from Lynette's hand on her way past.

"Hey!" exclaimed Lynette in protest, though she was laughing.

Courtney walked away from the table without a backward glance, trying to muster a swagger on the way. Lynette had said she'd have to kick it up a notch. That's exactly what she planned to do.

CHAPTER EIGHTEEN

Surprise Encounter

The next twenty-four hours passed in a something of a blur. Courtney had studied the items on her list until they were ingrained in her mind.

Ms. Krick had watched her carefully during English class. Courtney could sense her gaze, even though she never looked directly at her teacher. She was going to have to get creative if avoidance was going to be her only defense.

Sporting an innocuous smile, Courtney had ducked out of class the moment the bell rang, successfully averting any contact attempt by Ms. Krick.

On Friday morning, she again rose early enough to go for a run. She'd told herself it wasn't because she wanted to return to the fountain. Yet, as soon as she'd reached the sidewalk, she'd turned without thinking in the direction of the West Woods instead of onto her regular route into town. She just didn't want to run into Cole, she reassured herself. This wasn't about the fountain.

A chill came over her as she drew closer to where the trees flanked her path on to the left. Entering the woods was becoming easier each time. She'd never seen Ms. Krick out at this hour, but it was probably best to run all the way past the woods, then double back through the yard of the house on the other side. Kids called it the Taylor house, though she'd never wondered why before now. She supposed that must be the name of the family who lived there. She cranked up her music to distract her from entering the woods by a faster route.

Courtney's run had slowed to a jog. As she moved her foot forward to take the next step on the pavement, her foot hit something soft that gave way, landing Courtney in a heap on the sidewalk.

She'd just stepped on a bundle of fur. A dog.

Courtney yelped loudly and grabbed her right ankle.

A sandpaper tongue covered her with kisses as she pushed the dog off with her hands. Disoriented with the shock of her fall, Courtney reached up and yanked the earbuds out of her ears. She could still hear her music blaring from the ear pieces dangling loose around her neck. She scrambled to turn the music down from her phone. As she struggled to get her phone out of the pocket on her sleeve, the cord caught in her hair, pulling a chunk of frizzy red loose from her ponytail, leaving it hanging in a spiral at the side of her face. The wet tongue licking her then became small paws batting at her cheeks.

"Oh, Husk," Courtney groaned, rubbing her ankle where she'd fallen and as she struggled to sit up. "Now look what you've done."

Husk whimpered and snuggled in where Courtney lay crumpled on the pavement.

"Courtney!" Cole called, coming quickly toward her. "Are you alright?"

Cole grabbed Husk by the scruff of his neck and pulled him off Courtney. He wasn't dressed for running. He wore a heavy overcoat and what looked like plaid flannel pants – pajama pants. Slip-on boots completed his ensemble.

He'd probably never been a runner at all, Courtney realized. Hot fury rose on the back of her neck. Her ankle smarted. She turned her head away. She had nothing to say to Cole.

"Let me help you up," Cole offered, standing awkwardly over Courtney, who had pulled herself to a sitting position.

Courtney shook her head. She didn't want his help.

Was she all right? Courtney turned her head a little and wiped a tear from her eye with her sleeve. It didn't matter if he saw her like this. He'd made it clear he wasn't interested. She wasn't stupid enough to give him another chance.

Letting go of her throbbing ankle, she smoothed the escaped hair behind her ear. Cole had Husk in a firm hold and pulled him into his lap, as he sat on the sidewalk beside her.

"We really should stop meeting with you falling on the pavement," Cole said, with a slight smile.

Courtney looked away from him again once she realized she'd been staring. He didn't seem like the cruel person she'd been building up in her mind since he'd stood her up.

"Hey, uh..." he began, his voice cracking a little.

Here it came, the talk - the excuse. Courtney flexed her ankle, which screamed back in protest. If she could get up and run from here, she would. Instead, she needed a minute to recover. She was trapped. She turned her face toward Cole and squared her jaw. She had no choice but to listen to what he was about to say.

It wasn't like they'd been an item, she reminded herself. Sure, he'd made a good first impression, but the rest, well the rest she'd rather not think about. She might be stuck here, and she might have to hear what he had to say. But she didn't have to internalize it. Nothing he said mattered now. She listened to Husk's panting and resigned herself that this conversation was going to happen. She felt tired.

"Look, Courtney, I'm really sorry I missed our run the other day," Cole continued into the silence. "I uh, I slept in."

"Hmm," Courtney managed to say. She might not have had much experience with relationships, but she knew a line when she heard one.

"Well, the thing is, I uh..." said Cole, trailing off as he rubbed Husk behind the ear. "I actually couldn't sleep that night. I was really looking forward to seeing you again and I just couldn't get to sleep, so around five in the morning I finally dozed off and, well, when I woke up and realized the time, I just threw on my coat over my pajamas and rushed out to see if I could see you."

The hard kernel inside Courtney started to melt a little.

"I've been walking Husk every morning since, but I haven't seen you."

"I uh," Courtney stammered. "I haven't been running that way. I came here the other day, though, with a friend."

Cole's smile faded, just a touch.

"My roommate," Courtney added quickly. "I was here with my roommate."

That seemed to brighten him a little.

"I'm so sorry about Husk, Courtney," he continued. "We were just on our way back to the house when we stopped for him to do his business. I saw you over here, and I let him run to get your attention. I didn't mean for him to trip you, I..."

"I'm so sorry I wasn't there that day," he continued softly. "What you must think of me. I've been just sick over it. But I didn't even have your number."

Courtney looked at him curiously. Her fury had fled. In its place, she felt at ease with Cole and his awkward apology.

"It's okay," said Courtney, suppressing the smile that was trying to form. She wasn't ready to let him completely off the hook just yet. "But if we meet again, it would be easier if I knew where you lived, and we set a time – or I had your number."

A broad, slow smile spread across Cole's face.

Courtney's spirits lifted as she saw his relief. She tried to smile back, but winced with pain as she moved her foot.

"Here, let me look," Cole said, as he shifted the bulk of a

panting Husk under one of his arms with effort. He gently pulled Courtney's foot into his now vacant lap. "Where does it hurt?" He rotated her ankle slowly with his free hand.

"Ow, I uh..." said Courtney, as she shifted her foot out of his lap and pushed herself to a standing position. "I'll be fine."

She brushed off her legs nonchalantly. Her ankle was on fire. She felt a shiver ripple up her back. It wasn't below freezing this morning, but the pavement she'd been sitting on was ice cold and the sweat she'd worked up from her short run had cooled.

Cole hopped to his feet and set Husk down on the pavement beside him, holding tightly to his leash.

"Are you sure you're okay?" Cole asked, crinkling his nose, and with it, his freckles.

"Yeah, I uh, might need a hand, though," said Courtney. She tried to put weight on her foot but failed.

"No problem."

Cole quickly scooted to her side and wrapped her arm around his shoulders, supporting her as she walked. "I could piggy-back you to campus?" he offered.

"No, this is fine, thanks," she replied. Truthfully, she didn't want him to move his arm from around her, the warmth felt amazing. The wind had found the vent holes in her jacket and her skin crawled with gooseflesh underneath her sleeves.

"Here," Cole said, shimmying out of his winter coat and placing it gently around her shoulders.

"No, it's okay," Courtney protested, without moving away from the sudden warmth of his coat. "Then you'll be cold. And, uh..."

"I'm totally fine, really," he said. He was now standing on the sidewalk in just his pajamas. His flannel shirt matched his plaid pants, with white cording lining the lapel.

Courtney smiled despite herself and slipped the rest of the way into his warm coat. It smelled a little like cologne and, well, a little like Husk. The earthy mixture was calming, somehow.

Courtney drew in deep breaths, steadying herself.

She felt like she'd really done a number on her ankle this time. The dorm seemed like an impossible distance away. With Cole's help, Courtney gingerly started back to the edge of campus. Husk excitedly ran back and forth between them, though Courtney kept on eye on him. She wasn't about to let him make her fall again.

"So, uh," Cole began, walking beside Courtney and matching her slow pace. "Were you mad I wasn't there to meet you? Seems like you're mad..."

Courtney cocked her head to the side. What exactly did he expect her to say? Had she been mad? Yes, she'd surely been mad - or at least disappointed. Was she still mad? She'd only just found out he'd wanted to be there. She needed some time to process things. Looking up at the horizon, she noticed the sun was almost all the way up.

"I just ran like any other day," Courtney answered, watching the sun spread across the sky. Cole said he'd been looking forward to seeing her. She tried to focus on that.

"Oh, I'm so sorry," said Cole, turning toward her and steadying her with his arms. "Is there a doctor on campus who can look at your ankle?"

Courtney nodded.

"A nurse," she said. "But I'll just go back to the dorm and see her in a bit, it's still pretty early."

"We haven't totally missed the sunrise, at least," Cole said, looking straight at her.

He let go of Husk's leash. Husk was all too happy to wander away toward the edge of the woods. Courtney's gaze followed Husk as he poked around in a clump of trees. She didn't look at Cole. She didn't want to move, in case he took his arms away.

Without glancing in Cole's direction, she turned her attention back to the sunrise. The clouds over the campus shimmered with yellows and oranges, striped like brightly colored tufts of cotton candy woven together. She no longer shivered. Slowly, she looked back at him, standing less than a foot away from her, in his pajamas. No, she wasn't mad, at least not anymore.

They stood there for a moment smiling stupidly at each other, before he slipped his arms tighter around her waist and pulled her toward him.

"Let me make it up to you?" Cole asked, quietly.

Courtney nodded her head. She was hardly going to protest.

"I'll take you on a proper date," he said, looking hopeful.

Suddenly Courtney wished she'd taken more time with her ponytail that morning. She nodded again. She couldn't take her eyes away from his lips, so red against his pale skin.

As if he'd done it a thousand times before, Cole leaned in gently then and kissed her lips softly, slowly stroking the small of her back through his coat that she wore as his lips parted hers.

Courtney felt her knees buckle a little. This was the way a kiss was supposed to happen. Her hurried dare with Ethan flashed across her mind, but Courtney pushed the memory aside. Warmth spread through her - all the way down to her throbbing ankle. They stood there for a moment before Courtney had to shift her weight onto her bad ankle, faltering slightly and ending the kiss.

Cole leaned in to prop her up and planted one last kiss at the tip of her nose as he turned his back toward her and held out his arms.

"Now, hop on my back and I'll take you across the lawn. You need to get that ankle looked at. Where do you need to go?" he asked, looking around the wide campus.

"Over there," Courtney answered, pointing to the girls' dorm. She was sure her smile reached her ears.

Cole called Husk to his side and Courtney hopped up on Cole's back, pushing off the sidewalk with her good foot.

Cole ran playfully across the lawn, Courtney bobbing up and down on his back as he ran. They were both laughing and Husk ran happily beside them. Their laughter rang out over the deserted campus. Courtney didn't even care that the bouncing hurt her ankle.

"Over there," Courtney directed him.

They found themselves too soon at the door to the dorm. Cole carefully set her down.

"Are you going to be all right?" Cole asked. His voice was raspy from the exertion of carrying her. "I could help you to your room, if you like?" Courtney looked at him in alarm. Boys weren't allowed in the girls' dorm. Especially not at this hour. He wasn't even dressed.

"No," said Courtney, shaking her head, laughing at his forwardness. "You're still in your pajamas! I'll be fine, really."

"Okay, have it your way," he said. "But I do need your phone number, so I can call you and make sure you don't need a piggy-back anywhere else today."

Courtney laughed and accepted Cole's phone as he held it out for her. She typed in her phone number and handed it back.

"Get that foot looked at," Cole told her, touching her cheek.

Courtney nodded, but her thoughts wandered. Spraining her ankle was going to put a crimp in her plans. How was she supposed to make team captain if she couldn't swim?

"Your coat!" Courtney said, slipping out of it and handing the coat to him.

"I'll call you," Cole said, accepting the coat and stepping toward her until there wasn't any space between them.

And then were kissing again - smiling and kissing.

"I'd better go in," Courtney suddenly whispered, realizing they hadn't been talking quietly at all. "The house mother's room is right above us there." She pointed to the window just to the right of the door.

"I'll talk to you soon," said Cole, backing away and leading Husk with him.

Courtney nodded and went inside, hopping a little as she made her way down the hall. Quietly, she entered her shared dorm room, expecting Margaret to still be asleep. Instead, Margaret stood in front of the window, a towel wrapped around her body. Margaret had already showered. Courtney gave a start and looked at the time. She'd have to hurry.

"Courtney, what *happened* to you?" Margaret asked, rushing to Courtney's side, still clutching the towel wrapped around her. "You look like hell."

Courtney couldn't help but smile. Her hair was a frizzy mess, her knees were muddy and she was limping.

"Your jacket's torn!" said Margaret, helping her over to the bed, and tugging at Courtney's sleeve, which must have ripped when Courtney fell to the pavement. "Are you hurt?" Margaret helped her out of her jacket.

"I was with Cole," she said, lowering herself onto the bed.

"Cole!" Margaret exclaimed, her mouth agape. "He did this to you? Are you hurt?"

Courtney burst out laughing, but Margaret looked positively horrified.

"No, no – nothing like that!" Courtney assured her, smiling. "I fell, that's all. My ankle's hurt worse than it was the last time. I think it might be sprained."

"Coach Laurel is going to kill you," Margaret said, relaxing a little and looking down at Courtney's foot.

Courtney frowned. Margaret worried too much about Coach Laurel. Courtney doubted the coach would actually care if Courtney took some time off from the team. But that was a problem, in itself. It really was going to be tough to prove she could be team captain if she couldn't swim.

"So, what happened?" Margaret said. "Did you give him heck

for standing you up, or what?"

Courtney shook her head.

"Why are you smiling like that?" Margaret asked.

Courtney looked down at her runners and undid the shoelace on her injured foot as wide as she could, then slipped off her shoe.

"Well?" Margaret prompted. "What's he like? Did you guys talk?"

"Not athletic?" said Courtney, laughing, since it was the first thing that came to mind.

Margaret scrunched up her nose.

CHAPTER NINETEEN

Hurt

Courtney's ankle continued to swell throughout the day. By the time the last bell rang she found herself nearly hobbling back to the dorm.

"Ouch," Margaret said, furrowing her brow as Courtney came into their room. "Are you actually going to be okay to swim?"

"I guess so," Courtney answered, not feeling so sure as she pulled her swim gear out from under her bed. She had to try. She didn't have to put weight on it in the pool. She might be able to fake her way through practice. "But I probably won't be running for a while."

"Good," Margaret said, with a simple laugh.

"What?" Courtney asked, looking at her in surprise.

"No early morning alarm to wake me up!" Margaret answered brightly.

Courtney laughed as she scooped up the jeans and shirt she'd worn the night before from the floor. She stuffed them into her backpack to change into after practice.

She checked her phone. Still nothing from Cole, but he'd call. She felt sure of it.

Still clad in their kilts, Margaret and Courtney headed to the pool for practice. Courtney walked a fraction slower than usual, though it wasn't bad, considering what had happened to her.

"Uh, thanks, Margaret," said Courtney, as they walked across the campus to the shiny new sports complex, where the pool was located. She'd been meaning to thank Margaret for a few days. "For not making a big deal about the dare like Violet. I appreciate it."

"Never mind that," Margaret replied. "Violet just likes to talk. It wasn't that bad. But I *am* sorry if I shared too much about the fountain and all that. I'm just trying to help."

"I know," Courtney assured her friend. "It's just that I feel a little crazy chasing some story."

"It is *completely* crazy," said Margaret. "But fun too!"

Courtney smiled as she pulled open the heavy metal door to the Sports Complex, holding it open for Margaret. Throughout this whole ordeal, fun didn't really seem a good description. It felt more like her destiny to fulfill her wish.

The foyer of the Sports Complex was noisy as practices in the three gyms, which shared the building with the pool, were getting underway. The friends strode confidently through the students milling about, making their way past the gyms to the quiet hallway that led to the pool locker rooms at the back of the building.

The girls' locker room was abuzz, though the swim team didn't fill the large space. Margaret flitted off to visit with Sage, the current team captain. Courtney watched as Margaret turned on her charm. She'd made the team this year by the skin of her teeth. Sage had for sure influenced Coach Laurel on Margaret's behalf. Still, Margaret deserved to be here, Courtney had to admit. She added a lot to the team spirit with her never-ending positivity.

Courtney set her bag down on the bench beside Lynette and started to unpack her gear.

"Hey, how's your ankle?" Lynette asked. "I heard you were limping. You going to be able to swim?"

"Sure," Courtney said, nodding. She could manage. The cold water might even help, she tried to convince herself. Courtney grit her teeth as she pulled the knee sock from her bad ankle. She might have to tell the coach about her fall. From the sounds of it, most of the team probably already knew she was injured by now.

Coach would ban her from running for sure. She'd never liked Courtney running as much as she did. Easing up on running might be a smart play for Courtney. She'd show her coach swimming was her top priority. She was surprised that giving up running seemed like a good idea.

Courtney poked at her bare ankle, which was puffy to the touch. A faint purple tinged the edges where the muscle lay. It didn't seem bad enough now to be sprained. She hadn't bothered visiting the nurse. She knew what she needed to do to recover, but it wasn't going to be easy to shave off her swim times while she rested.

Courtney tossed the clothes she'd just removed, along with the rest of the contents of her backpack, into the nearest locker and pulled on her Owl's practice swimsuit. It was green, with a shiny silver owl covering the body of the suit. As she shifted her backpack in the locker so that she could close the door, a metal object fell with a clang to the floor, rolling under the bench in front of the bank of lockers.

Courtney scrambled down to bend under the bench, putting her head low to the floor tiles to see what had fallen out of her backpack. She reached under the bench and around a pair of her teammate's ankles to pick up the key she'd rescued from the lost and found.

"Hey!" the owner of the ankles exclaimed.

Courtney looked up to see Sage. Hadn't Margaret just been speaking to her?

"Sorry," Courtney mumbled sheepishly, scrambling to her feet, she looked around for Margaret, but she was nowhere to be seen.

Courtney opened her mouth to explain, but Sage had already gone back to talking with another senior – apparently unconcerned by what Courtney was doing on the floor. Just as well. She didn't want to explain.

Courtney brushed a fine layer of dust off her knees that had come from the floor under the bench. She felt the key she held scratch her skin lightly, leaving a pinkish line. She frowned at the line and turned the key over a few times in her hand. Its edges were rough. She shouldn't read too much into the scratch. Why did everything suddenly seem like part of a master plan? She needed to stay focused.

"Where did you come from?" Courtney asked the key, quietly.

The rusted outer layer crumbled slightly as she turned it, staining her hands where she held it. Courtney wiped her soiled hand on her towel, realizing too late as a rusty streak stained the white terry cloth.

"Crap!" Courtney exclaimed through clenched teeth. She looked around, but nobody had noticed her outburst. She moved to the sink to wipe the rest of the offending stain from her hands under the stream of water. Still holding the key, she ran it under the tap too, as if a quick rinse could wash away years of neglect. The result was a disappointing sink full of brownish water that looked like sewage. Courtney set the key on the counter. Half-heartedly, she splashed water around the sink to try to wash the stain down the drain.

"What's that?" Lynette asked, picking up Courtney's key from the counter.

"Careful," Courtney told her, an edge to her voice. "It's delicate."

Courtney's chest felt tight as she watched Lynette examine the key. She resisted the urge to snatch it back from Lynette's hands.

"It looks like it's seen better days," said Lynette, placing the key back on the bench.

Courtney knew her tone had sounded more threatening than

she'd intended, but she didn't apologize. Instead, she picked up the key and wiped it a little more, streaking rust across the white of the towel.

"What's it for?" Lynette asked, still watching Courtney carefully.

"I don't know what it's for," Courtney replied. "I found it in the woods."

She knew she was going to find out, the question was how. Courtney's mind had been working on the puzzle, but so far she'd come up short.

"Why don't you just throw it out then?" Lynette asked, eyeing the crumbling key.

"Oh, I don't know," said Courtney, glancing over her shoulder.

Most of the girls had made their way out to the pool. It was almost time for practice. She carefully placed the key in her locker, before shutting the door and fastening her lock in place. "Maybe it'll be useful."

"Useful?" Lynette repeated as the two hung their towels on hooks by the entrance to the pool and went out onto the deck.

Courtney bit her lip as she struggled to walk toward the starting blocks without limping. She didn't want Coach Laurel to make a big deal over her ankle. All she needed was a few days.

Lynette was still by her side as Courtney hopped into the water. As she spread her arms out in a wide arc under the surface, Courtney was keenly aware of their coach watching her.

Sage stood beside Coach Laurel at the water's edge.

Their coach was fully dressed in a St. Augustus track suit. Her pant legs were rolled up and her feet bare, as they always were. Her short gray hair was neatly parted on the side and combed down. She seemed to be scowling at Courtney.

I must be imagining that, Courtney told herself. Averting the coach's gaze, Courtney pushed off the wall with her good leg to start laps.

Her sore foot buckled underneath her with a shock of pain as she tried a flutter kick. Courtney clenched her jaw, then smoothly transitioned to the breast stroke without breaking stride. Breast stroke used the butterfly kick. It seemed to keep the pain to a dull roar.

As she neared the wall on her second lap, Coach Laurel called out to her

"Courtney!" the coach barked across the din on the deck.

Courtney looked up to see her coach waving her over to the side of the pool. She knew she'd been swimming slowly. Taking a quick breath, she ducked under the lane dividers and swam over to the edge, grabbing the side of the pool.

"Courtney, let me look at your ankle," said the coach.

"What?" Courtney asked, blinking at her.

"Sage told me," Coach Laurel said matter-of-fact. "Looks like you can't flutter kick?"

Courtney shook her head. Coach Laurel didn't miss much. Had Margaret told Sage, Courtney wondered? It probably didn't matter. Their coach would have noticed anyhow.

Courtney hoisted herself over the edge of the pool and onto the deck.

Coach Laurel took one look at Courtney's enlarged ankle and shook her head.

"Sit," Coach Laurel commanded, as she pointed toward a bench. "You're staying out of the pool until you get that ankle checked out."

CHAPTER TWENTY

I Spy

Courtney nearly bumped into Hanna as she rounded a corner in the Main Building later that evening.

"Hanna!" Courtney exclaimed. "Do you have a minute?"

Her sister's arms were full of richly colored fabrics. Costumes of some sort, from the looks of it.

"Sure," Hanna replied, looking at Courtney expectantly.

"Oh, um..." Courtney looked around the hallway. Not crowded, exactly, but not the right place. "Can I talk to you in private?"

Hanna shrugged, and led Courtney to a non-descript door just off the hallway. Courtney stepped unevenly after her, favoring her still sore ankle.

"What's this door?" Courtney asked, "I've never noticed it before."

Courtney had been cutting through a quiet portion of the building near the library when she'd bumped into Hanna. It was a shortcut to the Sports Complex that she took all the time. She'd been heading there to visit the team's physiotherapist.

"Shh...," hissed Hanna, with an edge to her voice. "We'll have to be quiet."

"Quiet? Why?" Courtney asked, following her through the open door. "Does this place have something to do with the map?"

"What?" Hanna asked, looking back over her shoulder. "Of course not. Why, did you find something? Courtney, are you limping?"

Courtney nodded, sheepishly.

"Can you climb the stairs?" Hanna asked.

Courtney nodded again. She'd made the decision to power through this injury. She wasn't going to let it slow her down, even if it hurt.

Ahead of them was a steep spiral staircase. Courtney looked back toward the hall. Where did this staircase go?

"I have to put these costumes away," Hanna explained. "We can talk upstairs."

Courtney fell into line behind Hanna, favoring her ankle up the stairs with a sort of hop.

As Hanna neared the top, which seemed more like two flights than one, she reached overhead for a string connected to a light bulb. Dim yellow light flooded a large, attic-like space cluttered with cardboard boxes and strewn about with gold embroidered fabrics.

"Wow," Courtney said, drinking in the strange room. "There's so much stuff."

The room was so cluttered that it reminded her of Ms. Krick's apartment.

They stood beside a tall shelving unit jammed with red faux flowers, helmets, swords and a bucket of candle holders. A large, ornate chest sat in one corner of the room, and multiple racks of clothing lined the far wall. Muffled sounds seemed to be coming from behind the clothing racks. Courtney looked at Hanna in alarm.

"That's why we need to be quiet," Hanna told her, in an exaggerated whisper. She walked over to the racks and pulled some of the clothing to one side.

Courtney hung back until she could see that nothing sinister lurked behind the clothing. Instead, bright lights shone through the rungs of a banister. The sounds had turned into voices, talking loudly. What were they saying?

Courtney edged toward her sister, who was watching something below.

"Is this the theatre?" Courtney asked, though she could see plainly that it was.

They were in a room somewhere above the stage. Courtney peered over Hanna's shoulder. A girl and a boy were rehearsing on the stage below. Their voices were raised. An argument was taking place.

"Is that part of the play?" Courtney asked, nodding her head toward the commotion below.

Hanna nodded, hanging the costumes she'd been carrying on the end of one of the clothing racks. Hanna wasn't in that year's play, but she'd volunteered as a stage hand. Hanna did an extraordinary amount of extra-curricular activities. So many, that Courtney could hardly keep track.

"What did you want to talk about?" Hanna asked.

It was unlikely they'd be heard over the commotion on the stage. Hanna had unloaded all the costumes she'd been carrying and had turned to face Courtney.

"The map," Courtney replied, needing to find out what her sister knew. "And the fountain."

"What fountain?" Hanna asked, her brow furrowed.

Drat. Her sister didn't know about the fountain.

"The map," Courtney repeated, figuring it was best to start with topics Hanna knew about. The fountain could wait. "What do you make of the symbols?"

"What symbols?" Hanna asked.

"With the sunrise," Courtney prompted, losing hope. "You didn't see the symbols?"

"Sorry, Courtney," said Hanna. "I only looked at the map briefly then rolled·it up again. I mean, it's nice and all, but Dad was way too wrapped up in it. I'm just not that interested in the history of the school."

Hanna seemed like the younger sister for the first time Courtney could remember. She wasn't going to be much help.

"Is there something interesting on the map?" Hanna asked.

"Well, there's a key," Courtney offered.

"To what?" Hanna asked.

"We don't know yet," Courtney admitted. "I was hoping you'd know."

"Sorry, no," said Hanna. "But you and Margaret will figure it out, I'm sure."

"If you find something, let me know," she added, "Sorry I'm no help." She began straightening some of the costumes as she talked. "Dad's going to be really happy you're taking an interest."

She patted Courtney on the shoulder.

"I've got to go," she said, turning for the stairs. "Bye!"

Courtney realized she needed to go too. She'd almost forgotten her physio appointment. Coach Laurel had insisted that she look after her ankle. She watched her sister leave, biting her lip in thought. She'd already learned more about the school than Hanna had. She paused at the top of the stairs before she carefully descended, but she didn't look back. This was a new feeling for her. The weight of trying to know as much as Hanna wasn't where it normally hung around her shoulders. It was freeing.

CHAPTER TWENTY-ONE

Headmistress Valentine

Courtney ran her fingers along the wall late on Saturday afternoon as she left the Sports Complex. She'd been unusually tired the night before and had gone to bed early, missing the epic truth or dare follow up game Margaret had raved about at that morning's practice. Courtney couldn't believe she'd ever participated in such a barbaric activity.

She'd hopped out of bed that morning to find her ankle had healed. Not just a little bit, but completely. Not even jumping, twisting on it or running gave her trouble. She'd run off to swim practice with a spring in her step. She arrived at the pool and had Coach Laurel clear her to swim a full half hour before any of the other girls had straggled in.

"Remarkable," Coach Laurel had marveled, examining Courtney's perfect ankle. She'd poked, prodded, and made Courtney bend it in all directions before finally deciding she'd be okay to swim.

Swim practice had run longer than usual, but still Courtney had stayed, swimming laps until her legs were shaky. Coach Laurel had ordered her out to go have lunch.

If she kept practicing like that, Courtney thought, she'd be in good shape for the upcoming meet. Still, making team captain a year early was proving to be tricky. She'd need more than just Coach Laurel to make it happen. The coach couldn't be counted on to break the rules.

Headmistress Valentine, on the other hand, had the power to influence.

Courtney didn't know what she was going to say, but she was on her way to the main office. Lunch could wait. She'd seen the headmistress in her office plenty of times on a Saturday, so Courtney hoped she'd be there.

She ventured off the path to make a beeline from the Sports Complex to the Main Building, straight past the teachers' residence. Two low windows at the side of the residence should be Headmistress Valentine's apartment, based on the door Giles had pointed out in the hallway the last time she'd been there.

Courtney hesitated, stopping beside a large oak tree on the campus lawn. Maybe the headmistress was at home. She leaned against the tree, hoping to appear casual as she strained to get a better look. A group of senior boys approached from the direction of the boys' dorm. Courtney pulled out her phone to try to look busy, while keeping an eye on the teachers' residence. There wasn't any movement, but even if there were, Courtney realized she wasn't in a hurry to visit there again. She might run into Ms. Krick. The thought of it made her scalp prickle.

No, she'd try her luck at finding Headmistress Valentine in the office instead.

Courtney looked down at her phone screen. She'd almost forgotten Cole was supposed to call, which surprised her. She'd been so looking forward to it. But she hadn't thought of it all today. As she looked down at her phone, there was an incoming call from a local number. Courtney pushed herself away from the tree and stared at the number. Her breath hitched. It could be Cole. What would she say?

As she straightened up, she felt a sharp pain on her foot.

"Ow!" she complained, loudly. She hopped on one foot, dropping her phone onto the frosty grass. It wasn't even the same foot she'd injured. "What on earth?" she mumbled, looking around.

She realized, too late, that she was yelling. The boys she'd seen earlier were still within earshot and turned to look.

They seemed just as surprised at her outburst as she was. Smiling sheepishly in their direction, she crouched down to retrieve her phone. The screen said that there had been one missed call. If it had been Cole, it had gone to voicemail.

She looked around in the grass for what had fallen on her foot. She caught sight of what looked like a white square of paper. Scrambling on her knees, she grabbed the object as her heart pounded. It was made from heavy paper, folded in two. A hole had been made on one end of it with a piece of string tied to a wedge-shaped rock. No wonder it had hurt.

Following a possible trajectory the rock could have come from, Courtney looked up at the tree she stood under, just in time to catch a shadow floating in swoops overhead.

"The owl," Courtney said aloud, as if she'd known he'd be there.

She watched as he made a graceful figure eight, then glided off into the low clouds, out of sight.

Courtney looked down at the paper. Her fingers trembling, she unfolded it. A note was scrawled in shaky handwriting, as if a right-handed person had penned it with his left. Or, as if Izzy had held a pen in his knobby beak.

GLAD YOUR ANKLE HAS HEALED.

HEADMISTRESS WILL HELP.

There was no other text. Instead, pasted below the note was a small square black and white picture of Headmistress Valentine and a second picture of Mr. Chase, with a plus symbol drawn between them, and a thickly inked heart surrounding the two images. The headmistress and Mr. Chase? Was the note trying to tell her they were an item?

Courtney dropped the paper as if it were hot. She felt a shock travel up her neck and into her skull, making her head swim.

Had Izzy delivered this note?

Rubbing her neck, she looked up into the sky that was darkening by the minute. There was no sign of Izzy, and it looked as if it might snow.

Bending down, she gently tore the note from the string that had secured it to the offending rock. She scrunched it in her fist and shoved it in her pocket.

HEADMISTRESS WILL HELP.

What did Izzy want her to do? Courtney's heart pounded.

She'd wanted the headmistress to help. If she could prove what the note said was true, she could make the headmistress help her, or reveal her secret love.

Mr. Chase?

Could that be true? Courtney sifted through memories of the headmistress and Mr. Chase, who was arguably the most well-liked teacher on campus. Was there really something there? And even if there was, so what?

"Think, Courtney," she said aloud.

She looked over at the Main Building.

She didn't need to figure out a plan all at once. She could start with a visit to the headmistress and go from there.

Tainted by her newfound suspicion that the headmistress might have a life outside of her work, Courtney slowly made her way across the lawn to the Main Building.

Once she entered, she could see yellow-tinged lights glowing from the stone ceiling in the wing of the Main Building that led to the office. Courtney slowed as she approached, looking into the outer office through the glass panel on the heavy wooden door. She was rewarded when she saw light spilling out into the main office from under the headmistress' door.

Courtney held her breath and tried to turn the handle to the main door. It was locked. Maybe the headmistress wasn't there, after all. Releasing the breath she'd been holding, she lifted her hand to the door and gave the glass a rap.

Her heart leapt as the headmistress' inner office door opened and Mr. Chase came out, flashing a smile of recognition as he approached, past Miss Samantha's desk.

Courtney narrowed her eyes as he unlocked the deadbolt to the main office door. Surely a teacher who didn't live on campus would have lots of legitimate reasons to visit the headmistress in a locked office on a Sunday. It didn't mean Izzy's note was true.

"Don't jump to conclusions," she chided herself, under her breath.

Yet the coincidence was uncanny. Had Izzy known Mr. Chase was in the office when he'd dropped the note on her?

Mr. Chase worked for the headmistress, of course. They had lots of reasons to be meeting on a Saturday that had nothing to do with romance. But the note implied something more. Was a relationship between them even allowed? She'd always assumed Headmistress Valentine was much older than Mr. Chase, but now she wasn't so sure.

If there was something between them, they probably wouldn't want that information to get out. They'd obviously taken care to keep the relationship a secret. If there even *was* a relationship, Courtney reminded herself.

Courtney felt her cheeks flush as the door opened. She forced herself to smile pleasantly as he let her in.

Mr. Chase pushed his hair out of his eyes and adjusted his wire framed glasses as he waved in greeting.

"Courtney!" he exclaimed, presumably loud enough for the headmistress to hear, if she was indeed in her office.

"Er, hi," Courtney said, looking past him to the headmistress' office door, which was now ajar. Her words seemed jumbled as she searched for the appropriate thing to say. "I just wanted to talk with Headmistress Valentine, if she's here?"

Mr. Chase nodded.

"She is, go on back," he said, reaching for his coat that hung from a nearby rack and pulling it on. "And I'm just leaving, so I'll see you later."

He let himself out of the wooden door into the hallway, whistling a jaunty tune as he left.

Courtney looked after him, wondering if she should lock the door. Deciding against it, she crossed the floor to the headmistress' inner office. She knocked gently on the partially open door, although she could clearly see the headmistress reading something intently.

"Headmistress Valentine?"

"Oh, come in, Courtney," the headmistress said, looking up and smoothing her hair back into its top knot.

"I was wondering if I could get some advice..." Courtney started, taking a seat in a visitor's chair facing the headmistress' wide wooden desk. "Advice on making swim team captain. Is there a rule that it has to be a senior?"

"Team captain?" the headmistress answered, looking thoughtfully at Courtney. "Well, no, there isn't a rule, exactly, though it is usually a senior who earns it." Her expression seemed to change slightly, her eyebrows knitting in the middle. "Sage isn't stepping down, is she?"

"No, no, nothing like that," Courtney replied, quickly, "I'm asking about next year." She paused for a moment before playing her ace card. "You see, my dad is really on my case to make sure my college applications are strong." Her dad carried weight, although Courtney had never tried using it before. "He's suggested I try for team captain a year early."

"Well, Courtney," the headmistress replied. A hint of a smile played at her lips. "That is definitely an ambitious goal for a junior."

Courtney shifted in her seat. The headmistress wasn't taking her seriously. She needed to take her seriously.

"Hard work is how Coach Laurel will choose the captain, I'm sure," Headmistress Valentine continued. "Along with achievement. Captain is reserved for those who inspire the rest of the team."

"Yes, of course, Headmistress," said Courtney. "I'm working on my times, but I've also been volunteering for the upcoming swim meet. All the girls attending will be getting an awesome loot bag. I came up with the idea myself and I'm providing the prizes." She hadn't exactly told Coach Laurel about the loot bags yet, but why would she say no? Judging from the headmistress' expression, Courtney would need her dad to make a call as well, but they had time. Team captain wouldn't be chosen until the fall.

"Well, that all sounds like a start, Courtney," the headmistress said, with a slight edge to her voice. "But I'm sure the loot bags aren't necessary. You can't buy your way into the position, you know."

Her words hung in the air over the desk between them.

Courtney felt her face go hot as the blood rushed to her ears.

"I'm sure Coach Laurel will take your contributions into account, along with the contributions of your senior teammates when the time comes," the headmistress added, more gently.

Courtney's puffed up chest had deflated. This meeting had been far from a slam dunk so far, though she hadn't brought out the big guns yet. She couldn't. Not until she had proof.

She was here now. Mr. Chase had just been here as well. Courtney's eyes darted around the office. Was there anything here that would prove their relationship was something other than simply professional? She drew in a sharp breath, as she spotted something on the headmistress' desk, sticking out from under a paper weight.

"Courtney?" the headmistress prompted.

Courtney quickly averted her glance away from what had caught her attention.

It was a card, with two flowers on the front, intertwined.

Courtney looked back over her shoulder to where Mr. Chase had gone. Then she looked back at the headmistress, who sat far back in her office chair, her arms crossed. How could she get a look at that card?

"Headmistress Valentine," Courtney said, sweetly. "My dad was wondering if you had a copy of his invitation to the admissions committee, he wanted me to give it to him."

It was a thin excuse. She should have waited a minute and thought of something better. It might not work. Too late now.

Headmistress Valentine's face brightened.

"Has he made his decision?" she asked, leaning in toward the desk.

"I think he's still considering," Courtney answered. "He just needs the letter."

Courtney knew Miss Samantha kept the headmistress' correspondence in the filing cabinets just outside the headmistress' office. Hanna was asked sometimes to come in and help with the filing. Courtney couldn't imagine anything more boring.

The headmistress pushed herself back from the desk. She looked like she was going to get up, then hesitated, looking back at Courtney. "I can just email it to him again. Does he not have the invitation in his email?"

"Beats me," Courtney replied, with what she hoped was a helpless-looking shrug. "He just said he needed the hard copy. He's pretty old-school," she added for good measure. "He'd rather have the letter, I guess." None of what she'd just said was true.

A beat passed while Courtney waited for the headmistress'

reaction. She'd heard the lies piling up as they spilled out of her mouth. There was no turning back now. She watched the headmistress carefully. Courtney replayed the story she'd just told, realizing it was full of holes. Was the headmistress going to fall for it?

"There should be a copy of the letter in the filing cabinet," the headmistress said, getting up slowly. "I'll see if I can find it." She crossed the room toward the door and stepped out into the outer office.

Courtney remained seated, trying not to fidget as she watched the headmistress exit the office. As soon as the headmistress was out of sight, Courtney sprang into action. She reached out and quickly snatched the card from the desk, stuffing it into her pocket beside the note from Izzy. She wouldn't be able to return the headmistress' card later, even if she wanted to. She'd crushed it in order to get it into her pocket.

Standing up, she went to the doorway. She had gotten what she'd come for.

"Thanks, Headmistress Valentine," Courtney said, lazily stretching her arms in a yawn, hoping it looked casual. She stood in the doorframe to the headmistress' office.

Headmistress Valentine had created chaos in the few moments she'd been at the filing cabinets. She had three separate drawers open and was rifling through them. Her sport jacket was hung neatly on the back of a chair nearby and she wore a white blouse untucked over her navy skirt. Come to think of it, her hair was pulled back, but not nearly as tidy as it usually was. Courtney hadn't noticed the headmistress had looked so disheveled, until now.

"It must be here somewhere," the headmistress said, looking up at Courtney. "Just wait a minute."

"It's okay," said Courtney. "No rush."

"When did you say you were seeing your father to give it to

him, dear?" the headmistress asked, frowning.

"Oh, I, uh –," Courtney didn't have any plans to see him. She didn't even know if he was in Boston that week, he travelled a lot. "I have some other things I need to mail home this week," she offered. Even if the headmistress asked, it was really none of her business what Courtney was mailing, was it? She felt a wave of nausea pass over her. These lies were coming easily. A little too easily.

"Well I'll be sure to have the letter sent to your room when we find it," the headmistress added, looking back at the files. "Miss Samantha will be able to find it much quicker on Monday."

"Thanks!" Courtney said, effectively ending the conversation. The office had suddenly become too small for both her and the headmistress to be there. Her chest felt heavy with the lies that had made the air thick. She gave a short wave and crossed the outer office to the door. Giving it a tug, she stepped into the hallway without looking back.

Courtney walked quickly through the corridors, then outside until she reached the dorm. She unlocked her dorm room door and stepped in, closing the door behind her. She'd wrested the card from her pocket by the time she reached her bed and sat down to read.

A grin spread across her face as she read the note inside, which was indeed from Mr. Chase. Courtney clasped the love note to her chest. It was simple, but its message was clear.

The headmistress would have to help her, or her secret would be exposed.

Moira,

I thank my lucky stars every day to have found you. Your love makes my world go 'round.

Love always,

Chase.

Wait, Courtney thought, reading the note twice more. Was

Chase his first name, or his last? Courtney put the note on her nightstand and lay back on her bed. It appeared some teachers had lives outside of school after all.

CHAPTER TWENTY-TWO

Violet's Wish

"Want to go shopping?" Courtney asked Lynette late on Sunday afternoon. They'd had a grueling swim practice, and were headed back to the dorm.

"Nothing good is open today," Lynette answered lazily. "It's Sunday."

"Target's open," said Courtney. Most of the stores in town were closed, but Target had extended hours. "I need to pick up some things for the swim meet."

"The next St. Augustus meet?" Lynette asked, giving Courtney a wary, sideways look. "It's not for months."

The headmistress had dismissed her idea of the loot bags. She'd then pitched it to Coach Laurel, who told her attendance to swim meets wasn't reliant on the swag they provided.

Courtney was convinced they were wrong. They'd see, if she gave them an example of just how over-the-top her loot bags would be.

"I'll take you for dinner after, if you come," Courtney said to Lynette. Target was a forty-five minute walk, and she'd have packages to bring back. She knew Margaret wouldn't be interested in coming.

"Are Margaret and Violet coming too?" Lynette asked, looking sideways at Courtney as they walked.

Courtney hesitated. She'd asked Lynette because Margaret was starting to lecture her about her obsession with team captain. It was getting on Courtney's nerves. Lynette also had better taste than Violet, who'd probably want everything in the loot bags to be purple.

"No," Courtney answered, without offering further explanation.

"Dinner at Luigi's?" Lynette asked.

Courtney smiled. Lynette would come. The coach would have to agree this was a good idea when she saw what Courtney had in mind.

Courtney opened the dorm room door softly as she returned after curfew on Sunday night. She'd just come from the student lounge, where she'd sat in her favorite corner, putting together the loot bags she was going to present to Coach Laurel. Bessie had come around to shoo the last remaining students to their dorms, but Courtney had convinced her she was working on a special project for Coach Laurel and it had to be done tonight.

To Courtney's surprise, Bessie had said she could stay until it was done.

Courtney had carefully scripted calligraphy notes that had given her hand cramps, placing the notes inside the bags. The blue ribbons that held the handles of the bags together had been tied and tied again until they were just right. Each bag had meticulously chosen gifts inside, each collection worth more than $100. She'd probably have to pare down the contents to roll out to the whole meet, but the coach would be able to see her vision. Any girl would be thrilled to get these, she was sure.

She juggled the three finished sample bags in her hands to reach for the light switch in her room, but Margaret's bedside lamp was already on. Blinking, she registered Margaret sitting up in her bed, but there was also someone sitting on Courtney's bed.

"Violet!" Courtney exclaimed, in surprise, "What are you doing here? It's past lights out!"

"Bessie told us you'd negotiated to stay out after lights out," Margaret said, drily. "How did you manage that?"

Ignoring Margaret's question, Violet rushed at Courtney and almost knocked her down with an enthusiastic hug.

Courtney held her arms out wide so Violet wouldn't crush the loot bags she'd worked so hard on and was holding in her hands.

Violet tried to squeeze the life out of her with glee.

"The most wonderful thing happened, Courtney!" Violet gushed. She spun around in a circle in front of Courtney. "Notice anything?"

Courtney's head hurt. She wasn't in the mood for guessing games. Besides, Bessie had said she could be up a few extra minutes, but all three of them being out of bed was pushing it.

"Stop spinning, Violet," said Courtney, pushing past her and setting the bags down on her desk.

"*Look* at me!" Violet declared, her arms wide.

Violet nearly vibrated with excitement. Her face glowed.

Violet had always been over the top. Courtney looked at her critically as she flopped back on her bed. She just wanted to go to sleep, but Violet wouldn't give up easily. Courtney decided to play along. It might speed things up. It was time for bed.

Margaret hadn't moved from her position on her bed since Courtney had arrived. She looked positively ashen. Alarmed, Courtney turned back to Violet and looked her up and down. Whatever it was, Margaret wasn't happy about it. Violet stood in front of them in green flannel footed pajamas, with sheep on the fabric and built-in slippers. Courtney wasn't used to seeing Violet in her pajamas. She did look odd somehow. Wait...

"You're not wearing purple," Courtney said, solving the riddle. Violet always wore purple.

"Exactly!" Violet squealed. She looked delighted that Courtney had guessed her secret. She quickly clamped a hand over her mouth and looked over triumphantly at Margaret. "I knew she'd see it right away!"

"Goodnight, Violet," Courtney said, starting to ready herself for bed. Whatever was wrong with Margaret, she was sure she'd hear about it anyway, but hopefully it could wait until morning.

As for Violet, it was good news she'd finally broken away from her all purple wardrobe. Courtney hadn't seen her in any other color since the third grade. Even in uniform she found ways to wear purple in her hair or on her jewelry, but that really wasn't newsworthy. Not tonight, anyway. There were bigger things on her mind.

"No, Courtney," Violet insisted, dragging Courtney to her feet and holding her by the shoulders. "You have to listen. We went tonight – we went to the fountain!"

"Great," Courtney told her, sinking back down onto her bed. She needed to think. Every minute Violet stood here meant Bessie could come and find them awake. Courtney needed to go to bed.

"Courtney, I *wished* for this!" said Violet. She started spinning around the room again.

Violet's words then began registering with Courtney. They went to *her* fountain? "You wished for green pajamas?" Courtney asked.

She looked over at Margaret for a sane explanation. Margaret just shook her head. She chewed on her lower lip. Courtney looked back over at Violet.

"No," Violet said, her voice dropping to a whisper. "I wished for *all* of it." Her eyes gleamed.

Courtney looked back and forth between the two girls. Her brain felt tired. She couldn't care less about Violet's new pajamas. But what were they doing with the fountain? If Bessie found them all still awake, she wouldn't be as lenient next time.

Courtney might need to stay out past lights out again sometime, and it was much easier to do with Bessie's permission. She looked over at the bedside table, where the lamp shone dully, but still bright enough to be seen from the outside. Courtney shivered and turned back to Violet.

"Violet," said Courtney, firmly, "you need to go."

Violet's smile faded a little, but she didn't move to leave.

"Courtney," Margaret said quietly, her face a sickly shade, "the fountain – it granted her wish."

"Isn't it wonderful?" Violet added, grinning from ear to ear. "And it's not just these, my whole wardrobe is changed! Every shirt, all my socks, even my underwear – all beautifully different colors, not just purple. I feel great!" Violet was almost shouting now, her arms in the air. "It works, it works! The fountain can give us whatever we want!"

Courtney felt as if the wind had been knocked out of her. They'd gone to the fountain and gotten Violet a new wardrobe.

"It's true, Courtney," Margaret said, coming over to Courtney's side of the room and sitting beside her on the bed. "Her jacket changed color to white, right while we were standing there."

"I wished for my clothes to be all different colors!" said Violet, with a giggle. "And then poof, they were! I'm going back into the woods tomorrow. I have a list of things I'm going to ask it for!"

Courtney looked at Margaret, their eyes were both wide.

"The way you've been feeling," Margaret said. "Your list - I think you can't help it. Even Bessie letting you stay out late. All of it."

Margaret's words came at Courtney like a freight train.

"Violet's ridiculous wish is proof the fountain works." Margaret added quietly.

"My wish was *not* ridiculous," Violet said, pouting. "It was a test wish, is all."

"Courtney," Margaret said, in a serious tone. "We need to get you free."

Courtney sprang to her feet and rushed to the bedside table, pulling open the small drawer where she'd stashed her now dog-eared list.

Get Home List

1. *Master the secrets of St. Augustus – know more than Dad.*
2. *Win at swimming.*
3. *Make team captain.*

Her heart raced, as she read the tattered page and reviewed her previous week. She'd made a detailed plan to help her become team captain, all but forgotten running to throw herself into swimming, and she was considering blackmailing the headmistress. She'd been trying to repress the feeling. The fountain was trying to make her wish happen. She'd been noticing things had come a little easier, but she hadn't really let herself believe that until now.

The moment she'd thrown her coin was suddenly crystal clear in her mind, and the rest of her week played through her thoughts as she sat with her mouth agape. Her hands felt cold. She dropped the list on the floor and turned to face her friends.

Margaret shook her head sadly.

"Isn't this great?" said Violet. "I love this school, and thank you, Isaac Young, or whoever put the fountain there. You don't think Ms. Krick has anything to do with it, do you?"

Courtney didn't move a muscle, though Violet watched her intently. Ms. Krick didn't even know where the fountain was - but they'd found it. And it had given them what they'd asked for – sort of.

"Did you make a wish?" Courtney asked, rounding on Margaret, the thought only just occurring to her.

Margaret shook her head emphatically.

"Violet," Courtney said sharply, pointing toward the hall. "You need to go." She pushed her exuberant friend toward the door.

"Did you finally meet up with that Cole guy?" Violet asked, wriggling out of Courtney's grasp.

"No, I wasn't with Cole," Courtney answered, her voice wavering.

"You could *wish* for him!" Violet exclaimed.

Courtney felt nauseated at the thought. "Violet, just go!" Margaret told her, jumping to her feet and helping Courtney ease their friend out the door.

"Fine," Violet answered, huffily, before tiptoeing down the hall.

Margaret and Courtney closed the door carefully together, then sank to the floor and looked at each other.

"I know," Margaret said, patting Courtney's knee. "We'll fix it. We'll fix it all."

"Margaret, I don't... I don't feel like myself," Courtney said, tears welling in her eyes. "I've got all these plans to make team captain. I haven't even thought about Cole in all this, though I don't even know if he even likes me. I haven't even checked my messages to see if he called." Now that they'd named what had been pushing Courtney to act this way, her gut ached. She blinked back the tears. Crying wouldn't help, she told herself. Now that she knew, she could stop. She could fix it. She could make another wish. But the tears fell anyway, not obeying Courtney's command. Soon, her body shook with racking sobs.

"I know," Margaret told her, putting her arm around Courtney and letting her cry. "I know."

CHAPTER TWENTY-THREE

Break the Fast

Courtney overslept the next morning and woke only when her phone buzzed with a text from her dad.

Tell Ms. Valentine I'll be on the admissions committee, if you want me to be? I'd like an explanation, though.

She'd left her dad a message after her visit to the headmistress' office, telling him she hoped he'd accept the school's invitation to the admissions committee, and that the Headmistress was sending him another copy of the invitation.

She looked at the time and slapped her forehead. It was later than she'd meant to sleep. The sounds of girls moving in the dorm hallway were already apparent and even Margaret was starting to stir in the other bed.

At some time during the night, Courtney had decided the best way to free herself of her wish was to make it come true - the whole list. Once the list was complete, the fountain couldn't push her will anymore.

Margaret was already leaving their room for the showers as Courtney rolled out of bed. Courtney couldn't remember the last time she'd overslept.

"And it'll give us anything we want!" Courtney overheard Violet telling the girls at breakfast later that morning as Courtney arrived at their table later than she usually did.

"Violet," Margaret said, cautiously, "we can't just wish for things! You're messing with something you have no business with. We agreed you'd make a small wish – like changing the color of a leaf or something. Your whole closet was totally over the top. Look at what's happening to poor Courtney!"

Poor Courtney? Is that what Margaret really thought? Courtney set her tray down loudly and slipped into her seat. She'd been awake off and on all night, and she felt like it. At first, she'd wanted to undo her wish, but the fountain was helping her. These were things she wanted. Or at least she thought she wanted, but it had to be on her terms.

"Courtney's been acting like a total lunatic and it's not even her fault!" said Margaret, to the girls at the table.

"Margaret!" Courtney exclaimed, sharply. She looked around the cafeteria, where the world around her seemed to be carrying on, without being aware of Margaret's soap-box speech. Even if it was true that Courtney was caught up in something, Margaret didn't need to say it for everyone to hear. Courtney was starting to regret having told Margaret anything at all. Courtney looked around at the girls gathered for breakfast. Since when had these girls become Courtney's judges? It felt more like a courtroom than a cafeteria this morning.

"No, no, we won't make wishes like *she* did," Violet told them, scoffing. "We'll *think* before we wish."

"I didn't know it would come true!" Courtney exclaimed, defensively. "If I'd known..." Would she have made the wish? Courtney knew she would have, but there was something there - something else. Now that she knew about the fountain's way of "helping", she'd be more careful. They needn't worry.

"Oooo, diamonds!" Violet exclaimed, seemingly breaking out of a deep thought and clapping her hands. "We should totally wish for them. What could go wrong with that? We could all get some."

"We'd probably end up having to steal them from some poor local merchant who never did anything to us," Margaret interjected. "We'll get arrested and won't even be able to enjoy the diamonds! No, no, no - absolutely not. No more wishes until we know more about what's granting them!"

"I thought you said it was an owl?" Hailey piped up.

Courtney looked at Margaret. Courtney had told her she'd thought she'd seen Izzy on Saturday. She'd told her everything the previous night after Violet had gone. Everything except about her plans with Valentine and Chase. She didn't think Margaret would approve of that.

Margaret wrung her hands, but she really needn't worry. Courtney wasn't worried. The fountain wasn't evil. It could be a tool for all of them to use if they were smart about it.

Violet had a point. If they learned to control it, they could have quite the year. The rest of their tenure at St. Augustus could be a breeze. This must be what her dad had meant. He and his friends had found the fountain. She wondered for a moment what they'd wished for and whether they'd gotten what they'd hoped for, or something else. And if that was it, why hadn't he just told her?

They'd been handed the keys to St. Augustus. Her thoughts reeled. They had to be smart about it. They needed time. They should take their time.

"That sounds right," Lynette agreed. "What do we know?"

"You're just scared," Violet taunted Margaret. "You haven't even made a wish, so you can't even know. Nothing bad has happened with my new clothes."

"I'm going to wish to feel more like myself," Courtney told the girls, not looking for their reaction. "I'm going to do it today. I don't see the harm in that. But I agree with the no more new wishes." Why had she said that? What did it matter if others got their wishes? Yet a cold chill prickled her scalp at the thought of a free for all on wishes, especially given the caliber of potential wishes Violet was considering.

"Why does she get to make another wish?" Violet demanded, looking at Margaret. "That doesn't seem fair. If Courtney can wish again, so can I."

Courtney was only half interested in Margaret's reply.

"No," Margaret said, shaking her head. "Who knows how you'll both have to pay for what it's given you? Nothing comes for free. No wishes for anyone until we know more. Especially you, Courtney. We can help you feel more like yourself without the fountain. If you go too far, we'll call you out and you can pull it back, right girls?"

Courtney looked around the table. The girls' earnest, nodding faces registered in a hollow way. She'd heard enough.

"The fountain takes our coins. That'll have to be payback enough. It's not up to you," Courtney said, pushing back from the table. "Do what you want, and so will I."

In the pit of her stomach was a pang she was just starting to recognize. It told her that her words hadn't been the right thing to say, but she'd said them anyway. An even stronger urge told her walking away from the table and leaving them all with their mouths agape wasn't the generally accepted way to treat friends, but she did that too.

"Sage!" Courtney called, as she approached the team captain's table at the far end of the cafeteria and sat down in the free seat beside her, at a table full of seniors she didn't know. "I've got some more ideas for the swim meet."

CHAPTER TWENTY-FOUR

Plan B

Courtney returned from classes that day to find Violet in her room with Margaret, yet again. She was starting to feel as if Violet was living there and it was getting on Courtney's nerves. Without addressing either of them, Courtney peeled off her uniform, including her white knee socks, and quickly put on jeans and a dry fit T-shirt.

"Um, hello?" said Violet, sarcastically.

"I just want to be alone," Courtney told them flatly. She didn't have the energy to deal with Violet. Obviously, Margaret could stay, but Courtney wasn't in the mood for conversation.

"Courtney," Margaret started, "we're worried about you."

Courtney looked blankly at her roommate.

"You don't really want to be alone, Courtney," Violet added. "It's your wish making you say things like that."

Violet's puppy dog expression triggered something inside Courtney. She wanted her room back.

"Violet and I have been talking," Margaret continued. "She's agreed to find out more before we make any more wishes."

Courtney studied Margaret more closely, as she leaned over the map – Courtney's map. She lunged forward before she'd had a chance to think about her actions, suddenly feeling a surge of energy.

"Courtney!" Margaret exclaimed, stepping in front of Courtney and blocking her access to the map. "The map could help us, we were just looking at it."

Courtney's limbs vibrated. The map was delicate. Margaret had it unrolled on the desk, text books holding the corners flat so they didn't snap back.

"Courtney," Violet said, her voice grating on Courtney's last nerve, "we're helping. You need our help."

Courtney whipped around to confront her.

"Relax, Courtney!" Margaret said, "Violet's right, we're just trying to help."

Something about Margaret's tone shook Courtney out of her trance. She had a plan. But she could use their help. There was no need to see them as the enemy.

Courtney took a deep breath. She'd been feeling off for the last few days. Maybe she was getting the flu. This couldn't all be from the fountain, could it?

She stepped forward, brushing past Margaret and putting her palms on the map. It was the calmest gesture she could muster, but it still felt forced. The parchment felt smooth and cool beneath her hands. Courtney gave her head a shake and traced the brown sketch marks with her right hand. Her plan hadn't involved delving deeper into Isaac Young's map. That suddenly felt like an oversight.

"Watch what happens when you hold it up to the window," said Violet, stepping forward and reaching for the map.

"I know that," Courtney replied sharply, slapping away Violet's hand. She lifted the books off the map and held it up to the window, where the thin evening light made the thin parchment glow.

"Well sorry," Violet snapped.

"Violet," Margaret said, studying Courtney. "Give Courtney a minute. It's her map."

But Courtney didn't need a minute. She'd barely registered their squabble. She stared at the map. Its symbols came to life more brightly than she'd remembered. When she'd first seen them, she hadn't fully understood. The symbols were part of the magic, the same magic she was trying to keep in check. It wasn't just a means to find the magic, but it was magic, itself.

"Okay," Courtney said, turning toward the others. "Most of the map's symbols are near the fountain. But this area here has a lot, as well." Courtney pointed to an area on the opposite side of the map from the woods, where a handful of icons were clumped together in the spot they looked at.

"That's a book," said Violet, pointing at one of the icons. "There's a tree, a squiggly line. What's that one?"

Not all the icons were easy to identify.

"Wait a minute," said Margaret, looking closer, "It's in the teacher's residence. Courtney, is that Ms. Krick's apartment?"

"Looks like it," Courtney answered. "Let's find out where the magic is coming from."

CHAPTER TWENTY-FIVE

Heading into the Eye of the Storm

It was well after dark by the time the three girls had run out of leads.

"Are we really going to Ms. Krick's apartment?" Violet said, with a giggle.

"It's no big deal, really," Courtney said, hoping she sounded convincing. "She won't even be there."

"I haven't agreed to this yet," Margaret piped up from where she paced the floor. She hadn't stopped since they'd started talking about how to best chase down the secrets of the fountain.

"That's fine," Courtney said. She'd already decided she was doing this with or without them.

"How will we get her to leave the residence so late at night?" Margaret asked. "Don't old people like to stay home?"

"We'll call her," Courtney said simply. "I saw a phone on her wall when I was there. Old people still have land lines. I bet it's been there long enough that it's a listed number."

Courtney pulled out her phone and did a search for M. Krick. Sure enough, the teacher's residence address came up, along with a number.

"Smart," Margaret said, with a nod to Courtney.

"And you think we can get in through the window?" Violet

asked.

"Ms. Krick said there was a drain pipe that my dad and his friends used to get in," Courtney replied. "Hopefully it's still there and we can climb it."

"But how will you get in?" Margaret asked.

Courtney noted that Margaret wasn't including herself in this caper.

"She leaves the window unlatched for Izzy," Courtney said. "We'll climb up."

"The bird?" Margaret asked.

"Izzy's an owl," Courtney corrected her, growing impatient. It seemed as if Margaret was losing track of the details on purpose, which sparked an idea for Courtney. A plan formulated in her mind as if it had been there all along. "I'll call her and tell her Margaret planned to go into the woods tonight," said Courtney. It was brilliant, and It killed two birds with one stone.

"You will not tell her that!" Margaret exclaimed, her hands on her hips.

"You don't actually have to go into the woods," Courtney told her. "Just be near enough to look suspicious. If I'm reading this right, Ms. Krick won't wait for you to explain. She'll march you straight to the headmistress and try to get you to tell them what you know."

"No, no, no," Margaret said, shaking her head.

Courtney felt some sympathy for Margaret, who took great pains to fly under the radar with teachers. She didn't have much of a reputation of being a good or a bad student, just nothing at all, and she probably preferred it that way. This move would throw her into the teachers' crosshairs, at least in the short term. This might even turn out to be a good thing for Margaret, a chance to make an impression on teachers and students alike. Courtney snapped herself out of a daydream where Margaret thanked her in the future for bring some edge to her existence at

St. Augustus.

"You won't have done anything she can prove, so you can't get into trouble for that. Would you rather come with Violet and me to Ms. Krick's apartment?" Courtney asked Margaret, knowing the answer.

Margaret shook her head, just as Courtney knew she would. Margaret was a liability as a cat burglar, but she was reliable and would do her best to keep Courtney and Violet out of trouble as a decoy.

"So, Ms. Krick will take Margaret to the headmistress' apartment?" Violet asked. "She lives in the teachers' quarters, same as Ms. Krick. Isn't that where you're going to be?"

"That's exactly where *we'll* be," Courtney corrected her. "You're coming with me."

"If we find out the fountain's intentions are good, I'm making all my wishes," Violet said, looking unimpressed.

"Violet..." Margaret began, seeming torn.

"Let's just find out what it's about," Courtney said, trying to sooth the tension in the room. "Then we can decide together."

Courtney looked from one girl to the other. Both nodded their heads. She'd been convincing. They would help.

"I'm hungry," said Violet.

It was nearly seven thirty and the cafeteria was already closed.

"I'm going to grab something to eat in the student lounge," said Courtney. "We should wait until a little later when it's really dark before we call Ms. Krick."

"We could just do all this tomorrow night," said Margaret.

"And give you time to tell everyone?" Courtney replied. "No, we're going tonight. Just the three of us. Are you in?"

"Coming!" Violet declared, grabbing her hoodie.

"Don't you think it'll seem suspicious that you're calling Ms. Krick at home?" Margaret asked, following them out into the hall. She seemed to be trying to catch up.

"She clearly asked me to feed her information," Courtney replied, in a non-committal tone. "So, that's what I'll do."

"Yeah, *false* information!" Violet said loudly, letting loose a laugh.

Courtney would have to settle Violet down considerably before they went anywhere.

"Shh!" said Margaret, as they moved down the hall. "You're going to jinx us."

"The fountain will help us," Violet answered, smugly.

Courtney looked over at Margaret, but she didn't need to ask if Margaret had just felt the same chill that she'd experienced.

Courtney and Violet had left Margaret shivering near the West Woods. She was wrapped in a blanket and reading a book by the light of her phone, which would serve as her alibi. They'd tucked her up against a brick wall of the West Building, so that she wasn't visible until a person was within yards of the woods. She'd had strict instructions not to move until Ms. Krick arrived. Then she was to walk toward the woods, stopping at the edge.

"What am I supposed to say when they ask me *why* I'm sitting here, reading a book?" Margaret complained as they left her. "Reading outside in the dead of winter is ridiculous. They'll know I'm lying." She'd been pushing back against the plan from the start.

"It doesn't matter *why* you're there. Just say you felt like it," Courtney replied, starting to walk away. "In fact, if she thinks you're lying, that's even better. But she won't be able to prove anything."

"Great," Margaret mumbled.

Courtney and Violet swept a wide berth around the Sports Complex, staying away from light sources. They only had an hour until lights out. It would have to be enough. Moving stealthy across the grass, they rounded on the teachers' quarters from the far side. Courtney pointed to the spire on the third floor where Izzy's window led to Ms. Krick's apartment, as they walked by from a safe distance.

"But it's so high," said Violet, losing the swagger in her step.

"We only have to make it to the second story roof," Courtney assured her, stopping near a tree.

Violet halted and shivered next to her.

The night was chilly. The roof did look higher than Courtney had remembered. The porch lights glowed with lemony light. They'd have to stay in the shadows at the side. She strained her eyes to see a thick line stretching up the side of the house, just behind the porch.

"That must be the drain pipe she was talking about," said Courtney, her voice low. "It's right next to the main floor porch. We can use the railing to get up to the porch covering then help each other up to the second floor roof." She realized that might be tricky to do and still stay in the shadows. They'd have to be quick.

She turned to Violet, appraising her partner in crime. Margaret would have been a better choice to hoist Courtney up, she was steady. Violet's white coat that used to be plum colored stood out like a ghost in the night, not a smart choice for staying under the radar.

"Please tell me you know how to climb a drainpipe," Courtney said.

"Like climbing a rope in gym class?" Violet asked, blinking.

"Yes, like that," Courtney answered sharply. "Can you?"

"I can climb a rope," Violet replied.

"You'll have to lose the mittens," Courtney said, starting to move again and motioning for Violet to follow. Violet wore fluffy orange mittens that Courtney thought might have been mauve the week before. There was no way Violet would be able to climb while wearing those. Violet nodded solemnly, stuffing the bright mittens into her coat pockets.

The pair ducked behind a maintenance shed on the east border of the campus that housed Giles' ride-on mower. Beyond the shed was more grass, then houses. The same line of houses that led to Cole's house. Courtney gave her head a shake. She couldn't let her mind wander. They couldn't get caught tonight. She couldn't afford to be distracted.

"Okay, be quiet," Courtney whispered to Violet, using her arm to brush the snow off a large wooden chest that probably held garden tools, so that they could sit down.

Violet nodded and sat beside Courtney, her bare hands tucked up into the sleeves of her coat.

Courtney pulled out her phone and opened the browser to where she'd googled Matilda Krick's number earlier that evening.

"Here goes," Courtney mumbled, holding the phone to her ear.

Violet huddled close to Courtney, pressing her ear to the backside of the phone. There was one long ring, then a second ring. Courtney glared at Violet, waving at her to back off. Violet smelled earthier than the usual lavender scent Courtney had always assumed was Violet's shampoo.

"Hello?... Hello?"

Violet pinched Courtney's arm hard through her winter coat. Ms. Krick was on the line.

"Oh, hi Ms. Krick," Courtney said. Her voice seemed loud in the night air after they'd been speaking in whispered tones, but whispering wouldn't do. "It's Courtney Wallis calling. So sorry to bother you tonight at home." Courtney paused a beat, thinking about how to make Ms. Krick believe she was ratting on Margaret. It had all seemed easy in her mind, but now she searched for the words.

"Oh Courtney," said Ms. Krick, "it's no bother at all. What can I do for you?"

Violet leaned in over into Courtney's field of vision and made a face.

"It's Margaret," said Courtney. She gave Violet a light push. "I didn't know if I should bother you with it."

"What is it, Courtney?" Ms. Krick prompted. "Does it have to do with, ah..."

"Yes, yes it does, Ms. Krick," Courtney replied, her voice quickening. This was going to work. She could feel it. "Margaret has been acting strangely lately, and tonight she said she was going to go to the West Woods. I didn't dare follow her, I... I-"

"You did the right thing, Courtney," Ms. Krick said. "Is she there now?"

"She left a few minutes ago," Courtney replied. "She was heading toward the West Building."

"You stay in your room, Courtney," said Ms. Krick.

Violet's silent laughter shook Courtney's shoulder.

Courtney shifted her body so she couldn't see Violet anymore. Ms. Krick assumed Courtney was in her room, by herself. Well, good. Now she had an alibi if Ms. Krick noticed anyone had been in her apartment.

Violet needed to be quiet. Her laughter would give them away.

"Uh, sure Ms. Krick," said Courtney.

She craned her neck around the shed that they'd sat behind so that they could see the teacher's residence. Courtney gasped as a wispy silhouette appeared in the lit window in the spire. Ms. Krick's face was clearly visible in the window.

Courtney quickly slipped back behind the shed wall, not daring to take another look.

"Courtney," Ms. Krick said, her voice low on the phone, "is Margaret looking for the fountain?"

"I, I don't know," Courtney replied. What was the best answer here? She needed to get Ms. Krick interested without getting Margaret in real trouble. "You just asked me to let you know if I knew anything. Margaret was acting strangely. I just thought you should know."

The lie had rolled easily off her lips. Courtney held her breath as she waited for Ms. Krick to take the bait.

"Thank you, Courtney," Ms. Krick told her. "I'll take it from here."

"Thanks, Ms. Krick," Courtney said, not having to fake her relief.

Courtney hung up the phone and waved at Violet to follow behind her to the edge of the shed.

Violet wasn't laughing now.

Courtney crouched at the edge of the shed wall, mashed up against its cold aluminum siding. Carefully, she peeked around the wall. Ms. Krick's shadow was no longer visible in the third-floor window, although the light was still on in the apartment.

"What if she doesn't go out?" Violet whispered, hovering in a squat right behind Courtney.

"Shh," said Courtney, raising her hand. "She will, just wait."

Courtney focused on the light coming from Ms. Krick's window.

"Yes!" Courtney whispered triumphantly as the light in the window went dark. She'd been right that Ms. Krick would want to go and see what Margaret was up to for herself. They'd have to work fast though. It was possible Ms. Krick wouldn't turn Margaret in, if she thought she knew anything about the fountain. But Ms. Krick really seemed to dislike Margaret. Courtney felt a pang of regret toward her friend. Margaret wouldn't have an easy time, but if she did a decent job of convincing Ms. Krick that she didn't know anything about the woods or the fountain, Ms. Krick should jump at the chance to take her to the headmistress. The plan should work and Margaret would be fine. Courtney hoped she was right.

"Ten, nine, eight..." Courtney counted under her breath. How long could it possibly take for Ms. Krick to get down the stairs? Just as her countdown neared its end, the front door to the residence burst open and Ms. Krick shot out, all dressed in black. She set out at a trot across the path through the lawn, in the direction of the Main Building and the woods.

"Ow," Courtney complained, shrugging off Violet. Violet had been holding her arm tightly and her fingernails had dug in through Courtney's winter coat.

"Sorry," said Violet.

Courtney rubbed the spot on her arm that had been assaulted.

"You ready?" Courtney asked. "We won't have much time."

"Yes," Violet replied, after a slight pause.

"Let's go, then," said Courtney. "But just walk naturally. Remember, we're allowed to be out at this time of night, even over here."

Violet nodded.

The pair stood up, brushing traces of snow off their jeans.

"We'll have to see if the drain pipe can even support us," said Courtney, as they sauntered casually together towards the large house. "If they haven't replaced it, the pipe would be really old."

Courtney took a quick look around the area, but there was no sign of anyone on this side of the campus. She zeroed in on the drainpipe as they drew nearer. It was light yellow, just like the siding on the upper part of the house, but it also bore markings that were too dim for her to make out from where they were.

"Is that the drainpipe?" Violet asked, pointing ahead.

Courtney nodded. They were now less than ten yards away from the house. She was pulled out of her concentration when the front door of the teachers' quarters slammed open. Without thinking, she grabbed Violet by the arm and pulled her to the snowy ground beside her. The two girls lay flat, with their heads raised to see who was coming out of the building.

It all happened too quickly for Violet to react.

Courtney put a stern finger to her lips.

Giles came out of the residence at a quick clip, holding his phone to his ear.

"I'll be right there," he said into the phone as he bounded down the steps.

Courtney pressed her body as flat as it would go, but they were woefully exposed. She let out a breath as Giles turned sharply, heading toward the Main Building.

Violet tugged at Courtney's arm, directing her toward the cover of a large tree at the side of the house.

"What was that, Courtney?" Violet whispered angrily. "It's not even lights out yet. What happened to 'just walk normally?' We'd have a hard time explaining why we were laying on the lawn."

"Shh," Courtney said, barely registering her complaint.

"Poor Margaret," Violet added. "Looks like Ms. Krick called Giles to come help interrogate her." Violet's voice had gone up a notch, with just a hint of hysteria creeping in.

They needed to act before Violet got cold feet.

"There's something covering the drainpipe," Courtney said in a low whisper. "I'm going in to see."

She didn't look back to see if Violet followed.

The two girls reached the drainpipe and Courtney reached out her hand to touch the dull metal wrapped around its trunk.

"Barbed wire!" Violet exclaimed, as Courtney pulled her hand back sharply.

Courtney looked at Violet, whose proclamation had sounded closer to relief than dismay. She looked up the length of the drain pipe, braided with aged barbed-wire tinged with rust. There was no way they could scale the pipe without shredding their hands in the process and probably contracting Tetanus.

"We'll have to go in the front door," Courtney said.

"No way!" Violet exclaimed, too loudly.

"Giles left too quickly to have locked it," Courtney explained. "It'll be much faster." She looked at Violet, who didn't move. "Suit yourself," said Courtney, starting toward the front door.

Violet was right beside Courtney as she reached for the doorknob and slowly opened the door. Once inside, the girls moved along the hall quickly in silence. Courtney tried to tell herself that comings and goings in the residence were probably commonplace and none of the teachers who lived there would take notice. In fact, if they got caught, she could just say she'd been there to see Ms. Krick.

They heard rustling from behind a few of the closed doors, signs someone actually lived in the residence.

The girls reached the top of the first set of stairs without incident, but Courtney's heart sank as they climbed up the second set of stairs. The front door had been open, but she hadn't even considered Ms. Krick's apartment door. If it was locked, they'd be forced to head back down the way they'd come. This was all happening too fast.

As they neared the door, she reached out and turned the handle, knowing full well it would be locked.

Violet wrung her hands. "What now?" she said, looking at Courtney expectantly.

Courtney looked around, spotting a lone window in the small vestibule in which they stood at the top of the stairs. She moved toward the window and leaned close to the pane, surveying the scene outside.

"Courtney, we should go," Violet said, in a harsh whisper.

Not missing a beat, Courtney yanked at the window frame to slide it up. The window squeaked, as it opened just wide enough for them to get out.

"Courtney," Violet said. "There's a two story drop below that window. There's no way I'm going out there!"

Cold night air stung her cheeks as Courtney stuck her head out the window. The second story roof landing outside Ms. Krick's apartment was no more than two feet to the right.

"We can make it," Courtney assured Violet, pointing to the roof landing. "I'll hold on to you to you and lower you down, then I'll jump."

If Courtney went first and left Violet at the window, Violet would chicken out for sure. At this point, Courtney lamented bringing her at all, but she couldn't risk Violet getting caught on her way out.

Violet stuck her head out the window to look at the drop she had to make, then turned back to Courtney, her eyes wild.

"Here," Courtney said, reaching out her hand. "You have to go now. We're running out of time."

After hesitating briefly, Violet took Courtney's hand. Violet's face was pale. Courtney gave her a gentle push on the back with her other hand to urge her toward the open window. Violet swung one leg over the sill, then the other, until she was half in, half out, of the teacher's residence.

"See anyone out there?" Courtney asked, peering out over Violet's shoulder, into the night.

Violet shook her head then slipped her body down feet first, gripping Courtney's hand tightly.

Courtney braced her feet against the wall and held onto Violet's hands until Violet could stretch and reach the roof landing by swinging her feet a short distance.

Violet dropped onto the roof with a soft thud, then rushed to the edge, looking out. Courtney watched with dismay as something fell from the roof to the ground. Violet's fluorescent orange mitten floated through the air and landed softly on top of the white snow just to the right of the porch steps. Courtney smacked her palm on her forehead. The bright mitten was plain for anyone to see. They'd have to grab it on their way out.

"Sorry!" Violet called, softly.

Courtney shook her head as she climbed up to sit on the window sill then flipped over onto her stomach and lowered herself down. She held onto the window sill with her hands until her arms were at full extension then reached sideways with her foot to position herself to drop onto the roof. Courtney let go of the window sill, but realized too late that she'd misjudged the angle. Her feet were going to miss. Panic rose into her throat as she fell, her feet passing the safety of the roof where Violet stood, frozen in her tracks.

"Help!" Courtney cried, grabbing at the air.

At the last moment, Violet's arms appeared over the roof. Courtney managed to make contact with a side of a sleeve before Violet hauled her onto the roof.

The two girls rolled back onto the roof landing in a heap, breathing heavily.

"Thanks," Courtney mumbled. Her body ached where she'd landed.

Violet had saved her from a very bad fall.

Courtney peered over the edge of the roof and shuddered to see how far down it was toward the mitten. There wasn't nearly enough snow on the ground to make it a soft landing.

Gaining her composure, Courtney crawled toward Ms. Krick's darkened window and lifted it, which thankfully didn't creak the way the hall window had done. Courtney climbed inside, reaching for the floor with her foot. Something soft brushed her shoe. Courtney lost her balance and stepped down.

An ear-splitting shriek erupted from the cat she'd just stepped on. Courtney jumped backward and hit her head on the open window pane.

"Ow!" Courtney yelled, her hand flying to the spot on her head where she'd bumped. It was rapidly swelling into a sizeable goose egg under her mass of hair.

"Are you okay?" Violet asked. She now had half of her body in through the open window, and was peering around the room.

"Shoo," Courtney hissed to Oscar, waving her arm at him to sweep him from her vicinity. Her eyes hadn't adjusted to the dark of the apartment, but the cat's glowing yellow eyes blinked before his outline scampered from the room.

Violet made her way into the apartment through the window and pulled it closed behind them.

"I assume we're not going back out that way?" Violet asked.

Courtney shook her head. They could go out through the door. She stood in the moonlight blinking at the scene around her.

"Whoa," Violet said. "You weren't kidding, Courtney. This place is a mess!"

In the dark, the apartment looked even more crowded than Courtney remembered. Ms. Krick's piles were stacked everywhere. How would they ever find anything in this chaos? Courtney didn't even really know what they were looking for. This whole thing suddenly seemed ill advised.

Violet turned on the flashlight on her phone and took a step forward.

"What's that smell?" Violet asked, wrinkling her nose.

"Cats," Courtney answered, pulling out her phone and following Violet's lead. "I don't know how many, but there's a bunch in here." She stopped for a moment and looked over at Violet. "Sorry, I just remembered you're allergic."

"This half-baked plan just keeps getting better," Violet grumbled. "Let's make this quick."

Courtney panned the room with her flashlight, illuminating each of the stacks of paper.

"Look for any papers that look old, like the map," she directed. "Or something that could open with an old key, like the one I found in the woods." They could search all night and still not get through the piles, Courtney realized.

"Wasn't there an icon of a book on the map?" Violet asked.

"Right!" Courtney said. She pulled up the pictures she'd taken of the map in the sunlight and zoomed in on the teachers' residence.

"There's the cluster," she confirmed. "But it's hard to tell where exactly the symbols are. The book looks the most promising. Let's find that."

"These stacks look like they're mostly student's assignments," Violet said, running her flashlight across a stack of papers in her hand.

"Thirty years of term papers, filed on her floor?" Courtney suggested. "Looks like she keeps everything, but a book that had something about the fountain would be really old, like the map."

The girls walked in a slow circle around the apartment and looked at each stack briefly as they passed. All were either papers or books, but every page was dog-eared. It was impossible to tell which stacks were the oldest. None had been preserved with care. Three cats followed them around the room, weaving their way in and out of their legs and generally making it difficult to move without stepping on them underfoot. Oscar wasn't with them.

"Ah-choo!" Violet let out a loud sneeze, burying her nose in her elbow.

Courtney gave Violet a sharp look.

"It's the cats!" Violet said, sniffling lightly and wiping her eyes with the back of her hand.

As they resumed their inspection, a tapping sound came from the window.

"That's Izzy," Courtney said, making her way over to the window. "He wants in."

"He's an owl," Violet said, looking toward the window.

Courtney stood up and strode toward the window. Izzy, tapped politely on the window again with his short beak as she approached.

"Does he bite?" Violet asked, sounding unsure. "Owls could carry disease or something for all we know."

"He seems tame enough," Courtney said, opening the window

to let him in then stepping aside to give Izzy access.

He hopped up onto the windowsill and paused. Courtney held out her hand for him to smell, like she would if he were a dog. She had no idea if that's how you were supposed to approach an owl. But, he was no ordinary owl.

Izzy spread his wings and glided to the floor, where he walked with purpose, or more accurately hobbled, on his short legs, to the other end of the room. The cats were suddenly nowhere to be seen.

"He clears out the cats, at least," Violet said, watching Izzy cross the floor toward her. "Though I have no idea if I'm also allergic to owls."

Violet took several steps backward toward the wall as Izzy approached, then passed, the couch and continued toward the deepest part of the room.

"Is he trying to tell us something?" Violet asked.

Courtney didn't answer her, watching Izzy intently. He ruffled his feathers a little, then hopped forward. Courtney followed him toward a stack of books where he finally stopped.

"We should look here?" Courtney asked.

Izzy touched his beak to the stack.

"Can he understand?" Violet asked, her voice shaking.

Courtney shrugged.

"The book on the map," she said. "Maybe it's here." She started sifting through the pile he'd pointed at.

Izzy turned his head around in its socket, the way only owls can, and looked at Courtney for several seconds. His gaze still fixed on her, he spread his wingspan to its full breadth. Courtney's breath caught in her throat. His feathers were a dull brown, but his wings looked positively majestic in the dim light, stretched to nearly five feet wide.

He glided easily over to the open window and landed on the sill briefly before heading down to the roof, where he stopped.

Courtney rushed over to the window and looked out. Izzy sat perfectly still on the second story roof. He looked out into the night, as though he were keeping watch.

"We don't have much time," Courtney said, turning back toward the stack the owl had guided them to.

Violet had already disassembled the stack of books and papers, spreading them out on the floor around her in a circle. She'd propped her phone up on a nearby cardboard box to shine down on the papers she surveyed.

"Everything here is related to building the school," Violet reported, indicating the mess in front of her. "There are newspaper clippings, letters and notebooks full of notes here. Isaac Young is mentioned in a bunch of places, but there's no way we can read it all tonight." She threw up her hands.

"We don't need to," Courtney assured her. "Just scan for what's there and we'll take anything that seems interesting with us. Is there anything there that looks witchy?"

"Witchy?" Violet asked, narrowing her eyes.

"Anything that looks like magic," Courtney answered her, sheepishly. She wasn't sure where the witch implication had come from, but she'd always wondered about Ms. Krick. "What's this?" she asked, reaching onto the top of the pile for a leather-bound book.

Courtney flipped the cover open to look inside its pages by the light of her phone.

"It's Isaac Young's journal," Courtney breathed.

"So?" Violet asked. "Isn't he just some rich old guy who founded the school?"

Courtney looked over at her co-conspirator. Had she not been following the line of thinking? This was exactly the kind of thing they'd come to find. It could even be the book the map had told them about. Before she could look away from Violet to take a closer look at the diary, a loud cooing sounded from outside the window.

Rushing over to the open window, Courtney looked out at Izzy, who hooted into the night then in the direction of some figures moving toward the residence.

"Ms. Krick is coming this way, with Margaret," she hissed at Violet. "Giles is with them too. Put it all back, we've got to go."

She tucked the journal under her arm and watched as Ms. Krick marched Margaret toward the residence. Even from this distance, Courtney could see Margaret's slumped shoulders as she walked. Margaret looked positively miserable. She'd better keep her mouth shut. Courtney bit her lip. Margaret was really bad at not telling things. But hopefully her aversion to teachers would help.

Courtney turned back and rushed over to Violet, who sat frozen in a sea of papers. She was vaguely aware of several pairs of eyes watching her from what must be the bedroom doorway, just off the kitchen. The cats seemed to have stayed at bay with Izzy still close by.

"How are we getting out of here, exactly?" Violet asked, her voice breaking. "Ah-choo! This place is *full* of cats!"

"With any luck, they're taking Margaret to Headmistress Valentine's apartment." Courtney answered. "We can go out the window and climb off the roof landing using the porch railing at the front if we're quick and quiet." Courtney stacked papers at random as she talked. "It's past lights out now, but if we get caught, we'll say we went out looking for Margaret."

Violet stared at Courtney, not helping her clean up.

"Here, stuff these in your jacket," said Courtney, handing her a few newspaper clippings instead of putting them back in the stack. "Does it look right?" She indicated how she'd piled Ms. Krick's collection. There was no time to fix it even if it looked wrong.

"I'm not sure," Violet answered, her lower lip protruding.

It would have to be good enough. Surely the cats messed things up around here all the time. Ms. Krick probably hadn't touched that pile in years.

"Come on," Courtney said, grabbing Violet by the arm and pulling her toward the window.

Voices floated up from the front porch. Courtney and Violet exchanged alarmed looks. Why weren't they inside yet? Several minutes had passed since they'd first spotted them approaching the residence.

"Moira, it would really be better if we could all go inside," Ms. Krick's voice rang out through the night.

"Whatever it is can certainly wait until morning. My, er, apartment..." Headmistress Valentine replied. "Well, I wasn't expecting visitors. So, tell me now what Miss Margaret has done wrong and we can all deal with it tomorrow."

There was a long pause in the conversation. The group stood on the covered porch and couldn't be seen from Ms. Krick's window.

Izzy still sat perched on the edge of the roof landing. Taking one forlorn look back at Courtney and Violet, Izzy hopped to the edge of the landing and spread his wings. Courtney watched him glide away into the night. He sailed over the Main Building, his silhouette outlined against the clouds shining with moonlight. He flew toward the West Woods, where Margaret had been.

"He's abandoning us!" whispered Violet.

"No," Courtney said, shaking her head. "He's making sure he doesn't draw attention to the fact we're here." She felt strangely sure Izzy was helping them.

"It was reported Margaret had gone into the West Woods tonight," Ms. Krick announced loudly below.

"By whom?" asked Headmistress Valentine.

"It was an anonymous tip," Ms. Krick replied.

Courtney could almost hear her straightening up as she

answered. The two girls exchanged a look. Ms. Krick had lied for Courtney.

"And," Headmistress Valentine added, impatiently. "Margaret, did you go into the West Woods?"

Courtney held her breath.

"No!" Margaret exclaimed. "I was just reading, that's all."

"I intercepted her just as she was about to enter the woods," Ms. Krick added, stiffly. "When interrogated, her answers were very suspicious."

"Giles?" Headmistress Valentine said, sounding tired.

"Ma'am, I can confirm that this student was at the edge of the woods when I arrived," Giles replied.

"But she didn't actually enter the woods?" Headmistress Valentine asked.

Courtney listened intently. They wouldn't have much time to get out the window before Ms. Krick came up to the apartment. They would have to be quick.

The headmistress' exasperated sigh was unmistakable. At least Margaret wasn't going to get in any trouble.

"Matilda, students are allowed to walk about on the campus. The fact someone told you she was planning to break a school rule is not evidence that she did," Headmistress Valentine said. "I won't have you working the kids up about the woods again. I thought we were through with that nonsense."

"But..."

Ms. Krick's voice could barely be heard from their vantage point at the window. Courtney held her breath. They couldn't leave now, not through the front door. Was there a back door to the house? Courtney didn't know.

"That'll be all, Matilda. Go to bed, we'll discuss this further tomorrow," the headmistress said.

Violet looked at Courtney, her eyes wild. Ms. Krick was coming upstairs.

"Giles, would you be so kind as to escort Miss Margaret back to the dorm?" Headmistress Valentine asked.

"Certainly," said Giles.

Courtney's gaze was glued to the stairs of the porch, which were just visible beyond the roof's overhang. The sound of the front door opening and closing seemed to shake the house. Moments later, Giles came into view, with Margaret not far behind. Courtney counted silently in her head. They didn't have long before Ms. Krick would be upstairs.

Margaret paused for a moment, beside the orange mitten. Her eyes widened and she looked up toward Ms. Krick's window. Courtney stood up in full view in the window frame and waved frantically for Margaret to grab the lost mitten, but Margaret only turned and walked away, so Courtney couldn't be sure she saw them. Courtney watched as Margaret caught up to Giles and followed him toward the Main Building and the safety of her bed.

"We've got to get out of here," Courtney hissed. "As soon as they pass that tree over there, we go out the window."

"Out the window?" Violet exclaimed. "I thought we could go back using the stairs!"

"No!" Courtney exclaimed. "Just get onto the roof and we'll figure it out from there."

They might be able to ease their way down onto the roof of the porch, then down to the ground, but they were running out of time. Courtney swung a leg out the window just as the front door to the teachers' quarters sounded, opening again. Courtney froze. Please let it be Ms. Krick following Giles and Margaret.

Instead, a man's form emerged from the porch, stepping slowly down the stairs. As he reached the path, he paused and looked slowly from side to side, as if he were looking for someone.

"That's Mr. Chase!" Violet said, crowding Courtney.

It was indeed Mr. Chase. Courtney felt herself smile, despite their precarious situation. Mr. Chase had clearly been the reason

Headmistress Valentine didn't invite the others inside. The girls watched from the window as he tucked his ironed shirt tail into the back of his pants and pulled on the down coat he had slung over his arm, zipping it up against the cold. He started off toward the teachers' parking lot.

Courtney watched with a knowing look. She could catch them here, at the house. Get proof. Mr. Chase stopped abruptly and doubled back toward the house.

"He sees the mitten," Courtney said, groaning.

Mr. Chase bent over and picked up the mitten from the snow, brushing it off. Then he turned and continued back in the direction of the teachers' parking lot.

"Is he taking my mitten?" Violet whispered. "I *like* that mitten!"

Both girls whipped around at the sound of distant footsteps climbing the stairs in the hallway. Mr. Chase was still less than 100 feet from the porch.

Courtney edged herself out a few inches, ready to drop. Three, two, one...

"He'll see us," Violet said, pulling Courtney roughly back into the apartment.

"Hide!" Violet hissed.

Courtney fell backward to the uneven floor of the apartment and looked desperately out at Mr. Chase as he made his way across the lawn. They'd missed their chance. She reached up and yanked the window frame shut in one fell swoop and turned to look for something to give them cover.

CHAPTER TWENTY-SIX

Hidden

"Violet," Courtney whispered. What was she up to?

Violet had moved quickly and was all the way over by Ms. Krick's couch, grabbing a thin knitted blanket off the overstuffed arm. She ran toward Courtney in the rounded window alcove. Violet reached a hand out to Courtney's shoulder and pushed her urgently to the ground, throwing the blanket over them both.

The door to the apartment opened with a creak, and Ms. Krick could be heard stepping inside.

The air under the blanket was stifling. Courtney tried not to move a muscle as the two girls huddled together in wait. The knit of the blanket was loose enough that she could see between the knots of yarn, but they were tucked away behind a wall, so they couldn't see the front door.

Mewing cats came out of their hiding places somewhere in the back of the apartment and rushed to the front door to greet their mistress.

The blanket shook as Violet stifled a sneeze.

Courtney raised her eyebrows at Violet and flashed a look she hoped would remind Violet of the situation they were in.

"Cats," Violet whispered back.

Violet's face was mere inches from Courtney's. Even in the darkness under the blanket, Courtney could tell Violet's eyes watered. The blanket must be covered in cat hair. This place was crawling with cats. They probably slept on the blanket all the time.

"Did you kitties open the window on the landing?" Ms. Krick cooed, as she snapped on the overhead light.

A wave of nausea came over Courtney. She'd forgotten they'd left the window outside Ms. Krick's door open. They were going to be caught. Light spilled into their hiding place through the holes between the blanket's yarn.

"I'll ask Giles about it in the morning," Ms. Krick continued, her footfalls heading toward the kitchen. "Very strange."

Courtney hugged her knees, making herself as small as she could. Her chest barely moved with each breath. Ms. Krick should be on high alert after finding that window open. Violet seemed to take up a gigantic amount of space under the blanket. Courtney willed the cats not to give them away.

"All that commotion, and now my tea's cold," Ms. Krick said, taking a noisy slurp of her drink. "What do you think, Oscar? Has Margaret found Great Granddaddy's fountain?"

Courtney gasped. *Great Granddaddy's fountain?*

Violet reached over and pinched her.

Courtney clasped a hand over her mouth, her eyes wide. What did that mean?

"And why would Ms. Wallis tell on her if she hadn't?" Ms. Krick continued. "She knows more than she lets on, I think."

A cat's purring could be plainly heard throughout the apartment. Courtney imagined Ms. Krick petting his shaggy black fur.

"She'll tell me soon enough," Ms. Krick said lightly, her sigh echoing through the cat filled room.

A cat could be heard jumping to the floor with a small screech.

He padded over to where Courtney and Violet sat huddled together, and rubbed his body along the blanket.

Courtney gingerly stuck her hand out for him to smell, hoping he'd remember her from the time she'd visited Ms. Krick. That time she'd been invited. Didn't that mean the cat would think she was friendly?

The sounds of running water and puttering about floated through the small apartment as Ms. Krick bustled around somewhere past the hallway behind the kitchen. She hummed a familiar tune Courtney couldn't place. Whatever it was sounded badly off key.

Oscar settled himself into a curled position nestled up against the blanket that covered the girls. This could even be *his* blanket, Courtney thought.

Violet shouldn't have pulled her back into the apartment, Courtney lamented, clenching her teeth. She tapped her fingers against her legs, pulled tightly against her chest. They could be on their way to bed now. Courtney felt an aggravated flash, something that was becoming altogether too common. She was being silly. If they'd gone out onto the roof, they'd probably have been caught. She closed her eyes and tried to breathe evenly.

The two girls sat in silence and waited. Courtney's mind raced. If they went undiscovered and Ms. Krick went to bed, it would still be at least an hour before it was safe to leave. What time was it, anyway? It felt like a long time since they'd arrived in the apartment. She'd been avoiding eye contact with Violet, though they sat facing each other. Violet didn't seem to be making an effort to communicate either.

Courtney looked at her now. Violet rested her forehead on her arms, which were propped up against her bent knees. Courtney prodded her gently with her toe. It wouldn't do for her to fall asleep.

Violet's head snapped up and she glared at Courtney. Her eyes were red and weepy-looking.

"*What?*" Courtney mouthed. She didn't dare make a sound. She pulled her phone out of her coat pocket and motioned for Violet to do the same.

11:06 p.m. flashed on Courtney's display. It was later than she'd thought. She unlocked the screen. There was a text from Margaret.

I'm fine, I covered for you. Did you find anything? Hurry back.

There was also a second message.

Where are you guys? I'm worried sick!

It had been sent at 10:45 p.m., not that long ago. Courtney quickly typed a reply.

Stuck in Krick's apartment. Hopefully back soon.

She hit send. Then she went back to her contacts list and typed in a new message.

We're going to have to wait here a while. She should go to bed soon.

She hit send again. Violet's phone buzzed to announce the incoming text. Violet typed furiously in response.

My eyes are burning!

And then her head was back on her arms and her whole body looked like she'd given up.

Courtney stared at her phone. The message indicator was on. She'd completely forgotten about the call she'd missed when she'd gotten the note from Izzy. She still hadn't picked up the message. *Had* it been Cole? Her finger itched to press the button and see if it had been from him, though of course, she couldn't do that in her current circumstance.

"Goodnight my sweet angels!" Ms. Krick called into the living room.

She was much closer than the girls had realized and they both jumped a little. Courtney shoved her phone under her rear to hide the light. Violet lifted her head and turned slightly toward the sound of the voice. Of course, Ms. Krick was talking to the cats, but it felt as if she knew the girls were there.

Courtney stared straight ahead, her breathing shallow. After a few long moments, the lights went out and they were in darkness again.

CHAPTER TWENTY-SEVEN

Escaped

"Where have you been?" Margaret asked, opening the door to the dorm room in one frantic motion.

Nearly an hour had passed after Ms. Krick had retired to her bedroom before Courtney and Margaret had felt safe enough to leave the apartment. They'd left using the door and had silently made their way through the teachers' residence to the lawn.

"Shh," said Courtney.

The hallway was dark. Margaret had the bedside lamp on, with a hoodie thrown over it, like they sometimes did after lights out. She quietly closed the door behind her.

"Where's Violet?" Margaret demanded, looking at the door as if Violet would walk through its solid form, like a ghost.

"She's fine," Courtney answered, taking Isaac's journal out of her coat and setting it on the nightstand. "She went to the restroom to wash off the cat hair." She'd known Violet a long time. Her allergy would subside once she washed.

"Oh, cats!" Margaret said, smacking her forehead. "Ms. Krick has cats! They make Violet sneeze, don't they?"

Courtney nodded. Violet had been a mess. To her credit, she hadn't complained, though maybe she'd been feeling too poorly to say much.

Margaret looked toward the end of the hall where the restrooms were located, her eyebrows knitted together with worry.

"She'll be fine," said Courtney. "Bessie's all the way at the other end of the hall and we get up to use the restroom in the night all the time. I've never seen Bessie come and check what we're doing, have you?"

Margaret shook her head, but didn't look convinced.

"What about Lynette, did she know where we were?" Lynette would have been worried Violet wasn't in bed at lights out.

"I told her when I saw you at Ms. Krick's apartment window," Margaret said. "It seemed inevitable you'd be late. You're not mad, are you? I had to tell her something so she could cover for Violet." Her lower lip stuck out in a pout.

"You did good, Margaret," Courtney assured her, patting her on the back. She'd asked Margaret to stay behind because Courtney had assumed she'd be a liability, but she'd turned out to be a pretty good decoy.

"Courtney, the fountain is dangerous," Margaret said, tugging on Courtney's arm. "Ms. Krick isn't going to stop until she finds it. You should have heard her questioning me tonight. She's nuts."

Courtney eased her arm away from Margaret, who seemed on the verge of a breakdown that Courtney was too tired to deal with.

"You were totally right about how she'd react," Margaret continued. "I really didn't think she would take me to Valentine. I wasn't doing anything wrong!"

Courtney pulled on her pajamas, rolling her eyes as she pulled on her shirt.

"I wasn't even in the woods," Margaret said, coming over to Courtney's side of the room and waving her arms in the air. "Just the suggestion that I might be, pushed her right over the edge. Courtney, we can't let Violet use the fountain again."

Courtney turned her back on her ranting roommate and crawled into bed. She'd had enough excitement for one night and there was still work to do. Margaret's ranting was tiresome.

"Goodnight, Margaret," Courtney said, closing her eyes.

Margaret grumbled in complaint. She clearly wasn't done talking, but Courtney didn't encourage her. Eventually, Margaret stopped fidgeting and settled in. She turned off her bedside lamp and climbed into bed, sighing heavily.

Courtney lay in her own bed, without moving a muscle. Margaret tried to initiate more conversation a few times, but Courtney feigned sleep. She waited nearly half an hour. When she was sure Margaret was asleep, Courtney grabbed Isaac Young's journal from her nightstand. She rolled over to face the wall and tugged her top sheet over her head like a tent. She then turned on her phone's flashlight and started to read.

Courtney rubbed her eyes, which were sore from a sleepless night. Her alarm clock flashed 5:30 a.m. She tossed and turned for twenty minutes, not being able to shake the list of things she had running through her mind.

She might as well get up. If she fell asleep now she'd probably just feel worse when her alarm finally went off. Isaac Young's diary had been a jackpot of information. Its slanted, cramped script spilled out his ancient thoughts on the pages. It had taken some concentration to unravel the messages he'd left. Had he known it would be read, or had he just written it for himself?

Courtney's brow creased as she thought of the journal sitting in Ms. Krick's apartment for who knows how long, its information withheld from the St. Augustus' students for whom he'd intended it.

She threw the journal under her pillow and dressed quietly. Courtney was getting good at opening their dorm room door without making a sound. She didn't meet anyone on her way to the student lounge.

Courtney went to her usual reading corner, a group of armchairs surrounding a low coffee table, beside a bank of windows. She set down her phone and the blank notebook she'd brought with her, on the table.

She'd made a wish and she could feel it was going to come true. She'd felt the fountain's power building within her since she'd made her wish. She'd made decisions that somehow felt as if they were being made by someone else. She still wanted the things on the list, though maybe she wouldn't push her dad to let her go home just yet. The faster she checked the things off her list, the faster she'd be in control of her own actions and feel more like herself. She might have to put herself first for the next little while. Her friends would understand.

A puddle of bright shone from the safety light hanging above the window, highlighting the notebook's smooth white pages where it lay open. She had some research to do on swim meets. Ideas from the best ones were what she was after.

She hadn't needed to finish the journal to know the fountain's power was real. She'd read every word anyway. Courtney sank further into the brown leather armchair.

Using her phone, she looked up pictures, news reports and results of swim meets across America. If she was going to make team captain, she'd have to do it with more than swimming. Her neck cramped from the odd angle she leaned at over the coffee table to jot down her findings. She'd plan a swim meet that wouldn't be easily forgotten. She'd be their only choice to lead this team.

Hours later, Courtney's stomach growled for breakfast. Her notebook was almost full. There was a lot she could do to help her wishes.

The lights still weren't on in the lounge, but sun streamed

through the windows, spilling beams of light onto her page. She'd have to leave soon if she wanted breakfast and she still had to put on her uniform. Courtney closed her notebook, pleased that she'd taken charge. But she had to get moving or she'd be going to class in her sweats.

Courtney ran at high speed to the dorm. It was all but deserted, so her path was clear. Most of the girls had already gone to breakfast. Thankfully, their room was empty when she arrived, even Margaret had already gone. Stepping inside their room, she stopped short. Her bed was neatly made, something Margaret did compulsively on a regular basis on days when Courtney wasn't around.

"Crap!" Courtney muttered, dropping her notebook and phone on the bedspread as she dove for the pillow. She knew before reaching underneath that that Isaac Young's journal was gone.

She quickly dragged a brush through her unruly hair and threw on a clean St. Augustus blouse.

"Ridiculous uniform," she mumbled aloud as she fought with the zipper on her kilt.

She reached for her knee socks and contemplated trying to put them both on at once. Shaking her head, she opted for putting them on the usual way instead. Every move took longer than it felt like it should. Even her loafers caught on her socks as she tugged them on. Margaret had probably shown the journal to Violet and the others by now.

Beads of sweat had appeared on Courtney's forehead by the time she burst out of her room and headed for the cafeteria. She slowed as she reached the wide entrance by the buffet line, looking back and forth between the food choices and her friends who sat halfway down the cafeteria at their usual table.

The clock on the wall made the choice for her. She grabbed the closest muffin on the way past the morning spread then headed to their table.

"Courtney!" Margaret exclaimed, getting up from the table and giving Courtney a hug. "Where were you? I woke up and you'd already gone!"

"Sounds like every morning," Courtney answered sharply, her eyes on the leather-bound book open on the table in front of Violet.

Courtney cringed as Violet took a bite out of her toast, spilling crumbs onto the journal's pages.

"You'll wreck it," Courtney cried, lunging forward and grabbing the journal.

Violet looked up in surprise, but didn't make a move to retrieve the book. Courtney stood at the end of the table, hugging the journal to her chest.

"We're all in this together, Courtney," said Margaret, shaking her head. "Don't worry so much."

Courtney looked at Margaret, then at the rest of the table, where the girls nodded their heads. They seemed ready to help, but how? She had the book now. But she might need help figuring out the map, and the key. Come to think of it, help was welcome, she realized, softening a bit. She'd have to tolerate them. She forced herself to smile.

"We're going to help you shake this wish," Margaret said, patting Courtney on the hand. "You really haven't been yourself."

Courtney narrowed her eyes. Margaret was starting to sound like she was stuck on repeat. There was nothing wrong with Courtney, she reminded herself.

"I'm fine," Courtney told the table, not moving to stay or go, simply watching.

"Courtney, you've always been bossy, so that's not really anything new," said Violet, laughing.

Her words didn't immediately register with Courtney.

"I can't believe it's all true," said Lynette. She looked at

Courtney as if waiting for Courtney to contradict her.

Courtney stared at Hailey, her mind reeling. "I could use some help actually," Courtney said.

"Will it help us figure out what Isaac Young wanted?" Rhoda asked, looking skeptical.

"You want to know what he wanted?" Courtney asked. What did that have to do with anything?

"To know whether it's safe to use the fountain," Rhoda explained. "We need to know why he made it, to know his intentions. Then we can decide."

Courtney looked at her blankly then noticed all the heads nodding again around the table. Their goal was certainly different from her own. She wasn't the least bit interested in how Isaac Young felt about creating the fountain, but their interest in it could be promising.

"Sure," Courtney replied. Her mind *felt* sharp. Puzzle pieces were starting to form. She could see three moves ahead. She sat down at the table between Hailey and Rhoda and urged Margaret to sit back down too. She was going to have to trust these girls. She put the journal on the table in the middle of the other five girls. "Here's what we're going to do."

After school that day, the girls assembled in Courtney and Margaret's room, where Margaret took charge.

Courtney looked around the room, wondering how much she should share. Not the note about the headmistress and Mr. Chase. That she would keep to herself. But what she had in mind needed all of them.

"Okay, we know from his journal that Isaac Young left the fountain for the students," Margaret recapped, pacing.

"And we think that's why Ms. Krick can't see it," Rhoda added, bouncing excitedly on Margaret's bed.

Courtney let them talk. They'd need time to catch up.

Violet had been the only one of the girls not at the noon swim practice, so she'd taken the journal and read as much as she could over the lunch hour. Courtney had quivered with anxiety throughout the practice, until she got back and Violet returned the journal.

"I could tell the headmistress you stole it from her apartment," Courtney had said as she got the journal back and tucked it under her arm. Her voice had sounded catty as she said it, certainly not like her own.

"You were there too!" Violet had exclaimed.

"Sure," Courtney had replied smugly, "but who do you think she's going to believe?"

Violet had flashed Courtney an odd sideways look and hadn't spoken to her since. That had been a few hours ago, now.

Courtney blinked at Violet, who sat across from her beside Rhoda on Margaret's bed. Why had she said that earlier? Of course, she wouldn't turn her in. Violet would forgive her. "I'm sorry, Violet!" Courtney exclaimed. Yes, that sounded more like her own voice.

"You can't help it, Courtney," Margaret said, coming over to pat Courtney on the shoulder, "Violet understands."

Violet gave Courtney a thin smile then got off Margaret's bed. Wordlessly, she picked up the map and unrolled it, holding it up against the window.

Courtney huddled in close behind Margaret and the others followed. She wanted to get a better look at her map. Each time she looked at the markings she learned something.

"It only works in sunlight," Margaret explained to those who hadn't seen it before. "So, get a good look now."

"Crazy," said Hailey, pulling out her phone and snapping pictures. "Is it magic?"

Margaret shrugged, looking over at Courtney as if she'd have the answers. Courtney looked away. She retreated to the closet and fished the key she'd found out of its hiding spot. She'd put it in a box of hats, mitts and scarves on the overhead shelf. She held up the key to show the other girls.

"And this is the key I found the night we got back from Christmas break and played truth or dare."

"You found it when you and Jake went into the woods, right?" Rhoda asked. "Was it near the fountain?"

Courtney thought about the question and shook her head.

"No, Jake and I barely went into the woods," she answered. "We went through the trees just behind the West Building. The fountain's in the middle, but maybe the entire woods are important."

Hailey took the key and held it for a moment before passing it to Rhoda.

Courtney peered over their shoulders at the map, which Violet still held up against the window.

"There," Courtney said, reaching her hand toward the map and pointing to a spot several inches in from where the pictures of trees began. She'd been looking for the key on the map at the edge of the illustrated woods, but the West Building hadn't been there then. It was built in the 1980's. It looked as if the woods had extended in the past to where the West Building now stood. The woods looked like they used to wrap all the way around the school to the other side of the teachers' residence. There was a smaller structure, like a miniature house inside the south border of the trees. Could it have actually been where Isaac Young had lived as a boy? Courtney wondered if it was still there. If it was, maybe they could find out.

"There's no key shape there," Hailey said.

"No, there isn't," Courtney replied. "There's only a box. I think it's the wooden one that the key was buried in. Things – well they seem to move."

"What things move?" Lynette asked.

Courtney knew it sounded a little crazy, even to her it did.

"The other night, the key symbol was there," she said, pointing at the school office. "That's why I went to the lost and found."

"I don't see it," Rhoda said, her face only inches from where Courtney had pointed.

"The key is part of the puzzle," Lynette said, pointing to a translucent key icon shining on an empty space inside a sketched building.

Courtney felt a chill rock through the group as they realized the location of the key icon.

"That's here!" Violet exclaimed, giving an excited hop, which shook the map. "It's magic! The map really is magic."

"Shh!" Margaret hissed. "You'll bring Bessie!"

"That's our room," Courtney said, tightening her grip on the key. "It knows."

"It knows?" Margaret asked, her mouth agape, as she leaned out from the map, looking intently. "Come on, Courtney. Keys don't know anything. It's a trick of the map, that's all. Like GPS." Her voice shook just a little.

Courtney knew Margaret didn't really believe the map worked using GPS. Still, the magnitude of what they'd discovered hadn't hit her when she'd seen the key in the office. She'd thought it was predictive somehow, but was it even possible that the map was somehow alive?

"The map knows we have the key," said Courtney. She felt frozen to the spot where she stood.

"That's crazy," Hailey said, giving a low whistle.

"So, if the picture of a key is actually a key," Lynette chimed in, "then the rest of these symbols must mean something too. What could the key open? Are there any doors shown?"

Courtney looked at Lynette. It was an obvious statement, and yet...

"Maybe there's a lock?" Rhoda suggested.

There was silence as the girls pored over the map that Violet still held against the window. The remaining five of them were crowded between Courtney and Margaret's beds, trying to see.

There were other symbols near their room, inside the dorm, but no door and no lock.

"The lucky room," said Rhoda, as she pointed to a spot just down the hall from where they were.

Courtney looked more closely at the spot Rhoda had identified. A fountain. There was a picture of a fountain. How had she missed that before?

"My arms are getting tired," Violet complained. She shrugged her shoulders, making the map ripple where it was held against the window.

Courtney took the map from her wordlessly and started to roll it up. She'd look at it herself, later. Who knew what other secrets it might hold? It all suddenly seemed too much.

"Wait!" Hailey cried, putting her hand out to prevent Courtney from rolling it further. "Put it back!"

Courtney gave a start and looked from Hailey to the other girls, then back at the map. There was no uncomplicated way to refuse. How could she explain what had just come over her? Reluctantly, she unrolled the map and slowly placed it back against the window. Outside, the sun was getting lower in the sky and the map's symbols looked faded.

"There!" Hailey exclaimed triumphantly, pointing to an area on the east side of the Main Building on the map.

Courtney squinted at the area Hailey pointed at, but it was hard to see the map and hold it at the same time. From her angle, the symbols were all but gone.

"Do you mind holding it?" Courtney asked Lynette, who was leaning in so much that her entire body was pressed against Courtney.

Lynette reached out and held the map at its corners. Courtney let go and took a step back so the symbols would be in focus. She needed a little space.

"It's a treasure chest?" Violet asked nobody in particular, pressing in at Courtney's shoulder.

"Looks more like an old trunk of some kind," said Hailey. "The kind a key like ours might open."

Courtney bristled at Hailey's insinuation that the key belonged to all of them. Was Hailey an expert on what a chest looked like, as opposed to a trunk? Weren't they the same thing?

Hailey stood so close that Courtney could smell her freshly washed hair.

They were only moments away from losing the light.

Courtney's gaze searched the area around the picture of the trunk that faded by the second as the sun sank below the horizon.

"That's near the library, isn't it?" Margaret asked.

"Who knows?" Courtney said, trying to sound nonchalant. "We'll have to look tomorrow in the daylight to know for sure. Thanks for holding the map, Lynette, but the light is gone. There's nothing to see, now." Courtney reached over and took one of the top corners of the map from Lynette, lifting her elbows high enough so that the other girls took a step back from the tight semi-circle. Courtney used the space she'd created to roll the map up tightly and snap the elastic back around it.

"I took pictures!" Hailey announced, holding up her phone.

Margaret took the phone from Hailey and zoomed in on where they'd seen the chest, or trunk, or whatever it was.

"It's sort of by the library," Margaret said, tilting her head. She moved the image around the screen with her finger so the whole area was visible. "But it's also by the theatre. I don't know what's over there, isn't it just a hallway?"

"Beats me," Courtney said, yawning wide. "I'm hungry. Let's hit the cafeteria," she announced.

Margaret handed Hailey back her phone and looked at Courtney. She seemed confused, but followed Courtney's lead.

"Yes, Courtney's right," said Margaret. "We can talk about it more over dinner."

The other girls didn't go without complaint, but they went. The promise of food was a good incentive.

After she'd ushered everyone out of the room, Courtney tucked the map back into its hiding place behind the umbrella in the closet. She'd have to find somewhere better to hide it, but it would do, for now.

CHAPTER TWENTY-EIGHT

Hidden Treasure

Courtney had eyed the door to the cafeteria all through supper, waiting for her chance to make an excuse. She'd managed to keep their minds off the hunt for the treasure chest by asking the girls to brainstorm ways to make the swim meet really over the top. Violet usually begged off all things related to swimming, but she liked party planning, so even she got busy with a list of possibilities. With an exaggerated yawn, Courtney made up a story about some homework she hadn't finished and left the cafeteria before the other girls had even stopped talking long enough to realize she'd gone.

Courtney made her way through the Main Building's stone hallways in the opposite direction from the Student Lounge. There was no sign of life or lights as she passed the office. The library was still open, its lights on, but Courtney glanced in as she passed and it looked deserted. She kept walking toward the theatre and paused at the plain wooden door to the costume loft Hanna had shown her. She turned the doorknob and entered, climbing the stairs as quickly as the narrow steps would allow without her tripping.

She reached the top and looked toward the far end of the room. It was just as she'd remembered - tucked under the costume rack and partially hidden by long garments that were hanging down. Courtney rushed across to the big old trunk, her hand in her pocket to draw out the key.

She knelt in front of the battered wooden trunk, focusing on the latch. She held the key in one hand, but the latch was smooth and had no keyhole. Courtney frowned. She'd been sure this was the room on the map. She scanned the floor for anything else that the key might open, but this was the only thing that looked like a treasure chest.

Turning her attention back to the trunk, she ran her empty hand over the brass latch, looking for a place to try the key. Finding nothing, she instead lifted the latch. It clicked, and released, springing the lid open to a ready position. Cautiously, Courtney raised the lid. As the hinges creaked, she heard the loud bang of a door slamming. Rapid footsteps on the stairs gave Courtney a start. There was more than one set of footsteps approaching.

Courtney wheeled around, still low to the ground.

"Where do theses stairs even lead?" Said a voice, as it floated up from the stairwell.

It was Violet's. She and Margaret emerged from the stairwell into the dimly lit room. Courtney felt her own heartbeat pulse in her ears. She'd checked the hallway before she'd entered. How had they known where she'd gone?

"Man, Courtney," Margaret called across the room. "You move quickly. We didn't see where you went, this was the last door we tried in the hallway, but as soon as we saw the staircase I knew this was it. What is this place, anyway? Have you been here before?" She looked around at the attic.

"My, uh, sister told me about it," Courtney replied. "I just came here to think. I'm fine, really." Her gaze darted back and forth, from one intruder to the other. They might still leave.

She could leave with them if she had to, then return closer to lights out.

"Ooo, you found the trunk," Violet exclaimed, clapping her hands. "The key worked! After all these years, the key still opened the trunk!" She hopped a little before joining Courtney as she knelt on the floor beside the trunk.

"It didn't," Courtney answered flatly, shaking her head. "It wasn't locked. The latch doesn't have a lock."

"But this is where the map said to go, right?" Violet asked, frowning before she turned to the contents of the trunk and starting digging, tossing the contents onto the floor. "Isn't that why you're here?"

"Violet!" Margaret exclaimed. "You're making a mess!" She bent to the growing pile of shiny garments behind Violet and filled her arms with the clothes. "You'll ruin them!"

Courtney peered into the empty trunk. The inside of the trunk was smooth, the wood weathered from years of use. The lid was lined with a deep chocolate colored satin, quilted in a diamond pattern. She ran her hand along the bottom of the trunk. She'd been so sure it was the one.

Violet had risen to her feet and circled the trunk, pushing the costume rack away by rolling it on its castors. She then proceeded to rap her knuckles methodically across the top of the trunk's lid, as if she were trying to find a stud in a wall. Violet's body was inside the trunk as she placed her ear only inches from its wall.

Courtney watched her intently, as she became aware of a noise coming from the corner. Momentarily distracted, she looked around to see what was causing the shuffling sound. Margaret was the culprit. In the corner of the room, she was busy shaking and folding each discarded garment with care and stacking neatly folded costumes on top of a nearby table.

"Margaret," Courtney said sharply. "Don't bother. The clothes weren't folded before."

"Well, they should be," Margaret replied. "The drama group really should take better care of them."

Courtney turned back toward Violet. Let Margaret do what she wanted. Courtney wasn't done searching the room.

"Hmm," Violet murmured, her ear bent to the top of the trunk as she tapped it lightly with the tips of her fingers.

"Did you find something?" Courtney asked, leaning in. The map had definitely showed this room. There was something in here they were meant to find.

"Violet!" Margaret exclaimed, rushing back toward the trunk.

Violet had reached into the underside of the trunk lid and was prying the shiny brown lining away from the edge.

"You're wrecking it!" Margaret protested loudly.

Ignoring her, Courtney reached out her hands and dug in beside where Violet struggled to free the lining. She gave the satin a tug, pulling it back with a satisfying rip. Margaret stood and watched, her eyes nearly bulging out of her head.

"Here!" Violet exclaimed, "Give me that key!" Violet had climbed into the empty trunk by now, and held out her hand to Courtney, who shook her head. She wasn't giving the key to Violet. Instead, she gripped the key tightly in her fist and stepped into the trunk herself, nudging Violet to the side.

"Hey!" Violet protested. "There isn't room for both of us!"

Squeezed in uncomfortably beside Violet, Courtney felt her way across the underbelly of the trunk lid, stopping when she felt a rough patch. It felt like a piece of metal encasing a hole. Her hands trembled with excitement. With a little difficulty, she managed to wiggle the key into the lock, its rusty edges needing some coaxing. The key slid snugly inside. Courtney turned the key a half turn to the right, and felt a click. She hesitated. What was supposed to happen?

Slowly, a panel began to separate, as if it were a cloud floating away from the lid of the trunk.

"Whoa," said Violet, with a low whistle.

Margaret had crowded close to Courtney and Violet, who were still crammed inside the bottom of the trunk.

"Stand back," Courtney told them, waving her arms out to the sides to push the other girls away. The panel continued to move toward them, until something fell out at her feet with a soft clunk. Courtney looked down, but couldn't reach her feet because the panel that had emerged was in her way. Gingerly, she stepped out of the trunk and turned back to access the trunk floor.

Violet beat her to it, bending down into the void Courtney had left, to retrieve the item.

"This looks old," said Violet, as she stood in the trunk and held the object in her hands. "It's another old book."

Courtney reached over and swiped it away from Violet. It was indeed a book that looked to be as old as Isaac Young's journal.

"Courtney!" Margaret exclaimed. "Stop it!"

Courtney took a step toward the staircase, the book tucked to her chest.

"Show us!" Violet demanded.

"We really should be going," Courtney said, ignoring their requests to be included, and taking another step toward the exit.

"We can't just go," Margaret said. "We have to leave this place the way we found it!" She gestured widely at the ripped lining of the trunk and the costumes that still lay on the floor.

The two girls had rounded her and blocked her path.

Courtney opened her mouth to tell them to get out of her way, but before she could say anything, Violet had snatched the book back.

"Hey!" Courtney exclaimed.

"Loosen up, Courtney," Margaret snapped, walking over to the costumes on the table. "You just did the same thing to her. Now help me put these costumes back."

"Who's Alexandrina Young?" Violet asked them. She'd moved

over to stand directly under the bare light bulb that hung from the ceiling. She squinted at the book, open to a page near the front.

"She was Isaac Young's mother," Courtney said, quietly. The book had belonged to his mother.

Margaret moved back and forth across the floor, filling the trunk back up with costumes. Courtney had joined Violet under the lamp and stood at her shoulder. She itched to take the book back, flexing her fists at her sides. Its loopy script was small and tightly written. It was very different to the handwriting in Isaac Young's journal. The page they'd opened to was titled Alexandrina Young. Under the name, in the same circular scrawl was one word and a date.

Grimoire -1901.

Courtney stared at the book.

"You girls really made a mess of this trunk," Margaret said. She removed the key from the lock and tried to shove the separated panel back in. She ripped the remaining liner of the lid and tucked it under the costumes she'd just replaced. "When is the next drama production?"

"They're rehearsing for it now, I think. They'll perform it closer to the end of the year." Violet replied, apparently losing interest in the book and letting the hand that held it fall to her side.

Courtney followed closely behind Violet as she wandered over to the trunk, running her free hand over the panel, which still protruded from the lid. It stuck out far enough so that the lid wouldn't close while it was in the way. How was she going to get the book back?

"Whoever's designing their costumes will have to come up here at some point," Violet said.

And Hanna, Courtney thought. Hanna would be up here, making it all work for them. Though she couldn't explain why, the thought of Hanna seeing the raised panel on the lid of the trunk, even though it was empty, unnerved her.

Unsure if she should go for the book or the key first, Courtney took a step forward toward the other girls.

"May I?" Courtney asked Margaret, holding her hand out for the key Margaret held.

Margaret stepped aside congenially and let her have the key.

Courtney slipped the key back into the lock and turned it a quarter turn to the left. The panel slid back into place as smoothly as it had opened. Courtney palmed the key into her pocket and closed the trunk lid. That was better. Now for the book.

She turned to Violet and steeled her stance.

"I need to see the book," Courtney said, holding out her hand in demand.

Violet shrugged and handed it over. That had been easier than she'd expected. Courtney flipped past the title page then scanned the first page. What exactly was a grimoire, anyway? She'd heard the word. Violet crowded her again, reading over her shoulder. Courtney had never been so sick of her friend as she was tonight.

Trying to ignore Violet, Courtney turned her attention back to the book. Its pages were filled with stanzas that looked like poetry, but seemed to contain ingredients. Was it a cookbook? At the bottom of each page were strings of words that looked suspiciously like nonsense. Another language, perhaps?

They're spells!" Violet shrieked.

Spells. The book was full of spells.

"Ridiculous," Margaret scoffed. "We can look at it back in the dorm. We've been up here a while and it's late."

Courtney looked up at Margaret who, despite her chippy voice, had made a good point. Besides, Violet would have to go to her own room at lights out. Courtney could handle having Margaret there, but Violet was twanging on Courtney's last nerve. She snapped the book shut and tucked it snugly under her arm.

"Could you get the light?" Courtney asked over her shoulder as she passed Violet on her way to the stairs, taking them quickly.

She heard Margaret and Violet scrambling to follow her then the light clicked off.

"Courtney, wait up," Margaret called down the darkened stairwell. "It's dark!"

Courtney reached the bottom of the spiral staircase and opened the door. Instead of the light flooding in as she expected, the hallway was dim, with only emergency lights casting a shadowy glow. She took a careful step toward the exit door.

"This whole wing shuts down at 9:30!" Margaret exclaimed, slapping the heel of her hand against her forehead.

Courtney pulled the book tighter under her left arm and tried the door that led out of the wing, into the Main Building with her right. It was locked. She checked the edges for a release, but it looked like one of the newer type locks that worked on a timer. There was no way out.

"It's 9:45," Violet groaned. "Lynette covered for me when we were at Ms. Krick's apartment, but twice in one week will be tough for her to pull off, even if she wanted to. She's starting to get uppity about it."

Courtney turned and made her way down the echoing stone hallway, back past the library and the theatre, to the outside door that led to the east side of the building. They used that door all the time to cut through from the cafeteria to the Sports Complex. Margaret and Violet followed closely on her heels.

"Courtney," said Margaret, tugging on her sleeve. "The other night I said you were in the restroom when Bessie asked. Tonight, we're both here. Who's going to cover for us? She's going to know we're not there!"

"There has to be a way out," said Courtney. "This is a school, not a prison. They can't just lock us in here."

The three girls had reached the end of the hall and stared at the sign written in big red letters.

EMERGENCY EXIT WHEN DOORS ARE LOCKED
ALARM WILL SOUND IF BARRIER IS OPENED.

A long black bar blocked their access to the handle. The bar had never been there before when they'd used this exit. Had the signs always been there? Courtney read them again. Of course they'd always been there, she decided. They couldn't just put up signs every night and then take them down. Yet it was strange that she'd never noticed them before.

"So, we open it," Courtney announced.

"But the alarm will sound!" Margaret cried.

"We weren't doing anything wrong," Courtney said with a shrug. "It's not our fault we got locked in. We'll be in more trouble if we miss lights out. Besides, they'd have to catch us first. By the time any of the teachers come to investigate the alarm, we'll be in bed."

"What if someone's just outside? What will we say if we get caught?" Violet asked.

Courtney was getting tired of answering Violet's questions.

"Simple. We'll tell them the truth, that we were checking out the costumes," Courtney replied.

"But we have nothing to do with the play," Margaret said, beginning to sound hysterical. "I don't even know what production they're doing this year. How do we explain that?"

"We won't have to, we're going to be fine," Courtney answered, confident what she said was true. She reached for the handle with her right hand, still hugging the book to her chest with her left. "Ready?" She looked from side to side at each of her friends' faces in turn. "Let's go."

Courtney pulled the black metal lever up then pushed the door open with her body. A siren pierced the air as the three girls spilled out into the night. The shrill alarm made Courtney's eardrums hurt, but covering her ears would only slow her down.

The West Woods

She ran, her heart pounding and barely aware of Violet and Margaret lagging, until she reached the dorm.

CHAPTER TWENTY-NINE

Second Chance

The following morning, Courtney's eyes fluttered open a full three minutes before her alarm was set to go off. Her stomach tightened as she realized the alarm was only her clock, not the door alarm they'd set off. What had they been thinking? Were there cameras on campus? She'd never noticed. Why hadn't she thought to look?

Courtney groaned softly. When had her life become so complicated? She might get to go home, after all, but expulsion wasn't the way she wanted to do it. Getting trapped in the costume room was an innocent mistake, right? But added to everything else that had happened lately, well – it was starting to be a lot.

Her alarm kept ringing, but Courtney was lost in thought.

"Courtney," Margaret squawked from her bed. "Make it stop!" She'd hopped out of bed to turn off Courtney's alarm.

Courtney looked over at Margaret, who'd collapsed back on her bed after she'd turned off the alarm on Courtney's clock.

"I'm not running this morning, sorry for the alarm," Courtney told her, rolling over. She closed her eyes.

Suddenly, Margaret was over Courtney's bed, pulling her up by the arms.

"Alright, honey," Margaret said, firmly. "You're getting up. You love running. Maybe it'll clear your head. Wasn't that the whole point of the whole wish? So, you could be on some silly track team in Boston?"

Courtney was reluctantly on her feet now, staring at Margaret in disbelief. What she'd said was absolutely true. Running would help.

"Uh, thanks," Courtney said, rubbing the sleep out of her eyes. She should run. It would clear her head.

"You're welcome," Margaret said, flopping back dramatically onto her pillow.

Now, where were Courtney's shoes? She was dressed and out of the room in no time. It had warmed up outside the previous few days and the ground had grown soggy with melted snow, though it was frozen and hard under her feet with the morning frost. It was still well before dawn.

Hitting the sidewalk, she high-tailed it toward town. She reached up to rub a spot on her lower rib that ached from exertion. She needed to relax. Watching her feet as she ran, she counted out two hundred of her evenly paced steps.

She looked up in surprise when she hit the long row of houses, one of which she assumed was Cole's. Why had she run this way? The last thing she wanted was to run into him and explain why she hadn't even picked up his message yet, if it even was him who'd previously called. Why hadn't she checked? She came to a cross street and made a quick turn to run down a new block. Ten steps in, she began to lose steam.

The run hadn't refreshed her like she'd thought it might. Giving up, she slowed to a walk and lifted her fingers to her neck to check her pulse. She came to a full stop in front of a small playground that was nestled between houses. Courtney crossed the park toward a row of swings. Gravel crunched under her shoes as she walked.

She just needed a minute away from the thoughts swirling in her head. That would help.

Sinking down onto a swing, Courtney felt the soft seat bend under her weight. Just a few short days ago, all she'd wanted to do was run. She'd had her first kiss, and then, she'd had a real first kiss. Everything had been happening in such a blur.

Her eyes widened as she replayed her kiss with Cole. She needed to know if he'd called. A sinking feeling settled in her stomach as she reached for her phone and checked her messages. There were two. The first was from her mom, which just asked her to call. She skipped over it without finding out if she'd needed anything else. The next was from Cole.

"Hi Courtney," he'd started, his voice cracking a little, "I was wondering if you knew how to skate. There's a winter carnival in town this weekend, and I thought maybe we could go together tonight. If you don't have skates, we can still go and do something else. I hope you can come!"

His voice sounded bright.

Saturday. That had been days ago. She'd missed their first date. In fact, she'd been so wrapped up in her own mess, she hadn't even known she'd been asked on a date. Courtney slumped into the swing. Cole had called like he'd said he would, and he'd completely slipped her mind. How would she ever explain? Tears welled up in her eyes as she stared at her phone. If she hadn't made the wish, she'd have been on a real date, with Cole, last Saturday. They might even have kissed again.

Instead, well instead she'd been on a wild goose chase to make team captain of a sport she didn't even really like.

She hung up the phone and put it in her pocket. Rocking her body back and forth on the swing, she pumped her legs until she flew up into the air then sank back down to ground again in a smooth arc. She swung until she felt lightheaded and her mind was finally clear.

Everything that had happened filtered through her thoughts as she swung back and forth. The choices she'd been making weren't like her at all. She couldn't date Cole, she realized. Not now. Not when she was going to make a mess of it. Not until she'd completed her wish. She could tell him she'd never gotten his message, but what about the next time? She really wasn't in control. Completing her list was always on her mind. Maybe by the time she saw him again, this whole wish business would be over.

Dragging her feet along the gravel, she slowed her swing to a sway. Courtney blinked to clear her blurry eyes as tears streamed down her cheeks. Dabbing her eyes with the back of her sleeve, she planted her feet on the ground to stop the movement, which was starting to make her feel ill.

When she looked up after a minute, she blinked several times. As if a mirage had appeared in front of her, Cole and Husk stood on the sidewalk in front of the park.

Courtney lifted her arm to wipe her drippy nose in a way she hoped was discreet. She'd decided to put things off with Cole. Until she... until she was herself again. He couldn't see her like this. She looked around the playground for an escape route, but there was nowhere to go. She was surrounded by houses. The only way out was by the path to the sidewalk, where Cole stood.

How long had he and Husk been standing there, watching her?

Cole smiled at her and lifted a hand in greeting. Husk sat beside him on the sidewalk, panting. Courtney could swear the husky had grown since she'd seen him last. It had only been a few days.

"I was just heading back to campus," she said, standing up from the swing and brushing off her pants. She felt as if she were intruding on his neighborhood. For all she knew, this park could be in his backyard. She still didn't know where he lived.

Courtney shook out her legs a little. They felt full of pins and needles when she reached solid ground after dangling them for so long on the swing.

"Husk and I will walk you, if you want?" Cole asked.

Courtney stared past him. Something was preventing her from engaging. Why wasn't he mad at her for not returning his call?

"Were you out for a run?" he asked, frowning.

She knew manners dictated she should say something in response, but she couldn't think of anything. She'd like to keep running - all the way down the street and past this really great boy, whom she couldn't think of a thing to say to right now. She'd just concluded she couldn't date him, although she really wanted to.

She watched him on the sidewalk, waiting for her to speak. He ran a hand through his orange hair in a nervous gesture. He was adorable. And she was, well, she was a mess.

She needed to get a grip. Her emotions weren't making a lot of sense right now. Of course, she could walk with Cole. She wanted to. She wanted to run right over and explain. Instead, she stayed rooted to where she stood.

"Walking's fine," she answered, still not moving toward him.

"Are you sure you wouldn't rather finish your run on your own?" Cole asked, looking at Courtney with a funny expression on his face.

How long had she been silent, Courtney wondered? Probably long enough for him to suspect something was wrong.

"No, let's walk," she said, joining him on the sidewalk and stiffly falling into step beside him as they walked toward campus. Husk walked ahead as far as his leash would stretch, sniffing the ground as he went.

The street around them was quiet. Much too quiet as Courtney realized they weren't talking.

"So, I didn't hear back from you," Cole said, after a few more beats than felt natural.

Courtney hadn't been looking at him, but now that she did, she realized he wasn't making eye contact, either. She didn't blame him. He must think she'd blown him off. Her body ached to grab his hand and tell him it was a misunderstanding. But she didn't.

"I wondered why you didn't call," Courtney said, lightly. "I didn't have your number."

Inside, she crumbled a little. She hadn't meant to lie about getting the call, it just came out.

"I, uh," Cole stammered, pulling Husk closer to him by pulling his leash. "I called you the day after we met. I was hoping to take you to the winter carnival."

"That's strange," Courtney answered, keeping her pace steady. "I didn't get a call. Maybe you had the wrong number."

"Courtney," Cole told her, stopping on the sidewalk. "It was *your* voicemail I heard. It wasn't the wrong number."

Courtney didn't answer. She wasn't sure what to say. Lying again would only make it worse.

"It's just that I really like you," he told her, slowing to a stop and taking both of hers hands in his. "You're funny and interesting. I wasn't sure what to think when you didn't call back."

He'd taken her hands. She was holding Cole's hands. The week before, she'd have been thrilled to be holding his hand. But it wasn't the same, somehow.

"Cole," Courtney said, lightly tugging her hands away and starting to walk again. "Things are very complicated right now."

"Oh," Cole said, falling into step beside her, skipping a little to keep up. "There's someone else? Listen, I'm sorry for..."

"No!" Courtney interrupted, shaking her head, and walking at a more normal pace. Why had she been walking so fast? She wasn't exactly in a hurry for anything, except to end this conversation. "There's nobody else. I just... I'm not really in a good place for dating right now, though I'd *really* like to."

By now, they were close to the edge of campus.

She could have said simply that there had been someone else. But somehow Courtney needed him to know she was interested. *Very* interested. She hoped he would wait until she was free from the mess she'd created.

Despite the feeling of a boa constrictor tightening its coils around her, Courtney smiled at Cole and they looked at each other at the same time. His freckles were amazing - clusters she'd like to memorize. She reached out to give his hands a squeeze. He was going to understand... They could pick this up again later. After. The pressure she'd felt on her lungs lessened.

"Okay, thanks for explaining," said Cole, letting his words express his disappointment.

But she knew she hadn't explained. She didn't want him to leave. Not like this.

"Come with me," Courtney said. She led him by the hand across the lawn toward the Main Building.

"Is this allowed?" Cole whispered back, following her, but tugging Husk behind. "I thought you said we shouldn't..."

"Can we tie Husk here?" Courtney asked, stopping by a tree. "We'll have to be quiet."

"Where are we going?" Cole asked, looping Husk's leash around the narrow trunk.

"Shhh..." said Courtney, with a finger to her lips. Maybe this wasn't such a good idea. It was in fact, a really bad idea, and she knew it, but she kept going, anyway.

"Stay," Cole said to Husk, sternly.

Husk put his head down on his paws and whimpered.

"Poor boy," Courtney said, patting him on the head. "We'll be back soon."

Taking Cole's arm, she led him to the stone steps in front of the main doors.

"We're going in?" Cole asked, hesitating on the bottom step.

"You wanted to see inside," Courtney reminded him.

"Sure, but..." Cole stammered.

"There's nobody even awake yet on campus," Courtney said. He could follow her, or not. But she hoped he did. She climbed the stairs with a spring in her step and tried the door, which opened with a bone-crunching squeak.

"Are you sure this is okay?" Cole whispered, wincing against the sound of the door echoing into the expanse of the foyer.

Courtney shrugged and sidled inside onto the slate floor, with Cole following closely on her heels. His presence fueled her, pushing down her sense of doubt.

The door swung closed behind them with a bang, making Courtney flinch. She looked around, her eyes adjusting to the dark.

"It's spooky for this place to be so empty," she whispered to Cole. Even her whisper sounded too loud. "It's usually full of kids."

"Maybe we should go," Cole said, softly. "You don't owe me anything, Courtney. It's okay."

Courtney shook her head. No, they weren't going anywhere. She knew Cole would like it here. She wanted to show him. Even if a teacher came by, they wouldn't know right away Cole didn't belong. She could make something up. She realized it was the first time all week she'd felt like doing something for someone else. She would do this for him.

Her heart pounding, she strode over to the wall at the bottom of the curved staircase and felt for a light switch. Finding only one, she flicked it up. Light flooded the foyer from dozens of lamps hanging from the ceiling, hurting her eyes.

"Wow," Cole said, with a low whistle. He spun slowly around in circle. "This is beautiful."

Courtney smiled as she watched Cole take it all in.

He looked up at the ceiling, mesmerized.

"I hoped you'd like it," Courtney said, without bothering to whisper anymore. Somehow it seemed silly to whisper with the foyer bright with light.

"I've seen pictures of this ceiling, in a book at the library," Cole told her, his eyes shining with excitement. "But the colors are so much more vivid in real life. There are eight separate scenes represented up there." He pointed to a section of the ceiling painted with a rolling field and fluffy white clouds in rich colors and a generous smattering of gold.

"The beams are covered in gold leaf, right?" Courtney asked, trying to remember what she knew about the paintings.

"Yes, that's right," Cole confirmed.

"And every painting in this room was commissioned by Isaac Young himself," she offered. She thought that was true anyway. The gray stone walls of the rounded room were lined with large portraits, all mirroring the same rich colors as the ceiling.

"Oh, those weren't in the book," Cole said, hurrying over to the nearest frame to study it in more detail. "They're original works," he called over his shoulder.

Courtney stood in the middle of the foyer and couldn't help but smile as she watched him. His thin frame was bent forward, his fingers outstretched to run them over the rough surface of the piece of art. His closely cropped red hair stood out against the top of the gilded frame. Courtney had never looked at any of the paintings up close. She'd never really noticed them before at all.

Sidling up beside Cole, she looked at the unsmiling lady in the picture, looking back at them. Had she been someone from Evergreen? She was shown standing by a willow tree in a wispy white dress. Courtney took Cole's hand and followed him as he walked slowly from one painting to the next. She reached out with her free hand and ran it lightly over the peaks and valleys of hardened paint.

"Do you paint?" she asked, looking at him sideways.

"No," he answered. "I wish I could though."

Cole stopped in front of the last painting on the wall and tilted his head to one side. He seemed perplexed.

"What do you see?" Courtney asked, looping her arm around his elbow.

"This is the only one in the room without a plaque," he replied, turning to face the other side of the circular room. "And there are five paintings on this side, when there are only four on the other. The stairs are the center of the room. That makes the painting placement asymmetrical. It's odd."

"Huh," Courtney said, looking around the room. Though he was correct that there were only nine pictures, she wasn't sure why it would seem odd.

"Do you see the arch above us?" Cole asked, reaching his arm around her shoulders and pulling her close to his side, pointing upward with his other hand.

Courtney looked up to where he pointed. They stood under a long stone archway. She walked through this foyer at least four times a day, but she'd never taken notice of it before now.

"Sure," Courtney said, looking up at the gray stone suspended over them in a rainbow-like arc. "The student lounge is up there, in the balcony."

"The triangular one is the keystone," he explained, pointing to the stone right in the middle of the archway flanked by other rectangular stones.

"Where did you learn all this?" Courtney asked, looking at him.

"I'm just interested in architecture, I guess," Cole replied, looking down at the floor.

"No, it's great," Courtney said, quickly.

He raised his gaze from the floor to meet hers. His deep brown eyes seemed to see right into her. How was it that she felt like he saw past what her actions had been? She wasn't in any shape to start something. She needed at least another week. She wanted him to kiss her again. Her body yearned to press herself against him. Instead, she took a step backward. Why had she done that, she wondered?

"Ahem," came a loud voice from the back doorway.

Cole's eyes widened, as he looked over Courtney's shoulder.

Courtney turned to see Ms. Krick standing with her hands on her hips watching the two of them.

"Ms. Krick!" she exclaimed, taking another step away from Cole.

"We were just... I," Courtney stammered.

"I was just leaving," Cole said decisively, raising his right hand in the air as if he were swearing an oath. "Bye, Courtney."

Cole looked at Courtney, who gave him a curt nod. She hated to see him go, but it would be better if she handled Ms. Krick alone.

Cole made his way across the floor in a stilted run, his footsteps echoing into the expanse. He opened the heavy door to the outside, letting in a thin stream of the light from the sun that had risen since they'd arrived.

Courtney watched the door close behind him, then turned to face Ms. Krick.

"Who was that boy, and what was he doing here with you?" Ms. Krick asked, her stance rigid.

Courtney's skin prickled. There really wasn't much to like about her spindly teacher.

"He, uh... I invited him here to help," she said, her instincts kicking in. "I... I thought the foyer might have something to do with Isaac Young's fountain, the paintings, maybe. He's a friend who knows a lot about architecture and paintings and things like that. I thought if he saw them..." She couldn't tell from Ms. Krick's expressionless face if she was buying Courtney's story at all. The lie she'd tried on Cole hadn't worked, but all traces of Courtney's earlier tenderness had fled. Suddenly, she felt like her heart was made of steel. The words coming out of her mouth seemed real enough in the moment that they weren't lies. Not really, anyway, she told herself.

"You haven't seen the fountain, yet?" Ms. Krick asked, narrowing her eyes.

Courtney shook her head vigorously. She couldn't see why she'd ever share the fountain with Ms. Krick. It was bad enough Margaret had blabbed about it to their friends. She couldn't do anything about that now. No, if the fountain hadn't let Ms. Krick find it in all these years, Courtney wasn't going to give it away.

"No," Courtney said, "but I had this idea that maybe there was a story or clue here somehow. In the pictures." She waved her hand toward the ceiling. "I thought there might be something Isaac Young left for us to find." Courtney sounded convincing, even to herself.

"And?" Ms. Krick asked, moving toward Courtney. "What did your friend find?"

"Well," Courtney said, licking her dry lips, "we hadn't really been here that long, but he pointed out the keystone up there." She was reaching for what Cole had said about the triangle stone. Ms. Krick did not look impressed. She'd have to think of something better. "And the paintings are asymmetrical," she added.

"What?" Ms. Krick asked, turning to look at the paintings on the walls.

"The paintings," Courtney repeated.

Ms. Krick seemed interested in this news. This just might work.

"He thought it was odd that there were five on this side and only four on the other," Courtney said. That, at least was true. Stick to the truth, it was easier to remember and less likely to trip her up. "And, there's no plaque on this one." She gestured to the painting of the lady in white.

Ms. Krick made a beeline for the fifth painting on the north side of the room.

Courtney watched intently, flexing her fingers at her sides nervously. She'd managed to distract her, but now what? What was the truth anyhow? Why had she invited Cole here?

"I can't date him. Not now," Courtney said quietly, so it could only be heard by her. "He wanted to see the inside of the main building. I thought it might leave the door open between us." Was that the truth?

Ms. Krick wasn't listening, anyway. Her hands were outstretched, feeling methodically around the perimeter of the gilded picture frame.

"Give me a hand, here, Courtney," Ms. Krick called.

The back doors opened and a few students trickled by, en route to the cafeteria. It wasn't early morning anymore.

Courtney joined Ms. Krick, and together they gently lifted the heavy painting off its hooks on the wall. The frame itself probably weighed more than Ms. Krick.

"Carefully," Ms. Krick cautioned as they set it on the floor and leaned it up against the wall. The frame now sitting on the floor stood as high as Courtney's waist.

Ms. Krick ran her hands along the stone wall behind the painting, periodically pausing to knock with her knuckles.

Courtney's eyes drifted back over to the keystone arch and she tried to remember the moment she'd shared with Cole standing there, just being together, but the moment was gone. Now the only thing filling her mind was Ms. Krick.

Ms. Krick's methodical inspection of the painting and the area surrounding it seemed to take forever. There was now a steady stream of students passing through the foyer, almost as steady as the pounding feeling building in Courtney's temples. Students going by slowed to gawk at her with St. Augustus' longest serving teacher, staring at a wall. None of them dared to stop.

"There's nothing here, other than the two picture hooks,"

muttered Ms. Krick.

As the foyer filled with uniformed students, Courtney shifted from one foot to the other. Ms. Krick showed no signs of ceasing her inspection. Would Ms. Krick even notice if she left? She was going to be late for class. Ms. Krick needed to stop – it was just a wall.

"Ms. Krick," said Courtney. "My friend only said it was odd. There's probably nothing here to find."

Ms. Krick didn't seem to hear her. Instead, she turned her attention to the bulky frame sitting on the ground.

"Hold this, Courtney," Ms. Krick told her, leaning the portrait out from the wall.

Courtney obeyed, eyeing the piece of history she was now supporting. It was very heavy. She leaned the painting against her hip to keep it from falling. The back of the painting was covered in brown paper that made a crinkling sound when Ms. Krick poked at it. What was she looking for? The painting did seem a lot more promising to Courtney than the wall. Were the lies she'd just made up about there being something hidden in the foyer actually true?

"There!" Courtney exclaimed, pointing to a corner of the backing. "Every other corner's secured, but this one isn't." Courtney smiled triumphantly. She'd been looking for something asymmetrical. Cole had taught her something.

Ms. Krick looked up at Courtney as if she'd forgotten she was there then turned her attention back to the painting. Slowly, as if she were peeling the covering off something that was steaming hot, she pulled back the corner of the paper. The backing gave way easily, coming off in one piece.

Courtney and Ms. Krick gasped simultaneously.

Under the brown paper, there was a sketch in dark strokes on the reverse side of the canvas.

Courtney blanched at the pair of eyes looking out at them – so lifelike.

"Izzy," gasped Ms. Krick.

"Ms. Krick, are you okay?" Courtney asked, reaching to hold her up, which was awkward with the heavy frame still resting on her hip.

What little color Ms. Krick normally carried in her cheeks had gone.

"It's him," Ms. Krick said quietly. "The light patch above his eye, the missing feathers on his right wing. It's him and this has been here all along."

"What does it mean?" Courtney whispered, her eyes darting around the now-busy foyer.

"Leave the painting," said Ms. Krick. "Come with me."

"But I have classes," Courtney protested, as Ms. Krick walked toward the back doors and left the foyer.

Taking one more look at the painting, Courtney pushed it away from her and leaned it as smoothly as she could back against the wall before rushing off after Ms. Krick.

"Ms. Krick, wait up!" called Courtney. She caught her elderly teacher by the elbow. "What does Izzy have to do with all of this? I've seen him. He's found me a few times."

"I knew it," Ms. Krick replied, stopping to look at Courtney, her eyes shining. "You're the one. Your father made a wish, you will too. You'll help me find it."

Courtney took a step back. She didn't want to be anything for Ms. Krick.

"What did my father wish for?" Courtney asked.

But Ms. Krick only smiled. He'd probably wished for dozens of things, Courtney realized, she would too, once she rid herself of this first ill-advised wish. It was too broad, yet too specific. It was changing her.

"You're related to Isaac Young, right?" Courtney asked, boldly.

"Yes," Ms. Krick agreed. "Though he never knew he had a son, who was my grandfather. He had magic. They all had magic. Magic that belongs to my family." Her gnarly hands shook as she grabbed at Courtney's arm.

Courtney blinked at Ms. Krick. Was she being serious?

"Do you, uh..." Courtney asked, stumbling on the concept of what she was about to ask. "Do *you* have magic?"

"No," replied Ms. Krick, shaking her head sadly. "Not yet."

Courtney let the words sink in.

"You can have your wish," Ms. Krick said to her. "Just bring me the magic." With that, Ms. Krick released her grip on Courtney's arm and gave her a push.

Courtney stared at the old teacher for only a moment before she turned and ran back toward the Main Building.

CHAPTER THIRTY

Magic

Courtney headed straight back to her room just as the late bell rang for the morning start to classes. She was still wearing her running gear, but she couldn't go to class anyway. Not now.

Opening the door to the girls' dorm, she nearly knocked over Bessie, who was coming out.

"Courtney!" Bessie snapped. "Why aren't you in class?"

"Sorry, Bessie," Courtney called over her shoulder as she blew past the house mother. "I'm feeling ill, can you let the office know?" Courtney clutched her stomach dramatically before ducking into the restroom at the end of the hall. Once inside, she rushed inside a toilet stall and slammed the door behind her, turning the lock. Standing behind its door, her mind ran through a thousand scenarios all at once.

"Are you okay?" Bessie's worried voice called from the hallway.

"I'll be okay," Courtney called back. "Just something I ate, I think. I'll be fine."

"Well, alright then," Bessie called. "I'll come check on you later."

Courtney waited in the stall, sitting on the toilet lid until she was sure Bessie had gone. She peeked out of the restroom door before making her way to her room.

Ms. Krick's wild eyes flashed in her mind. She'd been after

magic all this time. Was there such a thing? The fountain was real, so there must be some. She shook her head, hardly believing that seemed logical to her. But Courtney had already found the magic, in the fountain. She didn't need Ms. Krick.

Once in her room, Courtney looked at herself in the mirror that hung on their closet door. She almost didn't recognize the eyes that stared back at her under her flame-red hair. They looked tired, yet a little crazed, just as her teacher's had been. Courtney's hands ran over her gaunt face. What was happening to her? Margaret had been trying to warn her about something. Was she destined to pine after her wish forever, the way that Ms. Krick was devoted to finding the fountain? She had to get a grip. She needed to think.

The only thing that made sense after she and Margaret had read the journals was that it seemed only students could find it. Did Ms. Krick know that? Maybe she didn't want to see. Courtney shook her head sadly at the thought of her teacher's fruitless quest.

What Courtney wanted right now was to be free of the wish, at least so she could start again, make a more controlled change. She didn't want to be this person she was becoming. Something had started with Cole. She wanted to see where it went. And she could, if she completed her list.

Newly focused, she took out her phone and Googled "How to improve swimming performance". There were lots of suggestions for steroids and even caffeine. Courtney balked at the idea of steroids. She was hoping more for suggestions on diet, or training or something. Caffeine could be interesting, though.

Her mind reeled with possibilities. She'd try them all. She also had to figure out where Valentine and Chase might be in their evenings. Their help would speed things along.

CHAPTER THIRTY-ONE

Stalk

Instead of attending class that day, Courtney stayed as close to Mr. Chase's classroom as she dared, with no sightings of Valentine. By the time the last bell rang, she realized she'd have to work a little harder to prove there was something there. Of course, they wouldn't meet during the day. What had Courtney been thinking?

If their love-rendezvous spot was somewhere off campus, she'd have no way to follow them without a car. But they'd seen Mr. Chase at the teachers' residence. There was a good chance he'd meet her there again. She'd have to wait until after lights-out. She kicked herself for wasting a whole day following him when she could have been working on the swim meet.

Courtney's eyelids felt heavy as she headed to the dorm after school. She blinked, but it only made it worse. A headache brewed behind her forehead. As much as she wanted to use every moment she had available, she had to admit she was running out of steam. She hadn't slept much lately. If she was going to the teachers' residence tonight, she'd have to find a way to catch up on her sleep another way.

Entering her room, she paused a moment. Napping seemed like such a waste, but she had to recharge.

Izzy's note had pointed her towards exposing Valentine, and she needed to do that as soon as possible.

She fluffed her pillow and put her head down. She'd only rest for a little while, there was so much to do.

Funny that, before this week, she'd never wondered if Valentine had a boyfriend. Given that the headmistress lived and worked for the school as much as she did, Mr. Chase was probably an excellent choice. He was a catch, actually. He was good looking, nice and the students thought the world of him. Still – the headmistress seemed such a private woman. Courtney felt sure the headmistress wouldn't want this getting out.

Courtney would protect the headmistress' secret, for a price.

Courtney woke with a start. She was surprised to be met by darkness. Disoriented, she looked around to find herself in her room. She grabbed for her phone and looked in disbelief at the time. Margaret's outline could be seen across the room, fast asleep under the covers in her bed. Courtney sat up abruptly, brushing aside the fuzzy blanket she'd been sleeping under. It was the extra blanket from the foot of Margaret's bed. Margaret must have covered Courtney up.

Sweat plastered Courtney's St. Augustus blouse to her back. She'd slept that whole time in her uniform. Grabbing her pillow, Courtney gave it a few hearty punches then stifled a yell by burying her face in its softness. If Mr. Chase had been at the teachers' residence tonight, she'd missed him. It was well after midnight.

Courtney blundered through classes the next day, hardly absorbing a word. If she didn't correct this soon, she was going to have a tough time passing midterms. School just didn't seem important when she had so much else to do. Other than class and swim practice, she managed to avoid the girls completely. She'd taken her lunch and dinner to go.

That night, Courtney took no chances. She wasn't going to close her eyes for a moment. After lights out, she'd wait half an hour to see if Bessie was going to do a bed check, but then she was going to the teachers' residence to spy on the middle-aged lovebirds.

"Are you not getting ready for bed?" Margaret asked.

Courtney had been lying on her bed in her sweats, poring over Isaac Young's journal while Margaret readied herself for bed. She'd been over the brief description of the fountain more than twenty times, seeing nothing new.

"Uh, right," said Courtney. She had no intention of telling Margaret about the headmistress' extra-curricular activities. The headmistress needed to trust Courtney wouldn't tell on her and Mr. Chase for her plan to work. Asking Margaret to keep a secret from the other girls was like asking her not to breathe. It was really for her own good. She tucked the journal under her pillow and made herself busy putting her hair up in a pony-tail. She could throw her sweatshirt back on after lights out. For now, she needed to appear normal.

An hour later, Courtney eased herself off her bed and listened for a moment to Margaret's regular, deep breaths. Margaret was asleep. Courtney grabbed her coat and a hat before opening the door to their room and slipping out into the darkened hall of the dorm.

Though she stepped lightly, her footsteps seemed to echo.

"You do this all the time in the morning," Courtney reminded herself under her breath. "Nobody's listening."

When she reached the door to the outside, she pressed one hand against the frame and eased the door open with the other. She flinched as the door groaned. Thinking quickly, she ducked through the open door and let it float shut behind her with a click.

The campus lawn stretched in front of her, ending at the shadows of the West Woods. Courtney took a good long look at the outline of the trees in the thin moonlight. With a shiver, she headed down the stairs and onto the grass, staying as close to the wall of the dorm as she could.

She went the long way around the dorm at a steady pace, away from the Main Building. Too much light spilled from its windows, illuminating the lawn and making her path risky. As she rounded the corner of the building, her heart sank. The teachers' residence looked impossibly far away from her vantage point.

"Come on, Courtney, just go," she coached herself, under her breath. She'd been pushing herself since she'd made the wish, and nothing bad had happened, yet. The fountain was helping her. She could feel it.

She crossed the lawn at a sprint toward the boys' dorm. It was a plain, square brick building that had only been built fifteen years earlier. She crouched under a window, behind a scrubby tree. Looking up at the darkened glass, she wondered whose room it was. She'd never set foot in the boys' dorm. She gave her head a shake. Now wasn't the time to wonder.

Courtney darted from tree to tree toward the teachers' residence, until she found herself under the willow where she'd last seen Izzy. She paused beneath the tree and looked up into its branches. The moon's thin sliver peeked out from behind silvery limbs. Listening for any sign of the owl, she scanned the treetop, but all was quiet. There was no sign of anyone at all on campus at this hour.

The teachers' residence was close now. Sprinting one last burst, she didn't stop until she'd planted herself under the side window to what she thought were the headmistress' rooms. Breathing heavily, she pressed herself against the red brick on the main floor of the house and took stock of her situation. The house's wraparound porch afforded her some cover on one side, but looking the other way, she was completely exposed. The nearest trees were at least ten feet from the wall. Courtney looked back across the expanse of lawn. The only thing that way was the Sports Complex. There shouldn't be anyone there at this hour. She felt bolder than she should. Anyone coming along would see her standing here.

Why wasn't she terrified?

Courtney pushed down her doubt. There might be nothing to see inside Headmistress Valentine's apartment anyway. She turned her attention to the window above her, which appeared dark. Slowly, Courtney raised her phone above her head and pointed it toward the inside of the house. She positioned it to where there seemed to be a gap in the curtains and pressed the shutter button. Light from the flash bounced off the window and shone in Courtney's face, blinding her temporarily.

"Ack!" Courtney yelped. She clamped both hands over her mouth, still holding the offending phone. She pressed herself hard against the wall, squeezing her eyes shut and tucking her head under her arm. How could she have been so stupid? She listened.

There were no sounds of footsteps approaching. No urgent yells.

Being out of bed would get her in trouble at school, but this? Taking pictures through peoples' windows might even be illegal, Courtney thought to herself as she waited. Her stomach was in knots. Was it illegal? If it wasn't, it should be. Courtney shuddered at the thought of someone taking a photo of her through her window without her knowing. This was definitely crossing a line.

She took a deep breath. The headmistress might not even be in there, she reasoned. No harm done. She rested her head against the cold wood strips lining the wall. She should think about getting back to the dorm and rethink this whole thing.

Glancing at her phone to check the time, she saw the photo she'd taken on the screen. Courtney gasped. It was a little bright with the flash, but Headmistress Valentine was indeed at home. The window she now stood under led to the headmistress' kitchen. The picture had captured Headmistress Valentine, sitting in the dark with lit candles arranged neatly in the center of the round table. A glass of red wine sat in front of her at the table.

Courtney stared at the photo she'd taken. In it, the headmistress had no idea that someone lurked at her window. Courtney felt a pang shoot through her chest. There was nothing to see here. Headmistress Valentine was just having a glass of wine by herself at the end of her day.

What had she expected to see? She needed to go. She looked down one more time at the snapshot of the headmistress, her finger hovered over the trash can button on the screen. There was no reason to keep the evidence she'd been here.

Just as she was about to delete the picture, she hesitated. What was that? She tapped the screen to zoom in. A slow smile spread across Courtney's face. Across the table from the headmistress, was a second glass of wine. The headmistress was not alone. Courtney's heart pounded. This is what she'd come here to see.

At that moment, the faint sound of chatter could be heard from the direction of the window. Straining to hear, Courtney thought she heard the baritone voice of a man. She tingled with nerves from head to toe. Was it Mr. Chase, and was it enough to prove he was here, even with the candles and the wine?

Her hand shaking, Courtney pulled up the camera on her phone and tapped off the flash. She'd been lucky the headmistress hadn't seen the flash the first time, but she wasn't about to push it. Without pausing to think, she raised the phone for a second time above her head and held the shutter button down to take a burst of photos. Getting ready to run to the nearest tree's cover, she counted to three in her head. She hoped whatever she'd gotten would be enough.

She reached the tree easily and ducked around to the other side. She peered back at the teachers' residence. All was quiet. She should check if she'd gotten anything. She could always run back over there and try again if she hadn't. They seemed oblivious to what was happening outside.

Silently pulling up the photos she'd taken, she opened the first picture - It was clearly Mr. Chase, smiling and looking confident in the scene she'd captured. The picture was dim without the flash, but still clear enough. He stood behind the headmistress where she sat, his hands on her shoulders. The headmistress looked younger than Courtney had thought of her before. Pretty, even. Courtney held her breath. Was it possible she'd caught them in an intimate moment?

It wasn't like she was going to show the pictures to anyone but the two of them, anyway, Courtney told herself. She shouldn't need to, if the headmistress helped. Anyway, she hadn't caught anything intimate. Not really. It looked like Mr. Chase was rubbing the headmistress' shoulders. Courtney squinted at the picture. He could just be putting his hands there. It wasn't a smoking gun and could easily be explained away.

Quickly, she flipped through the remaining photos she'd captured in the burst sequence. Then Courtney saw them. Mr. Chase had his arm around Headmistress Valentine. The headmistress smiled widely, her eyes turning up at the corners. She and Mr. Chase appeared to be laughing together, looking into each other's eyes. Courtney felt a pang of regret for intruding on their night together. They looked genuinely happy. She hesitated a moment.

In the next few photos, Mr. Chase leaned in close to the sitting headmistress on the screen, smelling her hair, kissing her neck, and then the shot Courtney could have only hoped for of the two of them kissing. Perfect.

She looked around at the deserted campus, but there was nobody around to share her elation. She was alone. She had to get back to the dorm. Courtney looked from where she stood to the darkened dorm. Not even the porch light was on to light her way at this hour. The pale moonlight would have to be enough. This had been easier than she'd ever imagined. Clutching her phone in her fist, she ran off into the night, pumping her arms to get over the lawn as quickly as she could. The wind on her face felt exhilarating.

CHAPTER THIRTY-TWO

Into Thin Air

"Where were you last night, Courtney?" Margaret demanded.

"Mmm?" Courtney struggled to pull herself out of a sound sleep. When she opened her eyes, Margaret's face was right above her. She didn't look happy.

"You're out of control," Margaret said, her hands on her hips. "I can't cover for you every night, and for your absence in class, especially if I don't know what I'm covering for. Bessie's starting to get suspicious."

Courtney had a suspicion of her own, that Margaret was more upset about being left out of Courtney's plans than about having to lie to their pussy-cat of a house mother.

"I was sick," Courtney complained, trying to focus on Margaret. "Bessie let me miss school." Spotting her phone on the bedside table, she snatched it up and held it close. She rolled over toward the wall and pulled the covers over her head with her free hand.

"Courtney, you're not sick, you're skipping class, and I'm not going to let you do it again today," Margaret insisted, ripping the covers off her roommate in one motion.

Courtney groaned. She wasn't in the mood for a lecture. She'd gotten what she needed to force Headmistress Valentine in her corner. Now she just needed to figure out how best to approach her.

"You can't go on like this," Margaret continued, pulling open the drapes to let light flood into the room. "Missing class, staying out late... it has to stop."

"Hey!" Courtney protested, shielding her eyes from the sun by covering her face with her pillow.

"Don't bother arguing with me," Margaret said. "I know you think you don't need help. But you're obsessed." She gave Courtney's legs a shove and plunked herself down on the bed in the space she'd created. "I have a plan," Margaret announced.

Courtney looked out from behind the pillow with one eye. Margaret had Isaac Young's journal and his mother's grimoire stacked neatly in her lap. Maybe she'd found a way to help Courtney with her wish. Courtney sat up, propping her pillow behind her head.

"Fine," Courtney said, crossing her arms. "I'm listening."

"While you were napping the other night," Margaret told her, fumbling with the books on her lap. "Violet and I went through these, cover to cover."

Courtney narrowed her eyes at the thought of the girls poring over her books, but if they'd found something, she should try to let her feelings go.

"We've concluded that Isaac Young wanted the fountain to do good," she said. "But your wish is simply too big. You'll have to undo it."

"So, I'll undo it, then," Courtney said, though she had no intention of doing that. She was going to accomplish everything on her list. And then? Well, then at least she'd have options.

"That's the tricky part," Margaret explained, opening Isaac Young's journal to a page in the middle, marked with an orange post-it note. "The fountain awaits each student to grant one wish," Margaret read. "It seems clear everyone only gets one wish."

"That seems ridiculous," said Courtney, dismissing Margaret with a confidence she didn't feel. "How could it know?" But her comment seemed silly even to her. The fountain granted wishes. Of course, it would know who was making them. She'd read the journal herself, but had missed the implication. Maybe just like Ms. Krick hadn't realized the fountain was only for students.

"Courtney!" Margaret said. "Do you want to end up all crazy like Ms. Krick, never leaving campus with a room full of cats?"

Courtney shook her head. Margaret had a point. She should maybe listen.

"Good, then," Margaret said, with an approving nod. "Once we undo your wish, everyone but Violet still has a wish left. Maybe there's a different wish we could make for you that won't make you, well..." she trailed off, patting Courtney's leg in a motherly way through the covers.

"I thought you said I couldn't undo my wish," Courtney said, moving her leg out from under Margaret's annoying pat.

"Ah," Margaret said, her eyes lighting up. "That's where the grimoire comes in." She closed the journal, and then opened the other worn book in her lap. "We're going to call on Alexandrina Young for help!" she said, waving the open book in front of Courtney. "We're going to have a séance."

"What?" Courtney exclaimed, pulling her knees up to her chest. "Are you nuts? Listen to yourself."

"Courtney, there's definitely magic," Margaret continued. "How else do you explain what's happening? Everything we need to know about Alexandrina is here in this book. Even the fact she has a grimoire. She was a witch, and we think she'll help. We googled it, how to summon her. It seems easy enough. She'll for sure help us. It's her son's fountain that got you in this mess."

A witch. Alexandrina Young?

"No," Courtney said, throwing back what was remaining of her covers and standing up. "We are definitely not disturbing the dead. Especially dead people who can do magic." She had no intention of meeting any of Ms. Krick's relatives - dead or alive - especially not those who dabbled in witchcraft. "I'm fine, really. You don't need to worry about me. I have a plan, and everything I wished for will happen, and then I'll be fine again, and I don't want your help, I can do this by myself." She grabbed a uniform out of the closet, tucking it under her arm and started for the door, then turned abruptly and strode back to Margaret. Snatching the books out of her surprised roommate's hands, she left the room and headed toward the restroom, slamming the door behind her. She'd change there. Suddenly she felt suffocated being in Margaret's presence.

She changed quickly, heading for the cafeteria. She should probably go to class today. As she entered the foyer of the Main Building, her phone rang. Looking at the number, she froze. It was the same number that had called before. It was Cole.

Pausing in the hallway outside the cafeteria, she answered the call.

"Hello?" she said.

"Oh, hi Courtney," said Cole's voice. "I wasn't sure you'd pick up, but I thought I'd try you before class started."

"Oh?" Courtney asked. She cringed. She must have completely confused Cole the other morning. She'd confused herself, too. She wandered back outside and found herself standing at the top of the stone steps of the Main Building, with a clear view of the West Woods. The air had a crisp nip to it.

"Well, you said your situation was complicated," he barreled on. "But I thought maybe we could still be friends? I was serious about wanting to run more. I thought maybe..."

"Cole," Courtney interjected, looking off to the trees, "I don't really think..." she let herself trail off. Now, why had she said that? Her insides felt crushed. It was as if she was hearing someone else say the words. Someone who was making a huge mistake.

"Oh, I see," Cole answered, his voice flat.

"Cole..." Courtney said, choking on his name.

She tried to speak again, but nothing came out.

The fountain wasn't going to let her say what she wanted, what she felt. She wanted to spend time with Cole. The kissed they'd shared still made her tingle when she thought back. But somehow, she couldn't answer him.

"No, it's okay," Cole answered quickly. "You were pretty clear the other day. I'd just hoped... well, see you around, I guess."

"Yes," Courtney managed to say, her heart shredding into tiny pieces. "Thanks."

"Bye," said Cole, before he hung up.

Courtney stood alone on the steps, staring at the phone in her hand. A single tear made its way slowly down her cheek. Her vision blurred as she stumbled down the stairs and onto the grass. Before she realized it, she found herself in front of the West Woods. Wiping her eyes with the back of her hand, Courtney put one foot in front of the other, and stepped inside the line of trees. Seeing a relatively clear path open up in front of her between the trees, she broke into a run, heading straight for the fountain as she cried.

Several hours later, after being in the woods for the whole morning and missing a half day of classes, Courtney entered the cafeteria, zeroing in on her usual table. Her eyes were still puffy with tears that she hoped wouldn't attract any comment, but she was hungry. She'd skipped breakfast, and it was time for lunch.

Margaret was there, with Violet and Rhoda. Courtney sat down and looked around at the girls without a word.

"Courtney!" Margaret exclaimed, looking alarmed. "Are you okay?"

"I'm in," Courtney answered, putting both of her palms flat on the table in front of her.

"What?" Margaret asked, blinking at Courtney.

"I think..." Courtney started, choking on her own words. "I think I need help. The fountain – it wasn't even there."

"I've been trying to tell you," Margaret said, nodding her head, sadly. "We think once you make your wish, you can't see it anymore."

"I can't see it, either," confirmed Violet.

Courtney looked around the table. The girls had been back to the fountain, and it was gone for Violet, too. This was serious. They were serious.

"For real?" Rhoda asked. "I know you guys have been talking about magic and everything, but that can't be right."

"I can still see it," Margaret told the group. "But only if I go without Violet. I haven't used the fountain to make a wish, and I won't. Haven't you guys been listening? I've been trying to tell you."

"I want to summon Alexandrina Young," Courtney interrupted, before she lost her nerve. "I want her to end my wish. I can get those things on my own. I don't need the fountain's help."

"Okay," said Margaret, clasping her hands together solemnly and looking around the table at Courtney, Violet and Rhoda. "Let's do this."

"Thank you," Courtney said, looking at her friends around the table. The weight on her shoulders seemed to lift. Soon, she would be free.

CHAPTER THIRTY-THREE

Alexandrina Young

Later that night, Courtney and Margaret tiptoed out of the dorm and onto the lawn. It was just past midnight as they cowered under the eaves next to the stone wall. They huddled close to a large bush planted near the wall. The bush provided cover, but they hardly needed it. The campus and adjacent road were a ghost town at this hour. Courtney had her backpack slung over her shoulder, filled with the things they'd need.

"This feels wrong," Margaret whispered, expressing her second thoughts. "I hope Bessie is a heavy sleeper."

"She is, don't worry," Courtney answered her in a low voice. "How many times have I gone out running in the mornings? And then I've been out after lights out this week a bunch of times. Never once has she noticed." Courtney didn't feel worried at all. In fact, she felt like they could come and go as they pleased from the dorm. It was a bit of a frightening realization.

"I guess," said Margaret, shivering a little, though it wasn't that cold. "So, are you going to tell me what changed your mind? You were dead set against it when I suggested it this morning."

"Here come the others," Courtney said, nodding her head toward the dorm, where the door had just opened.

Violet, Hailey and Lynette crept silently down the steps from the dorm and came to join them. Violet carried a folded blanket in her arms. Lynette had brought her pillow.

"Margaret," Courtney said, turning to her as the other girls came down the dorm room steps. "What are Lynette and Hailey doing here?" They hadn't been at the cafeteria when Courtney had agreed to come. "And where's Rhoda?"

"Google said the séance works better in multiples of three's," Margaret replied, holding up three fingers in front of Courtney's face. "Besides, Hailey and Lynette are good, they won't squeal."

Courtney shifted uncomfortably on her feet. She didn't like surprises. Frowning, she checked the time on her phone. It was 12:05 a.m. The five girls huddled in a tight knot near the dorm room wall. If Rhoda didn't show up, then they didn't need Hailey and Lynette. Courtney could do the math.

"So, we're here," said Lynette, yawning as she approached. "And I'd like to get back to bed as soon as possible. What do we have to do?"

"Let's wait two more minutes for Rhoda," said Courtney, not answering Lynette's question. Margaret had said Rhoda was bringing the bloodworms. They were an ingredient in the grimoire recipe. Apparently, Rhoda's pet fish, which she claimed was a shark, ate them. Would they be able to call Alexandrina without bloodworms if Rhoda didn't show?

The dorm door opened again, much more quickly this time. Rhoda let the door slam behind her and looked around frantically.

Courtney stared at Rhoda, who scrambled loudly down the dorm's stairs. Was she trying to wake Bessie? Margaret stuck an arm out from behind their bush to reveal their thin hiding spot.

"Did you bring them?" Courtney asked, as Rhoda rushed over.

Rhoda nodded, handing Courtney a small, cold package. Courtney tucked it neatly into her backpack with everything else and slung it over her shoulder. Maybe Margaret was onto something, inviting Lynette and Hailey. If any of the girls got spooked, they could do the séance with only three and still have enough.

"Let's go," Courtney said and started walking toward the West Woods.

"Where?" Violet asked, as the group fell in line behind Courtney. "Where are we going? This isn't the right direction for the fountain."

"South of the woods," Courtney answered.

"The West Woods?" Hailey squealed. "But we're walking across the lawn in plain view. We're going to be seen."

Courtney turned sideways and looked at Margaret, who had invited Hailey. Had she not explained what was going to happen?

"We think Isaac Young's childhood home is marked on the map," Margaret explained, as the group made its way toward the edge of the woods. "The séance will be stronger where Alexandrina lived."

"Nobody's awake, Hailey," Courtney said. "So, if we're quiet, it can stay that way. Shh." She lifted a finger to her lips.

Courtney walked a little faster to lead the group. They climbed the hill to the edge of the woods, and then walked single-file along the tree line, heading south, away from the road. Once they were behind the West Building, Courtney reached out to touch the evergreen branches, dragging her hand along the trees as she walked. It hadn't snowed all week and there was none accumulated here on the grass. They couldn't be seen now from the Main Building.

Just a few short weeks ago, she hadn't believed in magic. Now she was planning to use it to summon the dead. Courtney's stomach churned. So much had changed. If only it would all go back to the way it had been before. Maybe after tonight.

"Do you think the house will still be there?" Margaret asked, trailing just behind Courtney.

"Well, if it isn't," said Courtney, looking over her shoulder, "it'll have to be good enough to get close to where it used to be."

"How far is this place?" Lynette called from the back of the line.

"We figure it's about ten minutes to get to the south end of the trees," Margaret called back to her. "We should be almost there."

There was no artificial light reaching them, now. The sky was ablaze with stars, which Courtney looked up at as she walked. She tried to imagine what the séance might be like. They'd watched a few online that afternoon, but they all seemed over the top. Is that really what this would be?

A stray breeze rippled the trees beside her and sent a draft through Courtney's coat. A shiver ran through her.

"How long are we going to be gone, Margaret?" Rhoda could be heard, asking behind. "You said we wouldn't be out here long. I want to help, but I really think we should be getting back to the dorm as soon as possible. It's very late."

"There's the end of the trees," Courtney announced before Margaret could answer Rhoda, pointing ahead and breaking into a quick jog. She hadn't bothered lowering her voice. They were a long way from the campus buildings now.

"Wow," said Margaret, keeping up beside her as they reached the end of the trees. "I had no idea the school grounds reached this far." The girls looked around at the vast field beyond the woods. There was no house in sight.

"We think the Young's house was here somewhere. I'd guess 200 yards from the edge of the trees," Courtney said, looking around at the field with dismay.

The other girls straggled in behind Courtney and Margaret to reach the corner of the woods.

"Spread out," Courtney directed. "Find anything that points to where the house was." She jogged what she estimated was about 200 yards. "Start looking here!" she called, snapping on the flashlight of her phone and waving the rest of the girls over.

Suddenly, she was happy there were six of them to bolster the search. "Look for anything that looks like someone lived there, once." She didn't wait for a reaction. Walking slowly away from the other girls, Courtney used the flashlight on her phone to search the area.

Six spotlights danced in the night like fireflies, scouring the ground for something from the past.

Courtney kicked the dirt beneath her feet as she walked. If there had been a house here, it would have been full of things. There must be something left. But her foot met nothing but long grass. She looked up to see Rhoda in the distance. She'd wandered too far away along the trees.

"Rhoda, it won't be over there!" Courtney called, beckoning Rhoda back to the group. "Come back!"

"Think, Courtney, think," she muttered to herself, well aware that they didn't have all night.

"Maybe it's all gone," Margaret said, coming up beside Courtney, her shoulders sagging. "We could just set up here, anyway. We must be close. It'll probably work."

Courtney was about to acquiesce when Rhoda called from her spot down the line, "I found something! Over here!"

The girls ran to join her, Courtney walking at a slowed pace, studying the tree line. Rhoda had gone too far. There shouldn't be anything over there.

"It looks like stones for a path," Rhoda showed the girls as Courtney joined them. She shone her flashlight on each flat gray stone as she stepped from one to the next. They were set deep within the knee-high grass. The girls followed Rhoda in a pack as the stones led diagonally into the trees, back the way they'd come.

Courtney and Margaret exchanged glances as they breached the tree line and the group stood inside the cover of the woods. A strange silence seemed to blanket them as they followed the stones between a thick spot of bushes.

"The trees here are shorter than the rest," Margaret whispered to Courtney, taking her arm by the crook of her elbow. "Maybe the woods grew up around the house after the Youngs left."

"Eureka!" exclaimed Rhoda, who'd been leading the group, as she kicked the bushes aside to reveal a low stone wall that might easily have once been a corner of a house.

"Can we just get started then?" Hailey asked. "We've already been gone a long time."

"I hadn't realized how long it would take us to get here," said Margaret, looking around the site. "It won't really be midnight anymore, it's nearly one."

"Let's get started, then," Violet said eagerly, reaching for Courtney's backpack.

Courtney held up her hand and pulled the pack away from Violet. She walked over to a clump of trees and stepped beyond them. There, in the grass, were three low, flat stones.

Margaret had followed her and shone her light on the stones.

"James Young, Alexandrina Young, Isaac Young," Margaret read, her voice wavering.

Courtney's eyes grew wide as she read the inscription under Isaac Young's name on his tombstone.

Izzy, to his friends.

"Are they *buried* here?" Margaret whispered.

It was clear that they were. There was no need for Courtney to answer the question.

"Is this where we should..." Courtney stammered.

Margaret shook her head vehemently, her eyes wide as she looked at Courtney.

"Seems disrespectful somehow," Margaret whispered.

"Come on!" called Violet from where they'd left the other girls near the wall. "We've found more stones. The house was here."

CHAPTER THIRTY-FOUR

Spirits

The girls had made a rough circle inside the outline of the small house. It was tough to make it perfectly round, as the ground was littered with piles of stones and small trees that had grown up through what was once a shallow foundation. Lynette and Hailey huddled together, sitting on Lynette's pillow, while Violet and Margaret sat on the blanket Violet had brought. Courtney and Rhoda each kneeled on the hard ground, having cleared the sharp rocks and twigs in their way. Each of the girls had their phones propped in front of them with the light on, casting an eerie glow illuminating their faces.

Courtney unloaded the contents of her backpack in front of her without saying a word. She took out six stubby white candles and handed five of them to Margaret, who kept one and passed the rest around the circle. They did the same with the glass IKEA candle holders Courtney produced. She'd swiped them from the props room over the theatre.

"We're going to call the spirit of Isaac Young's mother," Margaret said in a low voice, "Alexandrina Young."

Something was bothering Courtney. "Couldn't we call Isaac Young instead?" she asked.

Margaret was the one who'd done all the research and she was relying on her roommate knowing how this all worked.

"It's his fountain."

"We don't have anything of his," Margaret replied, holding up Alexandrina's grimoire. "We need something that was theirs. We didn't bring anything of Isaac's."

Courtney jerked her head toward the graves, locking gazes with Margaret.

"No," Margaret said firmly.

"So, we're going to see her ghost?" Hailey asked, giggling nervously.

"I don't know if we'll actually see her," Margaret told the group, setting her candle into its holder. "We'll summon her spirit, then ask her to end Courtney's wish."

"Is anyone else scared?" Violet whispered, looking around the circle.

"I've played Ouija," said Lynette. "Will this be like that?"

"I think so," Margaret confirmed. "We'll call her and ask her to release Courtney from her wish. Then we'll let her go."

Courtney found she didn't feel scared at all, just more regretful than anything. Throughout these past days, her connection with the fountain and her wish had given her purpose, though it had also cost her a chance with Cole. Courtney pushed her feelings down. Ending her tie to the magic was the right thing to do, and it would be over soon enough.

"There's nothing to be afraid of. Alexandrina should be a friendly spirit," Margaret said, addressing them all. "Her grimoire is full of things about nature. We're calling her spirit, not her ghost."

Courtney had no idea if there was a distinction between a ghost and a spirit.

"My mom claims she haunts the West Woods," added Lynette.

"What?" Violet said, "No, it's Isaac that haunts the woods."

"Shh..." hissed Margaret, silencing the two of them.

Courtney pulled out Rhoda's bloodworms and peeled back the blister pack, sprinkling their tiny frozen bodies on the ground in the middle of the circle.

"Violet, did you bring the food offering?" Courtney asked. Margaret had been very specific about the things they each should bring.

Violet nodded her head and opened the woven cotton cloth bag she had in front of her. Reaching inside, she pulled her hand out and tossed first one poppy seed bagel, then another on top of the bloodworms. The third bagel she tossed, which looked like it had raisins in it, rolled all the way over to Hailey, who sat on the opposite side of the circle.

Hailey reached out to stop the wheel of dough, tossing it into the middle of the circle with the rest.

Courtney stared in disbelief. "Bagels?" she asked Violet.

"Margaret said to bring bread!" Violet exclaimed. "It's all there was tonight at the cafeteria that resembled bread."

"It's fine," said Margaret, nodding. "Girls, turn off your phones. The only light should be from the candles."

The forest around them went dark as, one by one, the girls switched off their lights.

Courtney fished around for the lighter in her backpack as her eyes adjusted to the dark. She'd taken the lighter from Bessie's room earlier that evening.

The other girls had set up their candles like Margaret's, in the holders on the ground in front of them. The circle flanked the worms and the bagels in the center.

"So, after you've lit your candle," Margaret told them, handing them each a handwritten card, "we'll hold hands to close the circle and say these words together."

Courtney took her card from Margaret and read it over silently in the flickering light that spread as each girl lit her candle.

Margaret crawled on her hands and knees and placed the

grimoire on the ground in the center of the circle.

"The grimoire talks about summoning friendly spirits," Margaret explained. "So, I don't think she'll mind being called."

"Wait," Rhoda said. "It's the blood in the bloodworms that makes the séance stronger?"

Courtney nodded.

"My candle isn't lit," said Rhoda, holding out her hand for the lighter. Hers was the last dark candle. She nestled it into the uneven ground by grinding the bottom of the holder into the grass growing up between stones.

Courtney handed Rhoda the lighter without a word.

Rhoda flicked the lighter on. After she'd lit her candle, she moved the lighter over and held it an inch or so above the small mound of worms.

"What are you doing?" Courtney asked, frowning. Burning the bloodworms on wasn't part of the plan.

"Well, they were frozen," answered Rhoda, crouching over the worms. "It might help if their blood was thawed." She looked around the circle sheepishly. "If I'd known what we were going to do with them, I could have taken them out of the freezer sooner," she added.

"I don't think it matters," Margaret told her, gently. "Let's just get started."

Rhoda shrugged and sat back, placing the lighter on the ground.

Margaret silently placed her handwritten card on the ground in front of her and the others did the same. She then spread her arms and reached for the hands of Violet and Courtney, who sat beside her.

Courtney clasped her friends' hands and immediately felt at peace. The circle was closed.

CHAPTER THIRTY-FIVE

Séance

Courtney looked around at all of their faces. They were willing to do this thing for her, she thought, amazed. The trace of fear she'd expected earlier hadn't come. It felt as if she'd done it a hundred times before.

"Okay," said Margaret in an even tone. "So, we repeat the words until we feel Alexandrina's presence."

"How will we know?" Violet asked, snapping her gum loudly.

"If it works," Margaret said seriously, "we'll know."

Courtney hoped that was true. She knew Margaret probably had no idea. She admired her for leading the séance as if she did.

"Alexandrina Young," Margaret began the words she'd written out six times, as the other girls followed suit.

"Come be with us," they continued as a group.

"Bah!" Hailey blurted out, laughing. She released Rhoda and Courtney's hands to cover her mouth.

"Hailey!" Margaret exclaimed. "The circle has to stay closed!"

"Sorry, sorry," said Hailey, still giggling. "It's just that we sound absolutely ridiculous. It's not like it's going to work anyway."

She shared a conspiratorial smirk with Lynette.

Courtney glared at the pair. They clearly weren't taking this seriously. She'd been right the first time, Margaret had made a mistake inviting them. This would work. Courtney could feel it.

"It'll work," said Courtney, firmly. "Let's start again."

"Let's get this over with and get out of here," Lynette said, as she grabbed Hailey's hand.

Courtney looked around the circle at her friends. They looked as ready as they'd ever be, and it was getting late.

"Alexandrina Young," Courtney began again, before the others joined in.

"Come be with us," the girls added, in unison.

Courtney felt the nape of her neck prickle. How would they know if Alexandrina was there? Courtney wasn't sure herself if she believed this would work, even if she'd said it would. How many times had Margaret said they'd have to say this chant before they'd know if it had worked?

By the fifth time they'd repeated the chant, several of the girls squirmed in their spots, watching Margaret and Courtney for any sign that they could stop.

About the tenth time the group repeated the phrase, Courtney looked up into the nearby trees. She could feel something happening. Her voice grew louder as she started the next round of the chant. Branches above them had begun to sway, creating a swooshing sound that competed with the volume of their chanting.

Courtney stopped, as did the others.

"I think she's here," Courtney said, her voice barely a whisper.

The candle flames flickered higher than they should have been, swaying back and forth.

"Alexandrina," Margaret called softly up toward the trees. "We have called you here tonight to ask for your help for the students of St. Augustus. We have called you for guidance."

A great whirlwind suddenly came down at them, snuffing out all but one of their candles. The girls let out a collective cry, dropping each other's hands and hopping to their feet.

Courtney felt a crushing feeling on her chest as she looked up into the tree tops. Alexandrina was here. She tried to cry out, but her voice was strangled out by the swirling wind.

"Who's there?" called a man's voice from beyond the edge of the woods, his outline visible between the trees.

Courtney looked around at the circle, clutching her chest. The pressure was insane.

Margaret hurried around the circle, gathering the grimoire and the unlit candles then stuffing them into Courtney's backpack.

The other girls had already grabbed the blanket and pillow and ran deeper into the woods.

"Blow out that candle!" Margaret hissed at Courtney, turning and rushing off after the other girls, who could be heard crashing their way through the trees.

Courtney looked back at the shadow. She gasped for air. The man held something over his head that looked like a shovel. He approached her slowly. Courtney gasped. It was Giles. She had to get out of there.

With all her strength, she turned and followed the girls into the woods, leaving the last lit candle behind her on the ground.

As she ran away from the scene, a powerful gust of wind knocked her off her ˙ feet. She turned back toward their abandoned circle to see the lit candle tip over into a pile of leaves and a wall of fire blast up between her and Giles, taller than the Young's house that had once stood in that spot.

The last thing Courtney saw was a wide spread of wings soaring over the scene. She then turned and ran toward the campus as fast as she could.

Courtney didn't stop until she reached the stairs to the dorm. She'd sprinted across the lawn without a second thought of getting caught. The other girls were huddled by the bush.

"Courtney!" Margaret called. "We thought you'd been caught for sure. Was that Giles?"

"Yes," Courtney said, nodding. "But what are you doing out here?" Courtney dragged Margaret by the arm toward the stairs. "Get inside!"

"We weren't about to leave you out here," said Violet, pouting.

"Fine, well I'm here now," Courtney said, pushing the girls toward the steps. "Go, go, go!"

As she herded them up the stairs and into the dorm, Courtney looked out over the woods. Yellow flames licked the tops of the trees on the horizon. Billows of smoke belched up from the south end of the woods.

"The West Woods are on fire," Courtney said, stating the obvious. "Everyone get your pajamas on and blend in. The whole dorm will be up soon."

CHAPTER THIRTY-SIX

Woods on Fire

"**Margaret, we need** to look like we've been sleeping, and hide that stuff," said Courtney, pointing to the backpack.

"But Courtney, the whole woods will burn," wailed Margaret, going to the window and pulling back the drapes. The air, even near the dorm, carried a faint haze in the dark from the smoke. Flames in the distance flashed a warm glow on the horizon in the night sky. "The trees are made of wood. That whole side of campus is a fire trap."

"Giles would have called the fire department already," Courtney said. "There's nothing more we can do."

Courtney's alarm clock on her night table glowed 2:30 a.m. They'd been gone much longer than she'd thought. Alexandrina had been there, she'd known it. If she'd only had another few moments she might've gotten some useful help. But there was that crushing feeling. What had it been, she wondered.

Margaret blew her nose loudly into a Kleenex. She was openly weeping now. Courtney crossed to Margaret and pulled the neatly folded pajamas out from under her roommate's pillow, shoving them at her.

"Get your pajamas on. Bessie will for sure do a bed check once she's up." Courtney said. "We don't have much time." She shook her head. The other girls better be keeping it together better than Margaret, or they'd be sunk. At least all the other girls' rooms were on the other side of the hall. Their windows wouldn't have the view of the fire Margaret seemed to be drawn to. Courtney pulled her own pajama top over her head and wiggled into the bottoms as quickly as she could. Pulling back her covers, she looked over at Margaret who stood, transfixed, by the window.

"Oh, for Izzy's sake," Courtney mumbled, moving to the window and tugging at Margaret's hoodie in an attempt to get it off over her head.

"Courtney!" Margaret exclaimed, swatting Courtney's hand away.

"Get changed yourself, then," Courtney said. "Bessie will be here any minute."

Courtney pulled back her covers and hopped into bed, though not before taking one more look out the window. The fire still seemed close to the horizon. As far as Courtney could tell, it hadn't made its way any closer to campus.

She looked over at Margaret who, to her credit, had managed to get her pajamas on. She still stood by the window with a mesmerized expression.

"Margaret!" Courtney whispered loudly. "Get into your bed! We're supposed to have been asleep!"

Margaret briefly looked over at Courtney, her trance broken. She shuffled over to her bed and got in slowly.

"Doesn't it bother you that Giles is out there?" Margaret asked. "And where are the fire trucks, if he's already called them. How can you just lay there? I think I'm going to be sick. We should call someone. He might be hurt."

Courtney looked up at their ceiling. Margaret had left the drapes open. Flickering light played in front of her eyes, but that had to be an illusion. The fire was too far from the dorm to register here. She closed her eyes to shut it out, fighting the urge to panic.

"And how can you sleep? What if the flames take the whole woods? It'll light the West Building, too." Margaret said, sobbing. "What if the whole school burns?"

"It doesn't seem to be spreading," Courtney assured her hysterical roommate. "The trucks must be on their way." But where were the trucks? They really should be there by now. "Margaret," Courtney said, trying a different approach. "Stop crying or your eyes will be red and you'll have to explain."

This was not the time to worry about things that hadn't happened yet. The only thing they could do was wait. A surprising calmness was now directing Courtney's actions.

She needed to think and be smart. The candle she'd left, and the candle holder could tie them to the spot if the ones they'd gathered up were found in their room in the backpack. Courtney would have to dispose of them off- campus in the morning.

She methodically worked through in her mind all the moving pieces they'd put in motion. Did wax hold fingerprints? Courtney felt a cold sweat building. Surely the remaining candle would have melted to a puddle in the wall of flames that had engulfed the spot?

Courtney hoped Giles had been far enough away so that he wouldn't be able to identify them. Her bushy red hair was hard to miss, but she'd been wearing a hat. That would have helped to disguise her. She hadn't seen his face either, after all, merely recognized his silhouette. Yet she'd still known it was him.

Margaret's breathy sobs coming from the other side of the room interrupted Courtney's train of thought.

And then came the sirens. Distant at first and Courtney thought she might have imagined them - but then relief washed over her as the sound drew closer. The raging fire would be much safer in the hands of professionals.

The temptation was too great. Courtney got out of bed and

peered out the window, careful to stay in the shadows. Margaret joined her silently. Three fire trucks and several police cars lined up along the sidewalk at the edge of campus. One truck had jumped the curb and driven across the lawn toward the fire then a second truck had backed up and made a run for the curb, following the first one in. Soon, all the emergency vehicles had followed suit. They were headed for the southern edge of campus.

Courtney and Margaret exchanged glances. The noise of the sirens driving across the lawn in front of their window was deafening. Courtney counted five trucks. She hadn't known the town of Evergreen had so many fire trucks. Some might even be from nearby towns.

This was big. It wouldn't be dismissed. Courtney's mind kicked into overdrive as she tried to map out their story. Denial was the best course. They'd all been sleeping. She had to get rid of the candles in the backpack, along with the grimoire. Nothing else pointed to them. They'd all been in their rooms long before anyone was awake to notice.

Out of the corner of her eye, Courtney caught a glimpse of movement across the St. Augustus lawn outside their window. An unmistakable figure hurried along, hunched over, in the direction of the fire.

Courtney inhaled a sharp breath and withdrew behind the curtains. She'd know Ms. Krick's outline anywhere.

Courtney edged her way back to her bed, ignoring Margaret's persistent sobs. Courtney sank down into her bed and closed her eyes. Tomorrow was going to be a trying day. She was going to need some sleep. She knew she really should be feeling anxious, or even sobbing like Margaret was. But instead, she felt nothing.

Alexandrina had come, but they hadn't had time to ask her to release the wish. Courtney wasn't sure how she felt about that.

She hadn't finished anything that was on her list. But maybe that didn't matter. Had she completed what her dad had asked? She'd gone looking for the secrets of the school and she'd certainly found them, though they hadn't made her life better. Quite the opposite, in fact.

She was sure she already knew more about the secrets of the school than her dad ever had.

But there was still her wish, which bound her to do what it chose.

Margaret and the others still had wishes left. She could now get them to wish anything she wanted. The thought washed over her with sickening clarity. Ms. Krick would help her whether she asked for her help or not. Courtney had the pictures of Headmistress Valentine if she needed them. Everything was lining up. Was that because of the fountain, or because of the things Courtney had done? Maybe they were the same.

On the other side of the room, Margaret's sobs had quieted. Their room was still. The sirens were at the end of the woods now, barely audible.

"Bed check!" Bessie's booming voice rang out from down the hall.

"Don't say a word," hissed Courtney at Margaret.

CHAPTER THIRTY-SEVEN

Where There's Smoke...

The dorm had been thrown into chaos.

"What are you doing?" Margaret asked, staring as Courtney wrapped the candles with their holders in dirty towels and lowered them gently into her clothes hamper.

"Getting rid of the evidence," Courtney replied. "We'll have to get rid of them better in the morning, but this will have to do for tonight."

A flicker of understanding passed across Margaret's otherwise blank face and she silently reached for her own hamper and tossed her dirty clothes in with Courtney's.

As Margaret was bent over the now shared hamper, Courtney reached over and tousled Margaret's hair.

"Hey!" said Margaret, slapping Courtney's hand away. "What are you doing?"

"It has to look like we've been sleeping," said Courtney impatiently, as she surveyed Margaret's disheveled hair before messing up her own thick orange mane. They'd both had their hair tied up in tight ponytails which was much too orderly.

She hoped the other girls had their wits about them. The only thing she could help right now was what she and Margaret were up to, the others were on their own.

Courtney studied Margaret's crumpled expression. Hopefully she wasn't going to do anything stupid.

Bessie would be there any minute.

"Margaret," Courtney said. "Did you... did you feel Alexandrina's presence?"

"I'm not sure," Margaret said. "There was that wind, was that her?"

"Did you *feel* anything, though?" Courtney asked. "Like a sort of pressure?" Courtney tapped herself on the chest. She could still feel where the pressure had been, as if it was still upon her.

"No," said Margaret, shaking her head. "But Violet did say something on the way back about not being able to catch her breath."

Courtney looked at Margaret thoughtfully then moved quietly toward the door, which stood between them and the teeming squeal of girls in the hall.

Putting one ear up to the wooden door, Courtney closed her eyes and listened closely to the cacophony of conversations going on in the hall, trying to sort out the gaggle of voices. None of them sounded like Bessie.

"I can't hear Bessie out there," Courtney said in a low voice, looking back at Margaret. "We should go now. You ready?"

Margaret stood before her, her lower lip trembling.

"They're going to know we were there!" Margaret wailed. "Giles saw us!"

"No, he didn't," said Courtney, grabbing Margaret by the shoulders and looking at her sternly. "Get a hold of yourself. There's no way Giles could tell it was us, we were too far away. For all they know, we were sleeping. You were sleeping. *We were sleeping.* You got that?"

Honestly, Margaret appeared to have snapped. Courtney would have to do the thinking for them both. Margaret opened her mouth as if to speak, but was startled by a loud knock at the door.

Courtney feigned an exaggerated yawn as she reached for the door and opened it.

"Bed check," Bessie announced, standing in the doorway with her hands on her hips.

The last time there had been a bed check in the middle of the night was when some senior boys had been caught drinking in the woods the previous June. The boys had been expelled, just before graduation, without much fanfare. The staff had woken the whole campus up to make sure nobody else had been out. Courtney wondered what had happened to the three of them. Had they managed to go on to college? She shuddered involuntarily as she met Bessie's gaze.

Bessie wore a faded pink flannel nightgown. Her hair lay matted against her head in greasy clumps.

Courtney hoped her face showed confusion. She thought it probably showed something worse.

"What's going on?" Courtney asked in the best groggy voice she could muster.

"There's a fire in the woods," Bessie replied.

What was the right reaction to this news? Courtney searched her repertoire, but Margaret butted in.

"What? Really?" Margaret cried, running to the window.

Courtney just looked at Margaret. She'd not given her enough credit. Her reaction had been convincing. Courtney turned to see how Bessie had reacted to Margaret's performance, but she needn't have worried. Bessie had already moved on to knock on the next door.

"Come on," Courtney said to Margaret, nodding her head toward the hallway.

Margaret turned her tear-streaked face toward Courtney. "There's so many flames," she said. "We'll go to jail!"

"It'll be just fine," Courtney said, walking over and taking Margaret by the elbow. "The firemen will have everything under control in no time." She guided Margaret away from the window, toward the hallway, carefully avoiding looking anyone that was milling about the hallway in the eye. "Let's go find the others."

Margaret's puffy face fit right in when they arrived at the next room, where Jules shared with Amy. It seemed as if half of their floor was there, crowded in to look out the window, many hysterically sobbing.

Violet was in there too, huddled in a corner, hugging her knees to her chest. Her bright blue eyes were fixed toward the window, as if in shock. Courtney quickly rushed to her side, leaving Margaret to her own devices. Margaret seemed at least to understand the need to keep her cool around the others.

"Keep it together, Violet," Courtney told her in a low voice. "Just blend in."

"We need to say we were there," said Violet, her voice trembling. "They need to know it was an accident."

"We will do no such thing," said Courtney, in no uncertain terms. "We've been sleeping, like everyone else. No one will know."

"They'll know," Violet moaned.

Courtney scanned the room, but the commotion at the window meant nobody was listening to her and Violet talking quietly in the corner.

"There's no way for them to know," Courtney said, firmly. "But if you tell, you're on your own. I was never there. So, keep your mouth shut or it'll only be you who's expelled."

Violet's eyes were as wide as saucers as she looked at Courtney.

Courtney stepped away from Violet and waded deeper into the room that was filled with girls by now. She had to get to them all. They couldn't tell. Wish or no wish, that much she knew.

"Weird how it isn't moving any closer," Jules remarked loudly, her face pressed up against the window. "I guess it's lucky that there isn't much wind. I wish Bessie would let us get closer, to see what's really going on."

"Yes, closer to the firefighters, too!" added Amy. "They're cute, even from here."

"Well, that too," Jules admitted, grinning widely at the girls who'd assembled in the room. Jules' smile faded as her gaze reached Margaret's sullen expression. "What's wrong, Margaret?"

"What if the fire reaches the campus?" Margaret asked.

Jules just blinked at her.

Courtney held her breath. What was Margaret doing? Of course, the blaze wouldn't reach the school. They could barely even see it from here. Amy had been joking that she could see the firefighters. They were nothing but tiny specs against the blazing trees.

Could the fire spread this far? It had been a giant gust of wind that had created the wall of fire in the first place. If it really had been Alexandrina, surely, she wouldn't burn down the school her son had built. Courtney shook her head. She needed to get a grip. And Margaret needed to just lay low.

"Margaret, it's all the way at the other end of the woods. There are two fire trucks down there. There's no way it'll come here," Courtney said, putting a protective arm around Margaret's shoulders and giving her a squeeze. Maybe the squeeze was a little tighter than would be considered supportive.

Courtney quickly glanced around the room. Where were the others? She hoped they were holding it together better than this. She eyed the hallway, but before she could make a break for it, Bessie's disheveled frame appeared in the doorway.

"Girls, girls," Bessie said, clapping her hands in front of her. "That's enough excitement for tonight. I understand you want to watch the commotion, but you must get some sleep. Or at least watch from your own rooms. We're in no danger here, and the fire is contained to the south end of the woods."

There was a collective twitch, as the girls in the room all looked at each other at once. How could they be expected to go to bed with such a light show outside?

"Bessie," Courtney called, finding her voice. "Is everyone okay? I mean, are all the girls here?" Courtney's breath skipped a measure as she felt Bessie's gaze on her. She needed Bessie to say everyone had been in their beds, that she didn't suspect any of the girls had been summoning spirits in the woods in the middle of the night.

"Everyone's accounted for," she replied, eyeing Courtney. "But Giles was there when the fire started. There was a group there that fled. He thought they could be students, though he couldn't be sure. They could have been kids from town. I'm sure the police will get to the bottom of it tomorrow."

So, Giles was okay. No harm done. But the police? He'd told the rest of the teachers what he'd seen, which was nothing, or at least not enough to prove they'd been there. Courtney felt her eye twitch slightly as she met Bessie's gaze. She willed it to stop, but there it was.

Bessie looked away, sweeping her gaze over all the girls present.

"The headmistress will be speaking with you all first thing tomorrow," she said. "But if any of you have information about the fire, by all means, speak up tonight. I'll be available."

A small squeak erupted from Violet. Bessie's head snapped toward her. Bessie's hair hung crazily from its high ponytail.

"Violet," Bessie said, her eyes narrowed. "Did you have something to say?"

Courtney's gaze was all fire in Violet's direction.

"Um, no, Bessie," Violet stammered. "Just clearing my throat."

Bessie's expression softened.

"Of course, I don't expect it was any of you girls," Bessie said. "But you'd best be off to bed now, or I'll have to write the lot of you up. Tomorrow's going to come early."

Courtney nodded to Margaret and Violet as she left the room. The two girls followed her into the hall.

"Goodnight, Bessie," Courtney called.

"Goodnight Courtney, Margaret," Violet said, her voice breaking as she reached to hug the girls goodnight.

"We should do our own thing this weekend," Courtney said into Violet's ear as she pulled her in. "We'll meet in my room after school on Monday after school, but not before. Tell the others." Courtney tugged at Margaret and pulled her toward their room.

CHAPTER THIRTY-EIGHT

Solidarity

Violet and Rhoda waited outside her door, still in their uniforms when Courtney returned to the dorm after school on Monday. The faint smell of campfire still lingered in the air in the hall as well as in Courtney's hair, though she'd washed it twice since the fire.

Courtney silently opened the door to her room.

The girls filed in and took seats side by side on Margaret's neat bed, as if their entrance had been rehearsed.

Courtney pursed her lips. So, were they mad, or nervous, or what? She hadn't talked to any of them much all weekend, not even Margaret. Courtney had purposely avoided her friends. This talk she'd planned had to take place in a location they couldn't be overheard. She guessed she'd find out soon enough what they were thinking. She stared at them a moment longer before looking away, leaving them to sit in silence. This was going to be more difficult than she'd expected. She'd had time to think and her thoughts swirled about in a jumbled mess. She began to pace back and forth in front of the door as she tried to unravel the threads of her brain.

Margaret had been warning Courtney that she hadn't been herself, yet she'd never felt more like herself. She felt stronger somehow. She'd had a glimpse, however brief, of what she could have if she only opened up a bit with Cole, and she'd liked it. The rest of this, such as her father's challenge and the wish, it was all just a temporary distraction. She'd have it handled and then she could move on.

"Courtney," Violet asked from where she sat perched on Margaret's bed, "are you okay?"

"Fine," Courtney answered absentmindedly. She looked at the clock. Were the others even coming? She'd been clear they were to come straight here, she was sure of it.

"It's just that your face..." Violet didn't finish her sentence, scrunching her own face into a scowl.

Suddenly aware how sour she must look, Courtney tried for a more neutral expression and resumed her pacing without giving Violet a second look.

She'd really loved spending time with Cole and it pained her, what he must think. That's what had been painted on her face. She'd been okay, or at least it hadn't really hit her until the fire. She'd been scared. She'd felt alone and she'd wanted to call him and explain why she'd pushed him away. She knew it was a lot and he'd probably think she was crazy. She'd been thinking what she could say to him, anything that might make things better between them. Maybe she was really trying to convince herself. Somehow, she wished she could tell him she hadn't had a choice. She wanted him to know that, at least. But this was her punishment for being so flippant with her wish. She had to pay the fountain before she could move on.

She'd focus on completing the wish and on getting the girls on board.

Margaret let herself into the room without knocking. Lynette and Hailey were right behind her. All three girls sat cross-legged on the floor, snubbing Courtney's unmade bed. Hailey tugged awkwardly at her kilt, pulling it down over her knees.

"Okay," Courtney said, clapping her hands as she stood before them. She looked at all the girls.

Margaret flinched at the sound of Courtney's loud clap.

The knot in Courtney's stomach reminded her they could still be in serious trouble. She hoped they'd managed to erase all of the physical evidence. She'd gotten rid of the evidence of the séance in a dumpster in town. Courtney needed the girls to feel safe. They might not be willing to help her anymore and she needed them.

"What do we know?" Courtney asked the group. "Did anyone get asked anything about the fire this weekend?"

If there were any more loose ends to tie up, Courtney needed to know, and fast.

Hailey's lower lip trembled as if she were about to cry.

"Well?" Courtney said, as she studied the girls' faces. She hadn't meant to sound so harsh, but she had to know. Courtney pulled at the ends of her hair, springing a curl back.

"I did," Margaret said, raising her hand, timidly.

"Yes, Margaret?" Courtney asked, relieved to have Margaret's support.

"Jeff asked me in math class if I knew who the students were who'd started the fire," Margaret said.

"And?" Courtney asked, frowning, although she didn't really care what Jeff thought.

"I said no," replied Margaret, her eyes fixated on her hands in her lap.

"Anyone else?" Courtney asked, smiling for encouragement. She didn't let on she'd been asked about the fire herself, twice.

The girls all shook their heads in answer to Courtney's question.

Courtney had been called down to Headmistress Valentine's office. The headmistress told her she'd seen someone sprint across the lawn, on the night of the fire, toward the girls' dorm, before the fire trucks had arrived. Giles had called her immediately after calling the fire department and she'd caught a glimpse of the runner from her vantage point on the teachers' residence porch. She'd thought of Courtney, since she'd known Courtney ran. She asked if Courtney would be willing to speak with police.

If Courtney hadn't had the photos the outcome would have been very different. As it was, she'd had the photos, the headmistress did not call the police, and there would be no more questions from the headmistress' office, at least not for Courtney. But, she had to keep the others from suspicion as well. She could only control what Headmistress Valentine would report. If it got beyond her, well, Courtney would make sure that didn't happen.

"I think we should tell," said Rhoda, looking around at the other girls earnestly.

"What?" Violet nearly squealed, whirling around to face Rhoda. A vein pulsed on Violet's forehead, which it did only when she was very upset.

Courtney looked from Rhoda to Violet, then back again, feeling her blood pressure rising. The two girls were locked in a staring contest. Courtney couldn't let Rhoda tell. Headmistress Valentine couldn't protect Courtney if Rhoda went public. They'd all get expelled.

"I feel so sick," Hailey moaned, on the other side of the room. "We didn't mean to do it, maybe Rhoda's right." She buried her head in her hands.

Courtney looked to Margaret, who merely shrugged.

Did they all feel this way? Think, Courtney, think.

"Nobody's telling," said Courtney.

"Courtney, you can't decide what we do," Rhoda said, jumping to her feet. "Girls, I'm willing to go with you, if you feel we need to."

"I've got this under control," Courtney told them, holding up a hand. She'd have to tell them more than she wanted to, but their boy scout nature was getting out of hand. "There's nothing to worry about, no reason to tell." She took a deep breath. "Ms. Krick knows we summoned Alexandrina."

Rhoda remained standing, her arms folded defiantly. The other girls stared at Courtney in disbelief.

"Courtney!" Margaret exclaimed.

"I didn't tell her anything else," Courtney said. "Just that we'd felt Alexandrina's presence before we'd been interrupted. I told Krick we'd tell her the next time we tried to call her."

"What?" Margaret exclaimed, again.

Courtney faced the girls who all looked at her with alarm. "Don't worry, I have no intention of ever doing another séance," she added. Firstly, there had been that horrible pressure in Courtney's chest. Then Alexandrina had managed to start a fire. No, Courtney wouldn't try to call her again.

"I'd only thought the séance would help," Margaret said. Tears brimmed in her eyes. She pulled her knees up to her chest and used the hem of her kilt to wipe her eyes.

"We know, Margaret," said Hailey, putting an arm around Margaret's shoulders.

"And Courtney," Margaret added, her voice trembling. "All the things you've been doing, you've got to stop. That was the whole point of calling Alexandrina. We haven't fixed anything."

"I think we can finish my wish without her," Courtney said. "The fountain will help, but I'll need you all too."

"Sorry, guys, I'm out," Rhoda said, smoothing down her skirt with her hands. "I won't tell if I can help it, but you're on your own, Courtney." Rhoda took a step toward the door, but Courtney blocked her way.

"Take a seat," Courtney said, firmly.

Rhoda shook her head, but didn't make another move toward the door.

"I've also spoken with the headmistress," Courtney announced, looking around to take in their reaction.

The girls huddled closer together.

"She'll do as I ask," Courtney continued. She took a deep breath. Rhoda had forced her hand. "She's not going to have any of us questioned right now, but all that could change."

"You wouldn't," Lynette said, cringing

"Try me," Courtney said, folding her arms and fixing her stare on Lynette, whose lips were tightly pursed.

Lynette mumbled something unintelligible under her breath then sat back down next to Hailey, who patted Lynette on her knee with her free hand.

"Rhoda?" Courtney asked, looking over at her, since she was now the only one standing in the room besides Courtney.

"You can't make me help," Rhoda said through gritted teeth. After pausing a beat, she rushed for the door, roughly bumping shoulders with Courtney on her way past her.

Courtney threw up her hands. She'd have to deal with Rhoda later. Right now, she couldn't afford to have anyone else working against her. "Anyone else?"

"What if Rhoda tells?" Hailey asked in a small voice.

"She won't," Courtney said, firmly. "We'll make sure of it. But we have to stick together."

The girls all looked at her.

She still had enough girls left, even without Rhoda. She could get done what she needed.

"First, we'll deal with Rhoda," Courtney told them. "Then we finish my wish and end this."

If all else failed, these girls still had their wishes left. Courtney looked at Margaret, who stared forlornly at the door Rhoda had just exited.

"Do you trust me?" Courtney asked the group.

"So, you're saying," Lynette said, "that if we help you, Krick won't get us in trouble. But, what if we don't?"

It sounded threatening when she put it that way, Courtney reflected.

"It's not as bad as all that," Courtney said, trying to keep her tone light, as she made eye contact with each of the four remaining girls. "I was never there, that I'm clear on. But the rest of you, I suppose that's up to you and it's your word against mine."

Her words seemed to have the desired impact as the girls looked at Courtney in shock.

Margaret appeared the most put out, shaking her head sadly at Courtney.

Courtney looked at her roommate, surprised to find she didn't mind disappointing her. Not this time.

"Now, who's on board for making sure Rhoda doesn't tell?" Courtney asked.

Several moments passed before Violet put up her hand. Courtney waited them out. Soon, Margaret and Hailey followed suit. Lynette was last.

"Great, we'll meet in here every day after school to check in," Courtney told them, smiling broadly. They'd come around. She hadn't counted on what had happened with Rhoda, but that would be easily handled. "Just until we're straight on the plan," she added quickly, seeing the girls' expressions. "This could still blow up in our faces, we've got to stick together."

CHAPTER THIRTY-NINE

New Beginning

Several weeks later, Courtney moved through the West Woods on foot with ease on a warm Sunday afternoon. She preferred meandering between the tree trunks to taking the path. She'd learned which trees marked the way. The faintest odor of fire still lingered in the woods, or perhaps she just imagined that.

The new book she'd taken out of the library was tucked under her arm. She'd spent the better part of that morning curled up in her favorite corner of the student lounge and was more than halfway through. She'd only left because Ethan Roth had come and interrupted her quiet corner.

"Are you following me, again Courtney?" he'd asked, flashing her his dazzling smile.

"Maybe it's you, following me," Courtney had said, smiling back. She'd seen him reading in the lounge before, but somehow him talking to her pulled her out of her bubble she'd created and she no longer felt like being there.

Courtney knew she had a lot in common with Ethan. It was clear to her now why Margaret had thought they'd be a good match. She'd stolen another look at him once he'd settled in nearby with his book. He was going to make a great boyfriend to someone someday, but her heart was still with Cole.

"I was just going," Courtney told Ethan, giving him a friendly wave goodbye as she walked out of the student lounge.

She'd seen Cole by chance just the week before, walking Husk in town.

"Whoa!" Courtney had laughed as Husk jumped up all over her when she was just coming out of Luigi's with her friends. His muddy paws left marks on her jeans, but she was happy to see him anyway, scratching him behind the ears and hugging him close.

"Hi, Courtney," Cole had greeted her, not unkindly but not exactly warm.

"Hi," was all she could think to say in reply as Cole led Husk away down the road. She'd crouched on the pavement, where she'd been with Husk and watched the duo until she couldn't see them anymore.

"Snap out of it!" Margaret had said, clucking her tongue with pity as she pulled Courtney up off the pavement and they walked the short way back to campus from Luigi's pizza restaurant.

Her wish would be complete soon, but not soon enough. She'd reach out to Cole then. Her heart ached as she realized he might not wait for her. She clutched her chest, remembering the look on his face. His nod, as if they'd been merely acquaintances.

It seemed odd to Courtney walking through the West Woods, that the woods had once seemed so daunting and she'd first come in here on a dare. Now, she moved freely in the woods and didn't worry too much about being seen. She reached out to touch a tree and felt its rough bark. Her thoughts were clearer here.

She'd taken to walking in the woods after school, after she met with the girls in her room each day. The first few times she'd watched over her shoulder carefully before moving into the trees. After the first week, it didn't matter to her anymore if she got caught. Ms. Krick had been the only teacher to ever monitor the woods and she wasn't about to stop Courtney, though she peppered her with questions whenever they were alone, which was as infrequently as Courtney could manage.

Most days, Courtney's walks ended up in the empty fountain clearing. Other days, Courtney found herself walking straight through to the Taylor house. Twice, she'd even crept close and stared into the darkened windows. She'd wondered if the old woman whom she now knew lived there, had any idea there was magic so nearby.

Courtney was always careful to not venture too far south on her walks. She hadn't been back to the site of the ruined Young house and its graves. They'd unleashed Alexandrina's spirit out there and there was no way to know for sure that she'd ever left.

"Her spirit was released as soon as we broke the circle," Margaret had assured her, based on her research. Yet Courtney got chills just thinking about walking down that way. The trees would be scarred for many years and she wasn't ready to take responsibility for that.

Courtney had fallen into a bit of a routine lately, most of which felt normal. She'd been feeling less of the fountain's pull. She could only guess because the motions were all in place to achieve the items from her wish.

Taking a wide circle around a dense clump of prickly pine trees, she veered north and entered the fountain's clearing. Stepping past the last border tree, she felt the same pang of disappointment she did each time. The fountain wasn't there. It wasn't coming back, at least not for her.

She threw her running jacket down in the long grass. She'd never fixed the sleeve that had been torn by her fall with Husk – somehow it reminded her of what might have been. The ground was damp where it thawed. She sat in the middle of the clearing near where the fountain should be and closed her eyes, feeling the winter sunlight on her eyelids.

Her dad had come here, he admitted that now, though he wouldn't tell her what he'd wished for. She hadn't told him everything, but she'd shared enough that he must know she'd found the fountain and that she'd made a wish. He never asked about it.

"So," he'd said when they'd spoken the week before, "now that you know everything that St. Augustus has to offer, do you still want to leave?"

"I'm okay with staying for now, Dad," she'd said. If she left now, she couldn't become team captain in the fall and she'd be tied to the fountain forever. She had no choice.

Jim Wallis had chuckled in the way fathers do when their child has learned a lesson.

She all but had the appointment to team captain locked up. Violet had turned out to be her biggest asset in the group. The girl had an uncanny knack for knowing everyone's secrets and Courtney was becoming adept at getting what she wanted on campus. There wasn't a junior on the team who was putting themselves forward for captain next year, though there hadn't been any strong contenders in the group anyway.

When the time came, Valentine would have a well-placed word with Coach Laurel and it would be done. Courtney felt she might have earned captain anyhow. Her times had improved greatly since she'd ramped up her training.

Headmistress Valentine had repeatedly assured Courtney she'd broken it off with Mr. Chase, though that didn't lessen Courtney's hold. The headmistress was very keen on keeping their former relationship a secret.

All the changes were starting to take their toll though and Courtney found herself seeking more and more time away by herself, to process all that had happened.

The worst times were seeing what impact her actions were having on others. She'd twice been in a room with the headmistress and Mr. Chase. The former lovers kept their distance from one another, but the regret hanging in the air had been palpable, and made Courtney question the point of it all. Yet she couldn't back down now, not when everything was falling into place.

None of the girls had been questioned about the fire, either by the headmistress or anyone else, and it didn't seem like they ever would be. Courtney would never turn any of them in, not even Rhoda. She'd only said that to get them on her side.

True to her word, Rhoda hadn't tried to tell anyone that Courtney knew of, though, on the off chance that she'd change her mind, Courtney and the others had put in place an elaborate plan to discredit her, making up more outlandish stories that the headmistress had believed. Or had said she'd believed. Courtney had wondered which one it was.

She shuddered when she thought of all that had been done for her and her simple wish. She stared at the spot where the fountain had been. She reached into the jacket she sat on and pulled a quarter out of its pocket. It had been a long few months. Her college applications would be stronger with her swim times improving and her volunteer work for the meet. She'd met and lost Cole. If she'd known her wish would come true, she'd never have made it, that she knew. She'd have refused her dad's challenge. Had his wish been that much better that it hadn't taken over his whole world the way Courtney's had?

She toyed with the quarter in her hand.

Things were okay now. They were. She'd be okay if she stayed the course.

Courtney looked up into the tree tops, which were perfectly still. The sun shone down on the clearing, though there were clouds moving in. She searched for Izzy, whom she'd caught a glimpse of a few times lately, but for the most part he steered clear.

"You hear that, Izzy?" she called out into the empty woods. "I'd take it all back if I could!"

She waited, listening, but all she heard was silence ringing heavily through the woods.

Reaching her hand behind her back, she snapped the quarter in the direction of the invisible fountain. "I wish my family and I had never heard of St. Augustus!" she wished into the vacant space. "You hear that, Izzy?"

Of course, there was no fountain. She didn't get another wish. There was no answer from the treetops.

Grayish clouds had covered the sun that had shone down on the clearing.

Courtney sighed heavily and gathered up her jacket, sliding it on against her sudden chill. Rising to her feet, she turned and left the clearing, maybe for good this time.

ACKNOWLEDGMENTS

The West Woods wouldn't have happened without the support of incredible readers. Thank you from the bottom of my heart to everyone who read and loved The Fountain, which is where the magical world of St. Augustus began. This amazing community of readers and writers have blogged about The Fountain, reviewed The Fountain, and told their friends about it. Special thanks to The Canadian Science Fiction and Fantasy Association (CSFFA) members for nominating The Fountain for Best Young Adult Novel – it was an absolute thrill to have it recognized among Canada's best speculative fiction.

Thank you to my incredible group of The West Woods Beta readers, Avery, Abbey, Brooke, Elle, Jamie, Madeleine, Marj, Sofia and Tanya, who read drafts of The West Woods and gave the best feedback. Your love and care for the characters made them stronger and helped them do the things they were meant to do. I am so grateful that you let these characters into your lives. Your enthusiasm is the reason I write.

I also owe a debt of gratitude to the incredible Canadian writing community, When Words Collide and to my regular coffee and beer dates with fellow authors who have shared so much knowledge – you know who you are. I hope to do you all justice as I give back what I've learned to the writing community.

The folks at Evil Alter Ego Press have worked tirelessly to make this project a reality. You're the best little press a girl could ask for, and I thank you for taking a chance on this series.

Thank you to my publicist, Mickey Mikkelson of Creative Edge for believing in The Fountain Series and helping me shout about it from the rooftops.

The West Woods was written between moments of life, and I thank my family for giving me the time to work on something I love as much as this series. My husband, Jamie, is my wonderful rock – encouraging me when I wonder how it will all get done and inspiring me when I am ready to throw in the towel. Love you so much. Thank you also to our three wonderful kids for being almost excited about me being an author as I am – for not complaining when I write or attend signings during our weekends, and for always asking what's happening with the story. This book is dedicated to you.

ABOUT THE AUTHOR

Suzy Vadori is an Operations Executive by day, Writer by night. Suzy is an involved member of the Calgary Writers' community, serving as When Words Collide (a Calgary Festival for Readers and Writers) Program Manager for Middle Grade and Young Adult since 2013.

Her first novel, *The Fountain*, was short-listed for a Prix Aurora award.

Suzy lives in Calgary, Alberta with her husband and three kids.

Other Books in this Series

The Fountain
By Suzy Vadori

Other Evil Alter Ego Press Books

Mik Murdoch: Boy Superhero Series

Mik Murdoch, Boy Superhero
By Michell Plested

Mik Murdoch: The Power Within
By Michell Plested

Mik Murdoch: Crisis of Conscience
By Michell Plested

Scouts of the Apocalypse Series

Scouts of the Apocalypse: Zombie Plague
By Michell Plested

Scouts of the Apocalypse: Zombie War
By Michell Plested

Anthologies

Dimensional Abscesses
(edited by Jeffrey Hite & Michell Plested)